Change of Address

Rick Polad

CALUMET EDITIONS

Minneapolis

FOURTH EDITION NOVEMBER 2025

This is a work of fiction. Names, characters, places and incidents either are the product of the author's imagination or are used fictitiously.

ISBN – 978-1-960250-42-1

10 9 8 7 6 5 4

Cover art and book design by Gary Lindberg

Follow the author at:
www.rickpolad.com
www.facebook.com/spencermanningmysteries
@rickpolad

To Mom and Dad

Mom was blind at the end of her life –
Dad read the galley of this book to her every
night after dinner…

I miss you both.

Other Spencer Manning Mysteries

#2 Dark Alleys
#3 Harbor Nights
#4 Missing Boy
#5 Death's Door
#6 Drug Affair
#7 Cold Justice
#8 A Grave Matter

About the Author

Rick Polad worked as a geologist, taught Earth Science and Astronomy at a junior college for twenty-nine years, and volunteered with the Coast Guard Auxiliary on Lake Michigan. Rick edited the English version of *Living With Nuclei*, the memoirs of Japanese physicist, Motoharu Kimura, and currently works as an editor for his publisher, Calumet Editions. Rick also worked at Fermilab, the country's highest energy particle accelerator, and currently volunteers at Microtrace, one of the world's premier forensic chemistry labs.

Acknowledgements

This book would not exist without the help and support of several special people. Carol Deleskiewicz, who fills my life with joy, offered constant encouragement and convinced me to publish an e-book. To my brother, Mike, for a strong edit and several good catches after I thought the book was perfect. To my friend Tom Remec, who said, "I have a friend who published an e-book, and I think he had some success." That turned out to be an understatement, as I soon discovered that Tom's friend, Gary Lindberg, had the most popular thriller on Amazon during 2012.

Special thanks to Gary Lindberg, the best-selling author of *The Shekinah Legacy* and *Sons of Zadoc*, who graciously agreed to share his success story over breakfast. After reading *Change of Address*, Gary invited me to join his publishing company, Calumet Editions, designed the new cover and reformatted the book for print publication. Without Gary's expertise and industry knowledge and his willingness to devote his time, this book would not exist. And to all my friends who have read my story and asked for more Spencer, my undying thanks.

Change of Address

Chapter 1

When I awoke, the room was no longer filled with sunshine. The dingy furniture looked even more so in the sickly, late-afternoon light. I had fallen asleep again in my swivel chair, arms folded across my chest and legs crossed on top of my desk. There had been no knock on the door to wake me up. I uncrossed my legs and helped the left one down to the floor. It had fallen asleep. After rubbing out the pins-and-needles feeling, I walked over to the lighthouse calendar hanging on the wall and checked off another day. It had been more than a month since I had put the ad in the paper and there hadn't been one call, not one single knock on the door. I was beginning to wonder if I should take Uncle Lou up on his offer to make me a meat packer in Philly.

I had come back to Chicago not really knowing what I had wanted to do or why I was coming back. I had gone to college and graduated with a double degree in Psychology and Law Enforcement. Dad, a captain on the Chicago police force, had always hoped I would follow in his footsteps, and, after college, that seemed like the best bet. So, I took the exam and headed for the Police Academy. I was near or at the top of my class in everything, including firearms. When I was five, Dad taught me how to use a gun and how to respect it. The only problem was, when I left the academy I wasn't sure I wanted to be a cop so I joined the army.

That indecision came from three fronts. One, I didn't know if I could deal with the system. I knew that I couldn't handle the frustration of arresting someone on Monday and seeing him back on the streets on Tuesday. Dad said that was just part of an overcrowded system and all he could do was to just keep doing his job. Two, even though I could put as many shots as I wanted in the center of a bullseye, I didn't know if I could pull the trigger if my gun was pointed at a person. Dad said that was something no one liked but, again, it was part of the job and, if the time came, training would take over and the trigger would be pulled. If it was part of the job, maybe I didn't want the job. Third was a woman.

When I got out of the army, Dad suggested I take some time off and decide. So, I'd packed my camping gear and headed for the back woods of Yellowstone.

I had been gone for six weeks when a park ranger found me and handed me a telegram. My folks had been killed in a car accident. Two weeks had gone by since then. Suddenly, my decision was not so important.

I called Aunt Rose in Wisconsin and found out she and Sergeant Powolski had taken care of everything. According to their wishes, Mom and Dad had been cremated. They were waiting for me to hold the police service.

After the service, a group of people gathered at Antolini's, Dad's favorite Italian restaurant. After three hours of listening to people say they were sorry, Stanley Powolski, Aunt Rose, and I were the only ones left. Aunt Rose invited me to come up to Door County, Wisconsin and spend some time at her inn. I kissed her good-bye and told her I would even though I knew I wouldn't—at least for awhile. There were some memories up there I wanted to avoid. Stosh and I moved to the bar and spent another two hours talking about old times.

Some of my earliest memories were of Stosh Powolski, a big, tough man who got me addicted to hard candy. He was as close to an uncle as I'd ever have. And he was the only one I could have talked to about the accident. Both of us spent a few minutes quietly staring at our glasses before I brought it up.

"How did it happen, Stosh?"

He didn't seem surprised. It was like he had been waiting for me to ask. He took another sip of his beer. "Drunk driver, young kid."

"What happened to the kid?"

"Physically or legally?"

"Both." I raised my eyes and met his. His look was hard and official. It had to be. So did mine. Because just behind that hardness was a lot of pain that may not have stopped had it gotten started.

He looked down and sighed. "Physically, same old story. The impact must have thrown him sideways. There was a bump on the left temple and a bruised left shoulder. The kid at least had enough sense to put on his seat belt."

"Good for him."

Stosh looked back at me, and there was a warning in his look. He continued. "Legally, he was arrested and charged with DUI and manslaughter, two counts. He made bond. Case comes up next month. Seems pretty open and closed. But he's got some big-bucks lawyer."

"How old is he?"

"Twenty-two."

"Where did it happen?"

He pursed his lips and took a deep breath. "Well, you know your dad loved that drive along Sheridan Road. They had been up at the Highland Park Country Club for some political shindig. Instead of going back to the highway, he took Sheridan. Happened at the bend around West Park. Evidently the kid came up on him from behind and tried to pass. They hit the bend side by side, and the kid lost it. Your dad went almost straight over the edge and down into the ravine. The kid made it halfway around the curve to the left, spun and ended up facing the wrong way with the left side of the car against a tree."

"Rich kid?"

He swirled what was left of his beer in the bottom of the glass. "Nope. Not even close. Lives in a dump on Armitage. Has had ten jobs in the last four years."

"Then where did the lawyer come from?"

"Don't know yet. The kid wouldn't say. We're looking into it but we've got to be careful about rights, and it's not illegal to have expensive attorneys."

"No, just a little strange. It would be nice to know who's footing the bill."

"Sure would."

"Can't you do anything?"

"We're doing everything we can, Spence. I have a list of officers and detectives as long as your arm who volunteered to put in off-duty time to tail the kid, but that could open a can of worms. Last thing we want is a harassment charge. We did stake out his apartment. He never showed. Landlord said the kid stiffed him out of the last month's rent. We'll see if he shows for court."

"Any record?"

"None. Kid's clean. Not even a parking ticket."

"What about the car?"

"Registered to the kid. It was towed to a yard up on 41. It's still there."

I let the facts roll around and bounce off of each other. I liked things to make sense. This didn't. Stosh was watching the balls roll.

"Leave it alone, Spence."

I took a deep breath. "It seems a little strange."

"I know it does. But we're doing all we can. It's probably just a case of wrong place at the wrong time. And the kid is probably one of the thousands who hides in the cracks of society."

"And who has a high-profile attorney."

"I know. There are things that don't make sense. But that's only because we don't have all the facts. From the right point of view it will make perfect sense. We just don't have that point of view, and the kid wasn't talking. And he doesn't have to. He can plead guilty and get off with a slap on the wrist for a first-time offense. Or the big-bucks lawyer may find a loophole, and the kid'll walk." He shrugged his shoulders.

"It may be as simple as rich girl and poor boy fall in love, and daddy is helping to cover it up."

I thought some more. "Was Dad involved in anything big?"

I got another hard look that softened just a little. Stosh put his hand on my arm and said, "Leave it alone, Spence. We'll do our job. If there's something there, we'll find it."

I nodded. But I also knew how the system worked—with both hands tied behind its back.

The bartender asked if we wanted refills. We both declined. It was almost ten and, except for a couple at the table in the corner, the place was empty.

"You wanna tell me the kid's name?"

"Nope. That doesn't seem in line with my previous advice."

"It's public record."

Stosh nodded. "Yup. And if you really want it, go find it. But I'm not giving it to you."

I wasn't sure if I did, or, if I did, what my reasons were.

We talked about the Cubs for a few minutes, Stosh emptied his glass, and I put thirty bucks on the bar. He started to protest and then saw the look in my eyes. Twenty years ago, Stanley Powolski had saved my dad's life and, ever since, Dad had picked up the tab. Stosh's nod said more than words ever could have. We stood up and shook hands.

As I turned to go, Stosh put his hand on my shoulder and said, "You know, there's always a spot on the force for you, if you want it."

I smiled. "Thanks, Stosh. But I pretty much decided that I'd get a PI license and see how that goes. I think I still will."

"Well, whatever you do, you know I'm behind you. If there's anything you need..."

I smiled. "I'll be sure to ask."

At twenty-eight I was a big boy and thought I could take care of myself. But I was not above asking for help if I needed it, and I knew if I asked it would be there. I told him I'd be in touch.

Chapter 2

Six months later I had my license. The kid plea-bargained and was given probation. I looked up his name, but I didn't go to the trial. I was angry, but more so at life in general than at the kid. It just wasn't fair. I wondered how I'd act if I ran into him. I always thought I'd kill whoever harmed my family. And up close, I may have done something stupid. From afar I wasn't quite as angry as I may have been in person, so I stayed away. But the name Robert Dayton would forever be etched in my memory.

I'd rented a puny office with an adjacent room that I could pretend was an apartment on the top floor of an old three-story building on the south side. It was about as far from the old neighborhood as I could get and still be in the city, but it was only a couple of miles from the station. I'd eagerly hung up a little sign that said "Spencer Manning, Private Detective" and hung my diploma up on the wall. I figured it would be a fun and easy way to make a living. So far it hadn't been much of anything, except maybe bad for my health. I was getting fat and lazy sleeping behind that desk every day. If this kept up much longer, I'd be like one of those old walruses that can barely get off the rocks and back in the water.

My only visitor had been a friend who worked for Motorola who gave me a gift of a new-model pager, saying no self-respecting PI would be caught without one.

My stomach suddenly rumbled, and I realized I was hungry. I locked the office and walked down the hall and out the back door. I stood on the porch, wiped a few beads of sweat off my forehead and watched as a lonely, hot wind blew a single sheet of newspaper up against a rickety old fence. It was the third week of June and, as I walked down the stairs, I let out a sigh as I remembered how hot and muggy Chicago summers could be. So far, this one was even hotter than normal, and it had been a month since we'd had any rain.

Cutting across the backyards, I walked around to the other side of the block and opened the door of Beef's Diner. I had discovered it just a week ago on one of my strolls around the neighborhood. When Beef found out I had been in the army, he'd started giving me a cut rate on meals. I'd told him it wasn't necessary but he had insisted. He'd been a sergeant in Viet Nam and picked up his name there. Seems the officers in his outfit had told the guys that if they had a beef they could take it up with the sarge. No one ever did. I wouldn't have either. Beef was built like a bulldozer and looked like he had the personality to match. A jagged scar stood out like a medal someone had pinned on his left cheek. His arms were solid muscle, and his left forearm sported a tattoo of a flagpole. No flag, just the pole. He said the artist had a heart attack and died before he got to the flag, and Beef had decided to leave it as is.

His hair was almost white and cut in a crewcut that had probably been his cut of choice since birth. It topped his tough-as-nails exterior. But underneath there was a heart of gold. He always had something cheerful to say, and we passed the time telling war stories. All the interesting ones were his. And he always asked how business was. Unfortunately, he always got the same answer. I waved at Maria, who was busy in the kitchen working on the dinner crowd, and started toward my usual booth.

"Hey, Mister Detective."

"Hi, Beef. What's the special tonight?"

He grinned at me as he set down a couple of plates of meatloaf on the counter and said, "The special is, I got a case for you."

As I turned and walked back to the counter, I gave him a blank stare and tried to figure out if he was serious or had been at the rum again.

He set down a couple of beers and said, "You didn't get busy all of a sudden, did you?"

"Not since lunch, no. What do you mean, a case?"

He threw his hands up in the air and said, "A case, a job, something to do besides dust your desk with your legs."

"What happened? Somebody finally complain about your cooking and want to find out what this stuff really is?"

"Maybe that's why you're about as successful as the Cubs. You put out a sign that says 'Private Detective' but you really want to be a comedian. Last booth on the left. Go see what the young lady wants. I told her I knew this hotshot who was put on the earth for the sole purpose of solving her problem. Go on, I gotta close the joint in two hours."

A case. A real case. And a young lady at that. Of course, I had always pictured her walking in my door—long shapely legs, showing just enough under a tight black dress to let you know they were attached to more woman than any man would ever be able to handle. I guessed I could change the scenario to Beef's Diner. I peered eagerly down the row to the last booth on the left but there was nobody there.

My hopes dropped back to the ground with a thud, and I turned back to the counter. "Well, that figures, she's gone."

"What do you mean, she's gone? She'd better not be!"

I was starting to get angry. I didn't mind losing a client I never had as much as I minded being the butt of some joke. "There's nobody there, Beef. And it's not very funny."

He looked down the row and smiled. "Oh, I see. She's there. Just walk down there and see for yourself."

I shrugged and walked down the aisle. He was right. She was there, but she didn't have the long legs or the tight dress. What she did have was an adult-sized piece of chocolate cake, and she was shoveling it in faster than I would have thought possible. And now I knew why I thought no one was there. She couldn't have been more than four or five years old and didn't come within a foot of the top of the high-backed booth.

Beef had come up behind me and he introduced us. "Marty, this is Mr. Manning. He's going to help us find your daddy. PI, this is my niece, Marty."

She stopped eating long enough to give me a muffled "Hi" and then went back to the cake. She seemed much more interested in it than in finding her daddy. But then I'd tasted Maria's chocolate cake, and the cake *was* right there in front of her. Hard to ignore. Marty was a cute little thing. Long black hair framed a thin face with green eyes, a slightly upturned nose, and a mouth covered with chocolate. I told her it was nice to meet her and then noticed a Raggedy Ann doll sitting next to her on the bench with a white paper napkin spread across its lap.

"Who's your friend there, Marty?"

"That's Ann." She didn't take her eyes off the cake.

"She looks hungry. Did your daddy give her to you?"

"No. Uncle Ronny did."

I glanced over at Beef and saw the puzzled look on his face. I guessed this Uncle Ronny was a new addition to the family.

"Well, you see she gets something to eat, okay?"

"Okay."

I knew that was a lie. She wasn't about to share that cake with anybody. I took Beef's arm and steered him back toward the counter.

"So, you gonna take the case, PI?"

"How about you tell me what the case is first? Her father is missing?"

"More like we don't know who the father is."

"Her mother is your sister?"

"Was. She died six months ago." He pursed his lips and took a deep breath. "And to answer your next question, she wouldn't tell me who the father was."

"They weren't married?"

"They weren't married. But it's not what you think. She wasn't that kind of girl."

"I hadn't considered what kind of girl she was, Beef."

"Hey! How about a refill!" Down at the end of the counter, an old guy with a two-day growth of stubble held up his cup.

"Coming right up, Pops." Beef walked behind the counter and picked up the coffee pot. "I'm closing at eight," he said to me. "How about I get Marty settled with Maria and then come up to your hole in the wall?"

"Okay." I ate, put seven bucks on the counter, and headed back to the office. I wasn't crazy about the case. Missing persons wasn't exactly what I had in mind, but I felt I didn't have the right to be choosy. Things were a little slow and I had rent to pay.

Chapter 3

I unlocked my door, wondering if I'd ever get a real case so I'd have to use the old marker-in-the-door trick like I'd read about in the mystery novels. What was left of the sun left a sickly yellow pall over the few pieces of old wooden furniture that had come with the place, left behind by a tenant who didn't think them worth the trouble of hauling to the next address. If this worked out, I'd have to spend some of my inheritance and buy some real furniture. But, for the moment, I didn't want any of that money.

I was about to make the place a little more presentable when something about the room suddenly struck me as odd. A quick glance around showed me what it was. I must have noticed the blinking red light on the answering machine out of the corner of my eye. It was only the second message I'd had and the first one didn't count; that was me checking the machine, and what I'd said couldn't be repeated. I rewound the tape and waited anxiously.

When I heard the gentle voice, I sighed and shook my head. It was Aunt Rose. Another great expectation ground into dust. She said she was still waiting to see me and then went on to say she had run into Kathleen at the grocery store. Kathleen was one of the memories up in Door County I wanted to avoid, and the third reason I had joined the army. And now it seemed she was coming to Chicago to exhibit her paintings. Of course, Aunt Rose, who firmly believed I should have married Kathleen instead of joining the army, had given her my phone number and told her I'd love to see her. I could always count on Aunt Rose.

Kathleen Johnson was a beautiful, talented, sometimes addle-brained woman whom I had fallen head-over-heels for the first summer I was interested in that sort of thing. We had been spending summers up in Door and staying in Aunt Rose's inn for as long as I could remember. But, until the year I was fourteen, every summer had been spent down by the docks, out on a sailboat, or on one of the island beaches reading Mickey Spillane, Raymond Chandler, and Arthur Conan Doyle in the hot sun. Then, in June of one fateful summer, I had met Kathleen on my way to the boat and had spent the next month dreaming about her long blond hair and bright-blue eyes and following her around with about as much control over my destiny as a dog's tail.

She was almost a year older than me and at first wanted nothing to do with me. But I was persistent and, by the end of the next summer, she had fallen in love with me too. We were inseparable and, as the years went by, most everyone assumed we'd get married one day, especially Aunt Rose. Dad had laughed and said it was just puppy love. He said I'd go off to college and find out what love really was. Then I'd get married and find out once more; that's when Mom hit him. I'm not saying there weren't other girls in my life, but both Kathleen and I finished college without having found anyone else, and the next year I asked her to marry me.

It was then that the fighting began. Both of us had tempers which were quick to flare. And the main argument was over where to live. I had always wanted to be a detective and had planned on joining the force in Chicago. She was an artist and never wanted to live anywhere but Door County and she once said that, even if she were in a pine box, she would have found a way to keep herself from being shipped to Chicago. Evidently she was willing to sacrifice me for her art. But then I wasn't bending much either.

How had we spent seven years avoiding this issue to which there seemed to be no solution? But that wasn't true. There was a solution and I had found it. I broke off the engagement. A loving relationship spent watching fluffy white clouds and listening to tug whistles had gone south. We still loved each other, but that love was interrupted far too often by fits of anger. We were either in each other's arms or at each other's throats. And I never knew which was coming next. So I had eventually decided to put myself in a position where I wouldn't be able to change my mind. I joined the army. But a part of me missed her and had never forgotten her.

Evidently, neither had Aunt Rose. It was Tuesday, and Kathleen wasn't coming until next Wednesday. Eight days away. I'd have time to take care of Beef's problem and then run up to Door for a visit to Aunt Rose. I knew I was trying to avoid Kathleen but only because I knew I'd have a hard time saying good-bye if I saw her in person. I loved her—I probably always would. But love should be like a favorite old chair with lumps. If you know where the lumps are, you can settle down in the comfortable spots in between. With Kathleen, the lumps kept moving around.

I spent the next hour dusting my desk with my pants and wishing Aunt Rose hadn't reminded me about Kathleen. That was one clean desk.

Chapter 4

About 8:40, Beef knocked and let himself in. He dragged a straight chair to the other end of the desk and sat down. He had taken the time to put on his Hawaiian shirt and splash on some aftershave. Old Spice if my nose served me correctly.

"You going to a party?" I asked trying not to laugh.

"Nah. But I've heard about those gorgeous broads that are always dropping in on you PIs, and I thought I'd be ready."

But his Hawaiian shirt was already sweat-stained, and I didn't want to tell him what I thought he was ready for. He wiped his forehead on the sleeve of his shirt and said, "You know, I could do without this heat."

"You and me both. But I can remember Dad saying that same thing since I was a little kid, and he couldn't do anything about it either. You care for a cold one?"

He gave me a look that told me I didn't have to ask and, as I walked to the mini-fridge in the corner he said, "Ya know they invented air conditioning a while back."

"Yeah, I heard something about that. The crowd coming in the front door has kept me so busy I haven't had time to get one. Marty settled in okay?"

"Sure. I got her pj's on, and Maria's reading her a book. And not that trash you read either."

He was referring to the couple of hundred mysteries that lined the bookcase against the wall. There was also some Dickens and Steinbeck sprinkled in there for my more serious moods, not that Beef would have noticed.

He tipped back the bottle and took a long drink. "So, PI, you want the job?"

"I'm not too clear on what the job is, Beef. You want to fill me in?"

"It's not too complicated. My sister, Elizabeth, got herself pregnant some five years ago. She wasn't going to get married, and she wouldn't think of not having the baby. You know what I mean. So, nine months later, Marty is a member of the family, and I became an uncle. I loved that kid like I was her own father, changed her diapers, sang to her, took her for walks. I wouldn't give her up for anything."

My raised eyebrows got me a dirty look.

"Don't give me that look. Under this tough hide I got a heart just like you college boys. Just don't spread it around."

"She never told you who the father was?"

"Nope. She refused to talk about it, and after awhile I figured it didn't really matter so I stopped asking."

"Do you think she knew who it was?"

He set down the bottle and slowly turned red. "What the hell do you mean by that?"

"Nothing. Just trying to see how things stood." I had discovered one thing. You don't want to get Beef mad.

"Well, now you know. My sister was a good Catholic girl, and I don't want you to ever forget it."

I didn't point out that she had evidently taken at least one night off from being good.

He calmed down, took another gulp of beer, and continued. "She knew who it was all right. It was just some big damned secret."

"How can you be so sure?"

"Cuz the guy did the right thing by her. Aside from marrying her, of course. She got a check every month for support of Marty."

"You ever see the checks?"

A perplexed look preceded his "No."

"Then how do you know he sent them?"

"Because she said he did, and she wasn't hurtin' for money."

I finished my beer and asked, "Who's Uncle Ronny?"

The hardness returned to his face, and he sat up straight in the chair. "I don't know. That's the first I've heard of him."

"Not a relative?"

"Not in our family. And I oughta know. It was just me and Sis."

"Maybe the father's brother."

"Maybe."

"Or maybe a friend of your sister. You know how they always seem to get called uncle."

"Maybe. It really irks me. I figured Beth gave her that doll cuz she never lets go of it. Now I find out it's some slob. All the dolls I've given her, and she drags that thing from some stranger around."

"Doesn't sound like a stranger to me, Beef."

His eyes narrowed. "There you go again."

Crossing my arms on my chest and leaning back, I said, "I didn't mean anything by it. People are allowed to have friends you know." I hadn't noticed until now that the light from the setting sun had been replaced by lamplight from the street. I reached out and switched on the desk lamp.

"Yeah, I suppose," he said disgustedly.

I wasn't about to say it, but it crossed my mind that this big, mean junkyard dog was jealous. "He could've been the father, but your sister didn't want Marty to know."

"I don't think so. Sis was pretty firm about the fact that nobody ever needed to know. The guy is out there somewhere—he just doesn't have a name. That's why I'm hiring you." He looked perplexed and fidgeted in his chair. "There's just one thing."

"Shoot."

"Well, business is not that good. I've already got two mortgages on the joint. I—"

I waved my hand. "Don't worry about it. I'll do some nosing around and see what I come up with. If I get a line, we'll see where it goes from there." I didn't want to tell him that I was pretty well-off money-wise. With the inheritance and the insurance and the money I could get from selling the house, I could have afforded a much nicer office. Maybe even curtains on the windows. But I wanted to make it on my own.

"Thanks, Spence. But chow is on me." He gave me a quick look-over. "You could use a few pounds, you know." I thought my six-foot frame did okay at 190. Beef obviously disagreed.

"Throw in the chocolate cake and you've got a deal."

He laughed and we shook on it.

"I'll need to talk to Marty, Beef. When's a good time?"

"She gets home from camp by noon. Day care place. Any time after that. She'll be upstairs with Maria."

"Okay, tell Maria I'll stop by after lunch."

"Fine. Just keep it simple. I don't want Marty getting upset. And it's me that wants to know, not her. As far as she's concerned, she's got a daddy—me."

"Where did Elizabeth live, Beef?"

I got a hard look that would've melted lead.

"Why do you want to know?"

"Because I need something to go on here. The neighbors might know something."

He looked like he wasn't going to tell me and then gave me an address on Paulina. I jotted it down and then looked at him.

"Pardon my asking, Beef, but why do you want to know who the father is?"

"After Elizabeth died, the checks stopped. I had her mail forwarded thinking I would find out who it was. No more checks came."

"So whoever it was knew she had died."

"Right. And whoever it was could provide for Marty better than I can, and I'd like to see she gets it. She deserves more than what she gets from me." He squinted his eyes like he was thinking about something. I watched. It wasn't a pretty sight.

"I don't want you askin' her nothin' about that night—the night Beth died. She's forgotten about it. She spent weeks cryin' herself to sleep, and I don't want that startin' all over again."

"Okay, nothing about that night." I didn't want to upset her either, but I also knew that one day she'd remember. It wasn't something you could forget, no matter how old you were. And when she remembered, it would be nice to have something to tell her.

Beef pushed back his chair and stood up.

"Hey, Beef. How did she die?"

He turned and gave me a blank stare.

"Elizabeth, Beef. How did she die?"

"She just died, that's all. Everybody does sooner or later." There was no energy in his voice.

There was something here he was trying to stay away from, and I was going to have to find out what it was, but I knew I had to be careful. I wouldn't get any information out of an angry client and, at the moment, I was in need of some information.

"I have to know, Beef. I'm not going to publicize it for Christ's sake."

He stared at me for a good ten seconds, me holding my breath the whole time. About when I thought I was going to burst, he said, "She was killed."

I let out my breath. The barrier had been broken. I sat down on the corner of the desk, dangling one leg over the front edge, and asked softly, "What killed her, Beef?"

I watched as the look on his face went from defiant to puzzled. He was trying hard to find the right words. He remained quiet for a few more seconds and then said, "She was shot. Right through the heart. The coroner said she was dead before she had time to think about it."

I waited a minute while my shock wore off before I spoke. "That's not killed, Beef. That's murdered. Did they find who did it?"

He shook his head no.

"You know, the police don't look kindly on some PI nosing around in an open murder investigation."

He glared at me. "Nobody's asking you to. What I'm asking you to do is find the father. And anyway it's not open."

"Beef, it doesn't take much imagination to think that the father could be tied to the murder. Maybe they're one and the same. Maybe he got tired of paying the support or ten other reasons that we don't know about."

He waved his hand at me. "Nah. It was some jerk. That's all. She was in the wrong place at the wrong time and some jerk nailed her."

"Maybe, maybe not. What do you mean the case isn't open? It's not that old."

"Well, maybe—maybe it's open," he stammered. "But they're not doing much. They can't. It was just some jerk with a gun in his hand. Good luck finding him."

I stood up. "We'll see."

"We'll see, nothin'," he growled. "It's find the father or nothin'. If the two overlap, you come and tell me. I want this thing dropped. I've spent the last six months coming to terms with this and tryin' to forget that she's gone and I can't do anything about it. And now I want it left alone."

"Where did it happen?"

"At her apartment."

"The place on Paulina?"

I got another look. "No."

"She had two apartments?"

"No."

"Then?"

"Then, nothin'. She changed apartments. People move you know."

"Where was the new one?"

"You don't need to know."

"Maybe I don't, but I won't know that till I check it out. That's how this works. I don't have a magic ball. I have to follow all the leads I have, and her neighbors are a good place to start." I got the stare. "So?"

"So what?"

I took a deep breath. "Where was she murdered?"

He thought for a few seconds without changing the stare and then spit out an address on Hunter. I wrote that down too.

"Was Marty there?"

"No, she was with Maria."

"You went there?"

He let out a long breath. "The place was a dump. It was supposed to be a big secret but I knew about it. I finally got tired of knowing Marty was living there and was going to talk to Sis about it."

"You found her?"

"I walked in the door in the morning, and there she was."

"What did you do?"

"It doesn't matter. It's got nothin' to do with you."

"Beef. You dragged me into this. I can find out from the police report, but it'd be easier and somehow more meaningful if I get it from you."

He didn't respond.

"I'm not going to get in the way of an open police investigation. I'd just like to know."

He sat back down, his shoulders slumped. "I knocked and nobody answered. The door was unlocked so I went in."

He paused and looked up at me. I think he was hoping I'd be satisfied with that, but when I didn't respond he frowned and continued.

"I went in..." He took a deep breath. "It was a small joint. Just a living room and a kitchen stuck at one end, a small bedroom and a bath. She was lying on her side in the living room. First I thought she had passed out or something. Her back was to me. But when I got closer I saw the pool of blood and the look on her face. It was that blank stare that dead people get, you know like they don't give a damn about anything anymore, which I guess they don't."

His eyes had glossed over, and I knew he was looking at something that wasn't in the room with us.

"I saw the same look in Nam. Kids who got it without knowing it was coming didn't even have time to be afraid." He blinked and gave me a hard stare. "She got it quick—no warning." Then his jaw relaxed, and the lines around his eyes softened. "I couldn't stand that look so I reached down and closed her eyes." He said it like something someone would say in church during the sermon, quietly and reverently.

"Did the police come up with anything?"

"Nah. She wasn't important enough. They got better things to do."

"That's not true, Beef. Everything gets investigated. They just don't have the people to hit everything as hard. But I guarantee you if they found something it would be followed up."

His look said he didn't believe me. But it was true. Dad had always felt badly about the cases that didn't get solved and often complained that there wasn't enough money to hire the personnel he needed. Chicago was a typical big city with all the problems that come with it.

"Was the place upset any? Did it look like there had been a struggle?"

He got up again. "Find the father." He turned and stormed out of my office, leaving the door open behind him and my orders hanging in the air like sides of beef.

I took a deep breath, let it out slowly and went over to close the door. Until tonight all I had seen of Beef was a happy-go-lucky guy in a T-shirt and an apron. This side of him was a little unnerving and I had the feeling that there was something he wasn't telling me. Maybe it was none of my business or maybe I just didn't know how someone acted when their sister had been murdered. I'd just have to start digging and see what comes up. And sometime soon I'd have to have an off-the-record talk with Sergeant Powolski.

Chapter 5

I had a fitful night's sleep, tossing and turning and dreaming about winding roads when I was asleep and wondering why Beef didn't want me to look for the killer when I wasn't. It was a little before six. The night had not cooled things off much, and I lay in bed with the sheet twisted around my legs and tried to come up with another answer besides the two logical reasons that were written up on the wall in big letters. Either Beef was going to be on my tail waiting for me to find whoever it was and then plug him, or maybe he had killed her himself.

Statistically, the second made sense. Most people are killed by relatives or someone they know. But then he needed a motive and there didn't appear to be any. I knew he loved Marty, and, from the way he'd described closing her eyes, I knew he loved his sister too. I pulled my legs out of the sheet. And maybe he was nuts.

Knowing what I knew of Beef, the first option made more sense. I didn't buy Beef's story about coming to terms with his sister's death. He wasn't the type. He was the type for revenge. Either way, it bothered me and I considered turning him down. After all, I hadn't eaten any of the retainer yet.

But sooner or later Beef would run out of chocolate cake, and someday Marty might ask questions about her daddy and it might help to have the answers. And maybe someday her father would want to know about her too. I kicked off the sheet, swung out of bed, changed my shorts, and poured a glass of orange juice. The humidity had softened whatever finish was on the wood floor, and my feet made little thwack thwack noises as I walked across the room.

Marty got home from camp at noon. I'd have plenty of time to tie up some of the red tape my folks had left behind before I saw her. There were still bank accounts to be closed, insurance forms to be filled out, and a stack of mail I hadn't even opened yet. Then I'd talk to Marty and see if I could get a better feel for where this road was leading.

I grabbed a fast-food burger on the way to the bank. The temperature was 97 and they predicted it would hit 100. I liked the heat and tried as much as possible to live without air conditioning. But this was too much, so, on the way back, I stopped and picked up a window unit.

Back in the car, I turned the air to full blast, flicked on the radio, and pulled out into traffic. The first button was still set to AM 720-WGN, Dad's favorite station. I had grown up listening to the mostly talk format, and I still usually prefer that to music. Late at night they used to play big band music, and Dad and I would sit and listen and talk when I got home from dates. Now they had switched to all-night talk except for Saturday nights when Mike Rapchak still played the big bands. He always led off with "Girl Talk," Dad's favorite song. Dad had sent me tapes of the show when I was in the army. It was an anchor to home. Since I'd been back, I hadn't been able to bring myself to listen.

Me and this '65 Mustang went back to high school days. It was really Dad's car but he'd rarely used it. I can still remember how excited I was the day I turned sixteen and he handed me my own keys. Then, when I finished college, he signed it over to me for a graduation present and had it repainted my favorite color—just as light-blue as they could get, even lighter than a sky-blue popsicle. When I went into the army, we drained the fluids and put her up on blocks. Then, when I wrote that I wasn't going to re-up, Dad had her put back in street condition. She ran as smooth as ever.

I honked at some kids who were playing at the curb and pulled into a space in front of my building. When I got out and stepped into Mother

Nature's oven, I remembered why I didn't like air conditioning. The sudden shock of going from cold to hot and vice versa was like running into a brick wall.

The three kids who were usually raising hell in the yard were just sitting against the fence looking drained and beat. Score one for the heat. I lugged the unit up the stairs, installed it, and turned it to high. By the time I got home it would be cooled down, my feet wouldn't stick to the floor, and I could get a good night's sleep. After filing the morning's work on the pile on the desk, I headed for Beef's apartment above the diner.

Chapter 6

I climbed the back stairs and knocked on the screen door. In a few seconds Maria's smiling face appeared.

"Hello, Maria," I said as she opened the door.

"Hello, Mister Spence. Mister Beef tells me you were coming. Martha is waiting for you." She turned and led the way back to the playroom. As I followed, I admired the neat hair pulled tightly into a bun and streaked with gray and the bright, flowered dress that added to the warmth Maria brought into a room. I would have given about anything to have this happy, roly-poly Spanish woman for a grandmother.

Marty was sitting in the middle of the toy-covered floor coloring a picture. Next to her was her Raggedy Ann doll. I cleared a spot and sat down, but I wasn't quite sure what to say. How do you interrogate a kid?

"What are you drawing, Marty?"

"A house."

"Who is going to live in it?"

"Ann's mommy and daddy."

While she talked she stared at the paper and kept coloring.

"Isn't it for Ann too?"

She scrunched up her lips and furrowed her brow and, after a few seconds, said, "Sometimes. But sometimes she'll live somewhere else. And then they'll all move."

"Do you mean like you moved with your mom?"

She nodded yes and added, "And we were going to move again too."

I knew something was going on here. I felt like I was wandering down a dark, twisting path—one I wasn't quite sure I wanted to be on. I wanted to pick her up and hug her and tell her everything was going to be all right. But everything wasn't all right. This little girl's mother had been murdered, and she didn't know who her father was, and I had no magic to make her feel better. But she did have Beef and Maria, and I knew she would be well taken care of. She also had the shell she had built around herself, and she seemed to have transferred her problems to Ann. If I was going to get any answers, I would probably have to break down that shell and, as I looked at that fragile little girl at my feet, I decided that breaking down her shell wasn't something I was willing to do. For the moment she was nice and safe in there. Maybe at twenty-five or thirty she'd break into it on some therapist's couch, but that would be up to her. I didn't want someone breaking into my shell. I tried another path.

"Marty, last night you said Uncle Ronny gave Ann to you. Was she a present for your birthday?"

"No he just brought her one day."

"Did he bring you any other things?"

"He brought some coloring books and crayons too."

"Was Uncle Ronny related to your mother, like Uncle Beef was your mother's brother?"

She thought for a moment and said, "No, he was my friend."

"Did your mommy tell you to call him uncle?"

"No, he did. He said he was going to be our friend, and I should call him Uncle Ronny."

"Did Uncle Ronny come a lot?"

She got an angry look on her face and said, "One day Mommy told him not to come back any more. And he said he'd take me for a ride on a horse."

"Did he have his own horse, Marty?"

She shook her head no. "He said where he worked they had horses, and during the day they didn't use the horses so no one would know."

Finally she looked up, and I almost melted in the gaze of those bright green eyes. "Do you think you could get me a ride on a horse? Mommy isn't here to tell me no."

It was all I could do to choke out, "I'll see what I can do."

This was just great. Maybe I should have a new ad made up: PI will break down and cry if you get a kid to pull his strings.

"Do you remember what Uncle Ronny looked like Marty?"

She shrugged. "He looked nice."

"That's good. What color hair did he have?"

Another shrug.

"Was it like mine, or Uncle Beef's, or Maria's?"

She looked up at me and said. "It was your color, but longer. Uncle Ronny let me play with his ponytail."

"How big? Was he as big as me?"

"About like you."

I patted the top of her head and smoothed her black hair and told her to be sure to draw a good house for Ann and her family. She said she would.

I stood up and, as I walked out of the room, she said, "Don't forget about the horse."

I assured her I wouldn't. I couldn't. It was my only lead. That is if you didn't count a guy about my size with brown hair in a ponytail.

I said goodbye to Maria and walked back to the office thinking about horses. I had spent a good deal of my formative years at Linden Racetrack and Skyline Park. They weren't far from Elizabeth's second address. It might be a good place to start. But there was a better spot to get info on the track. I decided that tonight I'd pay a visit to the Blue Note Lounge and some of the sweetest jazz in the world. If horses were involved, old Blue Eyes Jackson would know about it.

Dad had taken me to the Blue Note ever since I was big enough to sit on a stool and had told me that there was so much blues in Mr. Jackson that, once he started playing, his brown eyes would turn blue right while I watched. To this day, I'd swear there were times when they did.

I had been avoiding the Blue Note and the memories that I knew would roll out when I opened the front door. But I had been avoiding long enough, and that would be the perfect place to start facing up to the past and start getting on with the present. I knew Dad would be there in spirit. I also knew that this time Mom wouldn't be waiting up for us with milk and homemade chocolate chip cookies.

I figured the next step was to see what the police had on the case. So, after making my way back to the office, which was too cold, I called the station to see if Stosh was free. He wasn't. I told the desk sergeant to tell Stosh I'd be in Thursday morning and to call if that was a problem. Then I took a nap.

Chapter 7

The Blue Note was located on south Stony Island Avenue. It opened at eleven for lunch and there would be music playing until they closed, and that was whenever the last person had gone home. During the day, pickup bands provided the entertainment, and they were worth hearing. Then at night, the quartet that had been there for as long as I could remember would take over. As far as I knew they didn't have a name. Blue Eyes called them the Four Play Blues. It had been awhile before I had figured that out.

Whatever they were called, they were simply the best in the world, and the people who dropped in to play with them proved it. Whatever big name was in town at the downtown clubs ended up at the Blue Note after they were done and joined the quartet on the little raised stage in the corner. I had seen Tony Bennett, Oscar Peterson, Joe Williams, James Moody, and many others. They played the big houses for money and the little one for fun.

It was nine thirty when I pulled into the parking lot and gave my five bucks to the boy sitting at the entrance outside of the shack. The kid started to reach for it when a voice came out of the shack.

"Hey, don't you be takin' that man's money. I slap you from here to Georgia, you take that five spot." The confused boy pulled away his hand like he had touched a hot stove and dropped back with wide eyes as Jesse shuffled out of the shack.

"You think I'd forget that baby-blue Mustang? How the hell are ya, Mister Spence?" he asked through a big smile as he leaned down through the passenger window.

I reached over and shook his hand. "I'm fine, Jesse. And you look great. There's not one more gray hair since the last time I saw you."

"That's cuz they was all gray last time you saw me. Been that way for twenty years. Stick her back there by the boss. I'll have the kid move Johnny's wreck." He yelled to the kid who moved pretty quickly for as hot as it was.

It was good to see Jesse again. And it was good to know that some of the good things don't change. He was still here doing what he did best and was happy doing it. I remembered what Dad had said when I first met Jesse: "That man is the best poker player you'll ever meet, and he can pick any lock in the city. It's a good thing he's on the right side." He was also one of the nicest people you'd ever want to meet.

I parked and let the heat in full blast as I opened the door. I could feel the beat of the music as soon as I got out of the car.

I walked in and got a strange look from the girl who took my ten for the cover. I stood at the edge of the foyer and looked the place over. It hadn't changed a bit. It was probably even the same smoke hanging in the air.

The quartet, drums, piano, upright bass, and sax, with soft-blue light dancing on its tarnished golden finish, was in the middle of "Satin Doll," and the muffled conversation was in rhythm with the music. As people nearest the door noticed me, they stopped talking and stared at me. As I remembered, Dad and I were usually the only White people in the joint. That hadn't changed either. Then a voice from behind the bar ended the stares, and the crowd went back to complaining about the weather.

"You gonna just stand there all night or are you gonna get your ten bucks worth and pull up a chair?"

I smiled and squeezed my way between the tables and over to the bar where Blue Eyes was balancing clean glasses three tiers high on the glass shelf over the liquor bottles. He put his tray down and held out his hand.

"Spencer Manning. I was about to come lookin' for you. I heard you were back in town, and I was startin' to think you forgot about us."

I took his hand and, by his handshake and the look in his eyes, I knew he was saying he was sorry about my folks.

"Could never forget, Blue Eyes. Just took a while to..."

"That's okay, kid. We all feel the same way. Your dad was one special person. Your mom too."

I just nodded. The last chord of "Satin Doll" hung in the air for a few seconds after the playing stopped, and the quartet took a break. The sax player, Lemon Walker, came over to the bar for his shot of Southern Comfort. His hair was all gray now, and he walked a little slower and a little more slumped than I remembered. I think these guys were around when the blues was born. He sat on a stool and then did a double take.

"Are these old eyes playin' tricks?"

"No tricks, Lemon," I said with a smile. "Nice to see you."

"You too, boy. Blue Eyes said you was done with the army. How did you get along all those years without the music?"

As far as anyone here was concerned, the Blue Note was the only place in the world where you could hear "the music." And they were right.

"It wasn't easy, Lemon. I listened to memories a lot."

"I hear that, boy." His grin faded. "Sorry about your folks. We know your old man is still listenin'." He angled his head back toward the corner booth.

"I know he is too. It's not somethin' you can just leave behind."

"That's for sure. That's plainly for sure." He threw back the shot and swung his leg off the stool. "You come over to the table and say hi, okay? The boys will want to see you."

"Sure thing, Lemon."

He winked and started to walk away. Blue Eyes stopped him, leaned over the bar and whispered something I couldn't hear but I knew what it was. When my dad had been coming here long enough, they had gotten to know him well enough to know that, even though he was a cop, he was just a level guy who liked good jazz, and they had consented to play his favorite tune, "Girl Talk." And after Dad got Johnny Ray, the bouncer and resident tough-guy, out from under a drug frame-up, they started playing it every night, whether Dad was there or not.

The DA had put together a case against Johnny that seemed airtight. But Dad had dug deep enough to find some cracks and the guy who built the frame. Since then, the quartet never missed a night. But I knew Blue Eyes had suggested that they skip it tonight. I said a silent thank you and put my elbows up on the bar. Little kids and old songs with memories attached. Some tough guy I was.

"The boys look the same, Blue Eyes."

"Now, Spencer, we both know that's a lie, but seeing as how I'm just as old as them, we'll keep right on pretendin'." He wiped the bar in front of me and set down a Schlitz. It was the first beer I learned to like.

"Thanks for remembering, Blue Eyes."

"Hey, a bartender don't forget, especially his friends. What you up to Spencer?"

I took a long drink. "Well, I've been tryin' my luck at the PI game."

"I heard somethin' about that."

"How'd you hear that?"

"Isn't much I don't hear," he said with a grin.

I laughed. "As a matter of fact—"

"Well I'll be damned," a familiar voice interrupted. "I thought I told that girl to watch who she let in here!"

When I was fourteen, Johnny Ray was the biggest man and had the whitest teeth I had ever seen. He still was. And, even though he must be in his sixties, it all still looked like solid muscle. I got off my stool and checked the teeth as I reached for his hand. They still sparkled. But I could squeeze harder now, so his grip hurt less than I remembered. Johnny was the bouncer and most of his bouncing was done with just a look. He let his 240 pounds do the talking for him.

"Let me look at you, boy." He moved back a step, rolled the cigar to the other side of his mouth, and shook his head slowly back and forth.

"I thought that army was supposed to make a man out of you. Hell, you're still White!"

I held out my arm. "Yeah, but I've got a helluva tan."

"Hey, come December, when you come around with my Christmas present, we'll see who's got a tan and whose is done faded."

I laughed and squinted as he held out his hands, palms down. I knew what was coming.

"C'mon, boy. Let's see if you got any faster playing soldier."

I took a deep breath. I was bigger and stronger, and my reflexes were army-trained to a fine point. I really didn't want to embarrass Johnny. "Not tonight, Johnny. I'm a little out of practice."

He showed his teeth and winked at Blue Eyes. "C'mon, Spencer. Wouldn't want word to get around that you run away from a contest."

I shrugged, held out my arms and put my hands in position under his with my palms up. I looked him in the eyes and waited.

"Go for it, kid."

"You know, those things work better when you light 'em."

He wiggled his fat cigar with his lips. "I'm tryin' to quit. But I gotta have somethin' in my mouth. Once a day I light up."

I went for it while he was talking. I missed. By the time I got my hands up and coming back down again, his were in his pockets. I was amazed. I also assumed that that meant he could handle a gun as good as ever. I tried again, and again, and then quit.

"That's it, Johnny. I don't want to embarrass you anymore."

"You try the top, kid."

I knew I couldn't escape so I held my hands out, palms down. And I concentrated—hard. And I got slapped—hard. "You win," I laughed. "If you like I'll take off my underwear and wave surrender."

He laughed. "Just once more, kid. You ain't tryin' hard enough."

I held them out again and concentrated—harder. I didn't get slapped any harder—he couldn't have. But this time, just for a little variation, he crossed his hands over and slapped my opposite hands.

"Get me another beer, please, Blue Eyes. If I'm this slow I might as well get drunk."

The crowd that had gathered while I was worried about embarrassing Johnny laughed and went back to their tables. Jazz and a sideshow for only ten bucks. Couldn't beat it. I let the foam hit me in the nose and took a drink. Blue Eyes set down a beer two stools away while a bartender I didn't recognize put the last drink on a tray for one of the waitresses. She smiled at me as she picked up the tray. It was one of those soft, warm smiles, full of things that don't go bump in the night. I smiled back.

I picked up my beer and slid off the stool. "I'm gonna say hi to the boys, Blue Eyes. When I get back I need to pick your brain a little."

"Sure thing, Spence. But pickin's about all you can do. Used to be you could have a whole meal in there but sometimes things just don't connect right anymore. Gettin' slow."

I laughed and followed the waitress across the room. She had on a tight, short, black skirt that left most of two dark, strong, well-shaped legs showing. They were a challenge. Not just to me, but to all legs everywhere. "Be like us," they said. "Just try." I had followed her a little farther than I needed when a familiar voice called my name.

"Hey, Spencer. She's pretty, but she don't know how to play the blues."

I smiled again as she glanced over her shoulder and barely puckered her lips. I turned and walked back to the table next to the bandstand.

"She doesn't have to, Bones. That's why they make records... so women who look like that don't have to play the blues."

He reached out and slapped me on the thigh. "You sure do know how to hurt an old man."

I shook hands with Bones Slattery, the bass man and then Marty Larkin, the piano player, and Lou Wright, the drummer. Along with Lemon they were known as "the Boys." Bones pulled up a chair and I sat down. When Dad had first introduced me, I thought Bones got his name from his physique. There wasn't much to him, and you could see every bone that wasn't covered. But, when we got back to our table, Dad explained that the name came from something Bones told every customer who was willing to listen. He said: "It sure would be nice of you folks to come back but you don't have to. From now on, you carry the music around in your bones."

We talked about old times and then, as some admirers stopped to say hello to the Boys, I excused myself and weaved my way back to the bar.

Blue Eyes made his way to where I was sitting and asked, "What can I do for you, Spencer?"

"Not much. Just a question about a case I'm working on. Can we go in the office?"

"What do you want to go in the office for?"

"Privacy."

He turned his head and looked at me sideways. "You still readin' those mystery books? There ain't nobody here who cares 'bout what we're talkin' about. Besides, I'm short-handed tonight. But, if you'd feel better, you can wait a few minutes till the boys start up again. Then I guarantee you nobody gonna be listenin' to *you*."

Chapter 8

A few minutes later, Marty sat down at the piano and started laying down some chords. One by one, the other three joined him and before I knew it they were well into "My Funny Valentine."

"You care for a refill?" Blue Eyes asked.

"No thanks. I'm the designated driver." I swirled the last swallow in the bottom of the glass.

"So, Spencer, what is it you think I might know?"

I took a breath, let it out through my nose, and shook my head. "It's not much. I'm looking for a guy named Ronny and so far the only lead I have is a little girl telling me that a guy named Ronny offered to give her a ride on a horse where he works. Brown hair, long enough to be in a ponytail, built about like me. He said he could do it during the day because they don't use the horses then."

"You got a last name?"

"Nope. That would make it too easy."

I got a look full of raised eyebrows and big round eyes.

"White?"

I pursed my lips, thinking that would have been an easy question to ask Marty. New kid in town. "I'm assuming yes."

"Care to fill me in?"

"Sure. I was hired by a guy whose sister was murdered not too long ago. She left a four-year-old daughter. She wasn't married and never told her brother, my client, who the father was. But the guy evidently sent checks every month to support the kid. After the murder the checks stopped coming."

Blue Eyes scrunched up his nose. He was thinking. "You're thinking the father did the sister? Got tired of signin' his name?"

"Maybe. Maybe not. I've got nothing to point either way."

"What'd the police come up with?"

"Don't know yet. I'm gonna have a talk with Stosh tomorrow morning."

"The brother wants to start the checks flowin' again?"

"That's probably part of it. The other parts haven't surfaced yet."

"Hmm."

We both listened to Lemon's haunting melody, and I wondered if Blue Eyes had forgotten what I was looking for. He hadn't.

"Where did this sister live?"

I told him—both addresses.

He grimaced at the second.

"Not the best part of the Garden City?" I asked.

"Kid, if that's part of the garden, it's where they store the manure." He thought for a few seconds. "'Bout your Ronny. How 'bout we figure he works over at Skyline. Post isn't till eight. If he works there he wouldn't have any trouble giving her a ride during the day."

"I was thinking the same thing. Name ring a bell?"

"Not to me. But I'm not the expert. Horses, yes. People, you'd better ask Johnny."

I turned to look for him and almost fell off the stool when I saw him standing right next to me. "You do magic now?"

They both laughed. Blue Eyes leaned close to me and lowered his voice. "We had some bad trouble a while back. Johnny was in back and some guy pulled a gun on me and cleaned out the register. Ever since, I got this gadget in my pocket with a button on it. Sends out a signal to Johnny that sets off a vibrator. Short push if I want to see him. Long if there's trouble."

"Nice." I explained who I was looking for to Johnny. "Sound familiar?"

He took hold of his cigar with two stubby fingers, pulled it out of his mouth and spit a wet glummy piece of tobacco leaf onto the floor. I always wondered how he managed to keep his teeth so white with all the damage those cigars must do. When he replaced the cigar, he said, "Maybe. But maybe the one I know ain't the one you're lookin' for. As a matter of fact, I hope he ain't."

"You got a name?"

The cigar rolled across his lips and settled in the left corner. "Ronny Press. Works at Skyline. And there ain't nothin' good about him. If you threw him in a pond, he'd float and you could scrape him off the top with the rest of the scum."

"White?"

"Yup. 'Cept he ain't got a nice tan like some folks I know." All of his teeth showed through his smile.

"What's his problem?"

He shook his head. "Just plain bad. Been arrested for a coupla things. Done time for some. Stab you in the back if you gave him the chance. If there's somethin' goin' down, he'll be close."

"Why do they let him hang around?"

"He don't hang around. He works there."

"Why do they keep him?"

"Cuz it ain't easy to find people to shovel shit."

"I guess not."

"Sound like your man?"

"I hope not. The one I'm looking for promised a horsey ride to a little girl."

Johnny grimaced. "All I got to say is if this guy promised somebody a horsey ride, it wasn't out of the goodness of his heart cuz there ain't no goodness in it."

Unfortunately, the guy sounded like a fit, but I hoped not. I'd trust Johnny's judgment on anybody. If he says somebody's rotten, they're rotten. And you can't get much more rotten than murder.

"Thanks, Johnny."

He put two fingers to his forehead, gave me a miniature salute, said to call if he could be of further use, and somehow managed to fade that big frame of his into the crowd.

"Nice toy, Blue Eyes."

"Yeah, Johnny's fun to have around."

"I meant the button."

"Yeah, that too."

I reached in my pocket and put a ten on the bar. Blue Eyes pushed it back. "Not in here you don't."

I knew I wasn't going to win, so I pushed it back and said, "Buy your grandkids some ice cream."

He picked it up. I had hit his weak spot. This was one sentimental guy. But I also knew about the sawed-off shotgun, which I assumed was now under the bar instead of in the office. And there was that slight bulge under Johnny's left arm. I sighed. Shit happens. Things change. The world goes on spinning, and the barrel of a gun still talks in capital letters.

I slid off the stool. "So long, Blue Eyes. Thanks for the tunes."

He shook his towel at me. "So long, Spence. Don't be a stranger."

"Not a chance."

When I got back to the entry, I got a smile from the girl behind what I guessed was bulletproof glass. I waved and walked out into the heat. If it would only cool off at night. The air was that heavy stuff that only moved when you forced your way through it. I was glad I had bought the window unit. At least I would get a good night's sleep.

I stepped back to the curb and stared at the big, blue neon lights above the door. It hadn't been as hard as I thought. But then that wasn't the hard part. That was just seein' old friends. Now I had to go home to an empty apartment. That was the hard part.

I got in my Mustang and turned on the Cubs game. They were losing to the Giants. It seemed like each game they invented a new way to lose in the ninth inning. The team that, on paper, was supposed to win the division, was fighting for last place. But this was what being a Cubs fan was all about. I was a Cubs fan because my father was a Cubs fan and his father was before him. Used to be it never mattered whether they won or lost. It was just a great place to watch a bunch of grown men playing a kid's game, drink beer, eat hot dogs, and soak up some sunshine.

But now there are big paychecks and something important is gone. The game had turned into big business. Ron and Ernie and Billy combined didn't make what some players make today. Used to be okay that they lost because they weren't supposed to win. But now the paychecks talk. They say this team is supposed to win. The dollar bill has taken over the Cubs. There will be no more great old names; there will just be big paychecks. The problem is, the big paychecks are still losing. Because the dollar bill can't change one thing—this is still the Cubs, and since 1908 they hadn't done anything besides lose. Must be something in the ivy.

I guess money talks. And I wondered if it wasn't talking to Beef. He hires me to find the father, then maybe he convinces the guy to start writing checks again, maybe pay off the second mortgage on the diner. Hell, there was some reason why the father wanted to be out of the picture. Maybe that reason still exists. Maybe it's still worth money. Maybe not. Maybe Beef was just doing it for the love of a little girl. Or maybe it was revenge. If some guy hadn't knocked up his sister, she wouldn't have moved to that dump and caught a bullet in the heart. Maybe. And maybe I needed some sleep.

Chapter 9

I woke up before six Thursday morning, felt the blanket pulled up around my chin, and thought I must be dreaming. Then I remembered I had turned the air conditioner to high when I got home last night. Sometime in the middle of the night I must have gotten up and thrown the blanket on the bed. The room was freezing. Stupid. I threw off the covers, turned down the air, took a shower, and pulled on a pair of jeans and a blue cotton shirt. Since coming home, I had been living in jeans. I had three faded pairs and one good pair in case someone invited me out to dinner. I laced up my running shoes and went to Beef's for pancakes. Sometimes I skipped lunch, but I never skipped breakfast.

I ate at the counter. Maria waved at me through the window of the kitchen, and Beef poured me a cup of coffee.

"You break the case yet, PI?"

"Sure, got it all wrapped up. You'll never believe it. So I won't bother telling you."

"Nothin', huh? Well, that's not surprising for a Cubs fan."

I dumped some cream in the coffee. "Hey, if you're going to get personal I'll have to say something about this coffee."

He leaned on the counter and looked tough. "I never said anything cuz you seemed like a nice guy, but we don't think much of you transplanted Cubs fans."

Several customers, all of whom I'm sure had "White Sox" tattooed on their rear ends, were waiting to hear my response. I didn't have any.

"Best thing you ever said," Beef smirked. "All I got to say is we got two series coming up with the Twins, and we're gonna make a run on first place." He walked back to the counter, picked up my pancakes and put them in front of me with a smug look on his face.

I took a bite. He turned back for some more orders. "I did get a lead on a guy who may be Ronny," I said. "I'll look into it today."

He nodded as he walked down the aisle.

I finished eating, walked outside, took a breath of hot air, and headed for my car. I waited for a minute after opening the doors before I got in. Only eight o'clock and the car was already an oven.

Twenty minutes later I pulled into the small lot next to precinct headquarters. It was usually tough finding a spot. This morning there were two. I took the first and the squad that pulled in behind me took the second. We got out at the same time, and I was pleased to see Rose Marie Lonnigan.

Rosie was four years older than I and had joined the force a year before I had joined the army. Her folks were friends of my folks, and Dad had taken her under his wing. But she didn't need much winging. She had a pretty face and a body that looked good even under that unflattering blue uniform. Underneath she had an attitude that said "Mess with me, and I'll break your legs." There were several guys staring at bars who hadn't bothered looking past the pretty face.

"Well as I live and breathe. If it isn't little Rosie Lonnigan."

"Hi, Spencer! I didn't get a chance to talk to you much at the dinner. I hope you know how sorry... I just wish... I mean I..."

"That's okay, Rosie. I know, thanks." I held out my arm. "May I escort you to the door?"

"I would be honored, sir," she said, taking my arm.

"How's the detective business? You doing okay?"

"Sure. I love it. Wouldn't want to do anything else." I didn't want to tell her something else was about all I'd been doing.

I opened the door and followed her in.

"You just visiting?" she asked.

"Yes and no. I need to see Stosh about a case I'm working on. I'm hoping he'll be able to give me some information."

She gave me a coy little smile and tilted her head. "Stosh?" She said it with a real long O. "Do you mean the respected Lieutenant Powolski?"

I shook my head. "Afraid I'll never be able to get used to that. He'll always be Sarge to me."

She waved to the desk sergeant, whom I didn't recognize, and said, "I've got to stop at the little ladies room. Let's have coffee, Spencer. Anything I can do let me know."

"Thanks, Rosie." I started to walk away.

"Hey, Spencer."

Rosie turned to me with her arms folded across her chest and a challenging look on her face. "Care for a rematch?"

For as long as we had known each other Rosie had made it a goal to shoot better than me. We hadn't shot since I left for the army but the last time she had come close. I would do everything I could to keep her from winning, but I would be thrilled if she did.

I laughed. "Sure, kick a guy when he's down. Do you know how long it's been since I've picked up a gun?"

"So practice. As much as you like. As a matter of fact, I'm going to the range this afternoon. Why don't you come along?"

I had nothing better to do, and I knew I should get some time in, so I accepted.

"Pick me up here at three." She turned and, over her shoulder, said, "I'll have them put up the big targets for you."

I watched her walk away and wondered for the hundredth time why we had never gone beyond friends. Maybe because we were such good friends. Why ruin a good thing? But there was something there. I'd kissed her once. A long time ago. She'd kissed me back, looking up at me with big blue eyes glistening with the start of tears. Then she ran away. We never brought it up and that was our first and last kiss. I took a deep breath and pulled my eyes away from the door where she had disappeared.

Before I went upstairs, I stopped to see Evelyn in records. She had to be close to retirement, but if they had any sense they wouldn't let her. She'd been there as long as I could remember, and anyone would readily admit that the place wouldn't run without her. Used to be that every case went through her hands. Anybody wanted to know anything, they asked Evelyn. If she didn't remember, she knew where to find it. Several years ago, when computers took over the record-keeping, Dad wrote that they'd hired her two assistants just to keep things straight. Evelyn wasn't happy about that but she had to give in to progress, not to mention an increase in crime.

I quietly opened and closed the glass door and tiptoed up behind her.

"Anything I can do for you?" she asked as she continued to type.

"You still got some candy for a kid with a sweet tooth?"

"Bottom drawer."

I opened the drawer and took two pieces of peppermint out of the jar.

She reached out and slapped my hand. "One piece. For cryin' out loud, won't you kids ever learn!" She stood up and gave me a bear hug. "You look great, Spencer," she said with a wide smile.

"Thanks, Evelyn. You look pretty good yourself."

"Stosh told me you were stopping by. I was hoping you'd peek in." Her smile turned into a frown. "If there's anything I can do... I know! You could probably use some home cooking. Just give me a day's notice, and let me know what you want to eat."

"Thanks, Evelyn, I'll do that."

"Well, back to my friendly computer. Don't be a stranger."

"Not a chance." I gave her a kiss on the cheek and let myself out.

Chapter 10

I took the stairs two at a time and bumped into Stosh as I rounded the corner. He managed to get out of the way of his coffee sloshing to the floor. He stared at me with a look that nailed me to the wall. I hurriedly got a paper towel from the nearby coffee cart and wiped it up. He was still staring.

I held out my arms. "Am I forgiven?"

"Kids. Everything's such a hurry. You know, when I was a kid..."

I held up my hand. "Yeah, I've heard. You want to continue this at your desk? You know, the one with the Lieutenant nameplate on it?"

He scowled. He had been happy being a sergeant and had turned down several promotion possibilities. A year ago, Dad had written that Stosh's wife was ill, and he finally accepted the promotion because he needed the extra money. She had died six months later. I half expected him to give back the promotion.

I stopped to shake several hands along the way to Stosh's office and had to run to catch up. His cubicle was at the far end of the room which had been organized into a maze. I would have lost him if I hadn't been on his heels.

"This business or pleasure?" he asked.

I smiled my "aren't I a nice guy" smile and said, "It's always a pleasure to see you, Stosh."

"Business. Okay, what can I do for you?"

"I'm looking for somebody, and it kinda overlaps a case that came in here a while ago."

He sipped his coffee. "Who you looking for?"

I screwed up one side of my face. "Well, I don't have a name. That's part of the problem."

"I'd say that's all of the problem. You're looking for somebody, but you don't know who it is." He shook his head. "And somebody pays you to do that? Boy, you PIs got it tough. You just hang out a shingle, come up with a fancy patter and a two-step that keeps everybody guessing and life's a piece of cake. Unlike us poor civil servants who gotta take tests to get our jobs and then get to sit behind a desk and watch you guys dance."

I crossed my arms and gave him my best disgusted look. "Is there a big finish to this number?"

"That's the trick about this job, kid. There's no big finish, just a new face floatin' in the water." He laced his fingers together around the cup and looked at me. "I assume you're gonna explain this a little."

I sat down on the edge of the desk. "A few months ago—"

"Hey. This is a Lieutenant's desk for chrissake. A Sergeant's desk, who cares? But this..." He spread out his hands over the old beat-up oak desk covered with piles of paper. "Let's have some respect." A smile spread across the tough, gravelly face, lined with years of seeing everything there was to see. "Pull up a chair from across the aisle. Maloney's in the hospital with an ulcer."

I did and sat down. "A few months ago, a lady by the name of Elizabeth Williams was shot to death in her apartment over on Hunter."

Stosh nodded, leaned back in the chair, and folded his hands on his stomach. "I remember. Not one of your finer residences."

"That's what I was told. Anyway, she had a four-year-old daughter named Martha. Evidently she was never married and was the only one who knew who the father was. The kid is living with her uncle now and he'd like to know."

While I was talking, Stosh pulled a file out of the cabinet next to his desk and leafed through it until he came to the page he wanted. I watched in silence as he refreshed his memory.

He had put on his glasses and now looked at me over the rims. "This uncle would be this Beef, right?"

"Right."

"Well, I'll be."

"What?"

Stosh stretched his neck and scratched his Adam's apple. "At the time, I didn't buy the story that the guy didn't know the father. He told us his sister got monthly checks that paid for the kid. Maybe that's what she told him but I doubted she got any checks. Didn't much wash with her hookin' in a rundown fire trap. This Beef had the mail forwarded to his address, but no more checks came, or so he told us."

"Doesn't mean there weren't any checks."

He folded his arms on his chest. "Okay, Mister bigtime PI, what's it mean?"

I shrugged. "Could be the father heard about the murder—read about it in the paper."

"Or it could mean the father did the murder," he said.

"Could. Or it could mean the father was hit by a bus the next day."

"Maybe he had dinner in Chinatown and got run over by a rickshaw."

"Too bad I'm not Charlie Chan," I said. "I'd have this solved in no time."

A detective stuck his face in the cubicle and waved a folder. Stosh held up a finger and nodded.

"I assume you checked her bank account," I said. "Any regular deposits?"

"Nope. We went back two years and there was no pattern. Doesn't mean much though. She could have cashed checks."

"Anything in her personal effects?"

"Nope. Besides some clothes and toys, the place was pretty empty. A drawer had drawer-type stuff, a checkbook with less than twenty bucks in it, and forty bucks lying on the desk."

"Doesn't that seem strange?"

"What's strange about it?"

"Where's all her stuff? Records, kid's drawings, stuff like that."

"You're talking about people with normal lives. People like that don't keep stuff. Life is too transient."

"But she wasn't like that. She had a normal life."

Stosh shook his head. "Not at the end she didn't."

I knew that. Something had changed her life, but it didn't have to change her, especially since she still had Marty.

"Can we back up to something you said?" I asked.

"Sure."

I didn't know how to ask without sounding dumb so I just said the word. "Hooking?"

Stosh's eyebrows raised. "Something your client didn't bother telling you?"

"I guess not."

"Yeah, hooking. That's mostly the profession of choice in that neighborhood."

"You sure?"

"That's what I would suspect. It was also confirmed by a neighbor who is in the same profession."

"Okay. Then it could have been a john looking for money."

"Sure. But there was the forty bucks, probably the night's take, sitting in plain view, so probably not."

"Where's the checkbook?"

He scanned the file. "Personal effects turned over to the brother."

"Do you buy Beef's story now, Sarge?"

"Lieutenant, kid. But between you and me, Sarge sounds better. I'm more likely to buy it since he hired you to find the father. If he's willing to shell out cash, then, yes, I'm buying it."

I didn't bother telling Stosh that the cash being shelled out was in the form of meatloaf and pancakes. I leaned forward and put my elbows on a pile of paper. "Any of the neighbors shed any light on it?"

"People in that neighborhood are like the three monkeys. Hear nothing, see nothing, say nothing. The broad next to her worked with her at a bakery. She claims not to know anything about making a living on the side. Not one of your finer citizens. We checked Ms. Williams' previous address. Nice place. Kind you wouldn't mind inviting your mother to dinner to. None of the old neighbors knew her well but they had nice things to say. Quiet, minded her own business, pleasant, dressed well, cared for her daughter. Seems she was somewhat of a loner. Nobody could remember her having friends over."

I sighed. "You sure she was hooking?"

"Fairly steady stream of men coming and going. I don't think she was serving tea." He shrugged, kind of apologetically. "We know it goes on there, but there's never been any trouble, and we're kept plenty busy dealing with what goes on in plain view out in the streets. As long as they keep it behind their doors..." He waved his hand.

"Beef seems to think his sister was a nun. He didn't like my suggestion that she might not be quite as pure as he thought."

"I bet. But I thought you didn't know about the hooking?"

"I didn't. I made the suggestion based on a child out of wedlock."

"Oh yeah."

"You got a name for the neighbor and the bakery?"

"This look like a library?" he asked snidely. But he gave me the names. "This Beef tell you why he wants the father found?"

"Said the guy can probably provide for Marty better than he can."

"You believe him?"

"I'd like to. Don't you?"

He blew air out his nose. "I don't believe or not believe anymore. I just find the facts. Is he taking care of the kid okay?"

"Sure. I don't know much else, but I do know that. He loves Marty."

"I hope so, Spence. It was my opinion at the time that she should have been left in the county home a while longer—see what turned up."

I straightened in the chair. "Why leave her in a home when she's got a relative. Why put her in a home in the first place?"

Again the raised eyebrows. "Seems like I know more about your client than you do."

I sighed. "What now?"

"Well, maybe that your client was—is, a suspect in a murder case."

Up till now, I'd had what I thought were some fairly good comebacks, but this time I was stumped. "Suspect?"

"Capital S. We had him in for questioning, but had to let him go. The bullet came from a twenty-two. Beef just happens to own one. We checked it. Not a match. But that doesn't mean he didn't use another gun. He gave us the description of a john he saw leaving the place but whoever that was was long gone. So, we got nothing concrete, but he's still the only one we've got and I haven't given up yet."

"All this just because he found the body?"

"No. All this because he had a huge fight with his sister the night of the murder, slammed the door and ran out. The next-door neighbor, uh..." he checked the file, "Brewer, heard them yelling and saw him in the apartment. One of the neighbors on the floor below said she was just about to call the cops. Said it was as loud as the el trains. A little exaggerated, I'd guess. Had her door open a crack and saw him come charging down the stairs. Coroner puts the time of death between ten and two. Beef was there between ten and ten thirty. The lock on the door was broken. Brewer says he broke it. He says he didn't. She says the door opened and this guy ran out."

"Did the neighbors hear a shot?"

"Nope. But when the trains go by you wouldn't hear a shotgun go off."

Stosh let his chair squeak back to straight. "Why do you think your client didn't bother telling you a few pertinent facts?"

I shook my head. "He seems to have his own agenda and doesn't stray from it."

"Listen, Spence. I know you are looking for the father. But you could get messed up in a murder investigation and with a client who isn't cooperative. I don't feel real good about that."

"Don't worry, Stosh. If it looks like the two cross, I'll get out of your way." I stood up. He didn't.

"Your getting in my way isn't what bothers me. Your ending up on a slab is."

I smiled. "That doesn't appeal much to me either. I promise to be careful. What was the fight about?"

"Don't know, he wouldn't say. But whatever it was could give him a motive. And if I find one I'm gonna get more serious about this."

He stood up and put his arm around my shoulders. "You wouldn't by chance have run into anything that I'd like to know have you?"

"Hey, I'm new at this. I don't even know where to start." I laughed.

He squinted his eyes and said, "Sure. If you do, call me."

"What do you mean, call you? You never saw Mike Hammer calling Captain Chambers with every piece of information that came his way."

He grinned. "No, but then Pat never changed Mike's diapers either. Seriously, kid. You're not some tough guy who grew up in the Bronx. You're too nice for this kind of thing. There's already one person dead in this case and, if there's going to be two, I don't want it to be you. I kind of made a promise to look after you if anything ever happened."

I laughed. "Just what I always wanted—a Polish baby-sitter. Okay, I'll call. And I won't do anything dumb." By not telling him about Ronny I wondered if I already had. But I didn't even know if it was the right Ronny. And I had to do some things for myself. Besides, if I had to, I could stop being nice for awhile.

He steered me out into the hallway. "You got a gun, Spence?"

"No. Haven't gotten around to it yet."

He shook his head. "Just remember, the bad guys do. If you'd like to get some practice in, give me a call and I'll take you over to the range. I'll spot you fifty points."

"If we shot today that wouldn't be enough to make it a fair fight. But you're going to have to stand in line. Rosie already threw down the gauntlet. I'm going to practice with her this afternoon."

"Good, I'd hate for anyone to say I took advantage of you. You can use all the practice you can get."

He knew I was as good with a pistol as any man on the force and had a slew of army medals to prove it. He also knew I was out of practice and I knew he was telling me that, if I was going to be in this business, I'd better get some.

We walked to the main hall. He looked around like he was looking for someone. There was no one there. "By the way," he said, "I put your dad's personal revolver and a box of ammo in the wall safe at the house. It's cleaned. Do the paperwork if you're gonna use it."

"Thanks, Stosh." We shook hands. "Let's have dinner one night soon."

"You got it, kid. Any time you want."

"So long, Sarge."

He winked.

I was halfway to the stairs when I heard a loud crash and the sound of breaking glass. I turned and saw Stosh running down the hallway. I followed. The sound of a man yelling was getting louder. I could make out something about not knowing they were cops and they had no right keeping him.

I was right behind Stosh when he rounded the corner of the cubicles that opened out into the main room full of desks and chairs. A group had gathered over by the windows. We got closer and, as Stosh pushed people out of the way, I saw what the problem was.

A young kid in tattered jeans and a T-shirt, unshaven and seedy-looking, hands cuffed behind his back, was standing by one of the windows. The window was smashed with jagged shards still hanging in the frame and pieces of glass scattered on the floor. Blood running down the kid's face didn't make it too hard to figure out what he had broken the window with.

A detective I didn't know stepped toward the kid and reached for his arm.

The kid twisted, pulled his arm away, and yelled, "Don't touch me, asshole."

The next yell came from Stosh.

"Don't touch him, asshole! Where the hell's your head, Barker? Everybody back off and give him some space." Without taking his eyes off the kid, Stosh asked, "This your arrest, Barker?"

"Yes, sir," Barker answered sheepishly.

The kid watched warily. Nobody moved, including him.

"What's the charge?" Stosh asked.

"Possession—cocaine."

"User?"

"Yes, sir," said Barker. "He was shooting up when we entered."

"So we know the holes in his arm aren't from volunteering as a pin cushion at the senior center. My suggestion would be to stay away from that blood. Call an ambulance." He addressed the kid. "You've made a helluva mess here, kid. That's a taxpayer's window you broke. Why don't you have a seat."

"Bullshit. They broke into my place without due cause. I know my rights. I'm gettin' outta here if I have to jump out of this window."

"If you want out of here so bad, I guess you gotta try, but I wouldn't recommend it. In case you haven't noticed, you're two stories up and, at the moment, you don't have the use of your hands."

The kid tried to look at his hands like he wasn't aware of that, but he couldn't find them. He seemed to have no idea they were behind his back.

Stosh continued. "If you're going out the window, at least wait till the ambulance gets here. I'd rather not have to deal with the crowd all your broken bones in a hump on the sidewalk is going to attract. And if, by some miracle, you're unlucky enough to be alive, you're still gonna have to come back here somewhere along the way. So, how about sitting down and getting it over now?"

The kid tilted his head and squinted his eyes but said nothing.

Stosh pulled out a chair and sat down. "Okay, I can wait."

I could just make out the sound of a siren in the distance.

The kid flinched as he noticed the ambulance. "Okay, okay," he said haltingly. "I'll sit, but I don't want that asshole near me."

"Fine," said Stosh as he stood up and offered the kid his chair. "Rodriguez, take over here, please. Let the medics do whatever they have to do, and somebody get Mac up here to clean up this mess. Tell him there's blood."

Stosh turned and walked toward me as everyone else went back to work. I walked with him back to his office.

"Nice job, Lieutenant."

He sighed and shook his head. "I don't know what I'm more mad at, that screwed up kid or my stupid detective. Glass and blood and he chooses that time to stop thinking. If I wasn't getting rich off this job I'd quit."

"Right. And the Pope's going to convert to Judaism. Me, I'm going hunting."

He gave me a long hard stare. "Watch your ass. You never know when there's trouble waiting around the corner. Sometimes, from a distance, it looks like fun. But, when you get closer, it just makes you wanna puke."

"Thanks for the pep talk and the wonderful imagery. If I get to that point, I'll call."

"Oh, you'll get to that point, all right. It's not a matter of if—it's a matter of when. And after you're done puking you can decide how you like the taste that's left in your mouth." He turned into his cubicle and disappeared.

On my way to the car, I thought about my next move. The race track was the next obvious step, but first I wanted to have a talk with Beef. And on the way I wanted to drive by Elizabeth's two addresses.

Chapter 11

Her old address was a large, U-shaped apartment building that took up the whole end of the block. It was nicely landscaped and had a high, wrought iron fence across the courtyard in the center. There was a gate in the middle with a callbox on the right side. The gate wasn't closed. The building was brick with wood trim and had a nice homey look to it. Stosh was right in his assessment. I assumed he would be right about the other place too. He was.

About four blocks away from 2415 S. Hunter the neighborhood started to change drastically; garbage in the streets, boarded-up buildings, tough guys pitching pennies on the sidewalks, and old men with brown paper bags rolled up in the shape of a bottle. Ragged kids played in front yards of dirt and weeds.

I stopped across the street from 2415 and felt like I had been kicked in the stomach. It wasn't the worst on the block; as a matter of fact, it was one of the best. But still, it was not pleasant knowing Marty had lived there. It was an old, stone three-flat and, compared to the previous residence, it was a slum. If Elizabeth was the nice person Beef and her neighbors thought she was, then I had a puzzle to solve. What would make a nice girl desperate enough to move into this dump?

I put the Mustang in gear, did a U-turn, and headed north to the restaurant.

There was only one customer in the joint, and Beef was chatting with him at the counter. I walked in, headed for my booth, and motioned for Beef to join me. He did. The guy at the counter threw down some coins and left.

"You like some coffee?" he asked.

"No. I'd like an explanation."

He slid into the booth. "Of?"

"Of why you forgot to mention a few things."

"Like?"

"What is this, *Password*? Like, imagine my surprise when I discovered that the police had a suspect in your sister's murder and that suspect was, and is, you."

"Oh," he sighed. Then he got tough. "I thought I told you to stay away from that."

"Yeah. And now I know why."

He stared at me for a few seconds before he continued. "I got nothin' to hide. I sure didn't kill my own sister. So I figured it wasn't worth bringin' up."

"Anything else you didn't figure worth bringin' up?" All I got was a cold stare.

I nodded. "Sure, I get it. If you didn't bring it up before and I haven't run across it, then you continue with the clam routine. Mind if I go over what you told me last night?"

He shrugged.

"You said you went there in the morning and found her dead. Now I know you were there the night before. You had a fight sometime between ten and ten thirty. Was she alive when you left?"

"If I say she was, what's to make you believe me?"

I tried the shrug routine. I wasn't as good as he was. "Not a thing. But at least I'd have the current story."

"She was alive. I wouldn't kill my own sister, for chrissake. She was all I had left."

"Wrong, you had her and Marty. Now all you've got is Marty."

He fiddled with the salt shaker.

"What was the fight about, Beef?"

"Nothin' that makes any difference. It was a family problem."

"Like with her making a few extra bucks at night?"

He slammed his fist on the table and knocked over the salt shaker. "I told you she wasn't that kind of girl. She never—"

"Cut the crap, Beef. I'm tired of this holier-than-thou routine. She was turning tricks at night to make a few extra bucks. That doesn't make her bad. She was probably a good kid who got in a jam and needed extra money and saw that as a way out. Her morals don't interest me. But I just took a tour of her last two addresses, and what does interest me is what happened to bring her from somewhere in the middle of the ladder to the bottom rung."

After a deep breath that let out the toughness, he said, "Yeah, I wondered about that too." He pushed the shaker around the table with his right forefinger. I watched. "I figure the father quit sending the checks for some reason, and she had to move."

That seemed like the logical answer. If so, what had happened to stop the checks? Could be the father was dead too. Now that Beef had calmed down, I figured I'd try again. "Was that what the fight was about, Beef? Her night employment?"

He looked puzzled for a second. "Oh yeah, sure."

I had the feeling I had just given him an easy answer, but I played along anyway. "Did she say why she did it?"

"She said she needed the money and was looking for a night job when some friend at the bakery told her about this building where she lived that would save her a lot of rent and give her a chance to make some easy money. When I asked her why she didn't come to me, she said she knew I had taken out a second mortgage on the joint and was having money trouble myself. I told her I would've sold the joint rather than have her live in that dump. She said that's why she didn't ask. I shoulda known something was wrong when she asked me to watch Marty overnight more often. And she used to have me and Maria for dinner. That stopped when she took the night job."

"She told you she was taking a night job?"

He nodded. "She said she needed some extra money and was going to work nights at the bakery."

"Did she tell you she was moving?"

"No. I found out by accident one night. Marty had forgotten her doll, and I told her I'd drive her home for it. We got to the old place and she said she didn't live there anymore. She said her mommy taught her a new address. She rattled it right off. We drove over there and I couldn't believe it. My sister and Marty living in that... that..."

I could see the disbelief and the pain in his face, and I could tell how tough this was for him. Whether his sister was a "good girl" or not, Beef sure had thought she was. And that was all that mattered. After a minute, he continued.

"I wanted to shake her and ask her why the hell she had moved there. If only I hadn't been crying 'poor me' about that second mortgage. Maybe she would have asked for help. I figured she had a good reason for moving there and hadn't told me cuz she was embarrassed. And she would have been even more embarrassed had I walked in on her. So, I did what I figured was the next best thing—I kept Marty at my place as much as possible."

I let him sit in silence. I could tell he felt guilty as hell but nothing I could say would do any good. Guilt isn't something someone else can wave away. All I could do was try and get at the truth. I had to keep giving him little pushes, but not hard enough that he'd tell me to go to hell.

"So the night of the murder you finally went over to talk to her? Did you know then she was hooking?"

He gave me a blank stare. "What?"

"The night she was killed," I said emphatically, "You finally thought it was important enough to talk to her to risk her knowing that you knew about the new place?"

Knowing I was putting words in his mouth, I watched his face carefully. The vague look suddenly left when he remembered what the new story was. I figured anything he said was better than nothing and maybe one of these times the truth might come out by mistake.

"Yeah, that was it. I decided that wasn't a good place for Marty, and, no matter what Sis thought, they were moving in with me."

I had no doubt he would make that offer, but I figured he would have made it before and there was still something he was leaving out.

"So, what happened that night?"

"I drove over there and knocked on the door. Nobody answered so I knocked again. Then she asked who was there. When I told her, I heard a noise inside, and she said she'd be right there. She sounded afraid. I was about to knock the door down when it flies open and this jerk comes runnin' out yankin' up his pants." He turned sideways in the booth, his knee up on the cushion and stared out the window. "If I hadn't of been so shocked, I would've killed the guy."

Beef was breathing hard and his face turned red. His left hand was clenched in a fist and the veins were popping out on his forearm. The guy was lucky that Beef had hesitated or he'd be dead.

I needed to push a little more. "Could it be you broke the lock on the door?"

He banged his fist on the table, drawing looks from the clientele. "Who the hell are you working for? You're supposed to be on my side."

"Hey, if I'm going to help you I need the truth. And the lock is a big part of the story."

I got a blank stare. I also realized that if he didn't kill her but did break the door down, he left an easy in for whoever did. The guilt tied to that would be huge and he may never admit it. But Stosh was right— Beef was certainly capable of the deed.

"Okay, so what happened after you got in?"

"I told her to pack her things, that she and Marty could move in with me." He turned to meet my gaze. "She refused and the fight started. I told her there was no question—I'd be back in the morning to get her. That's when I found her." The red had drained out of his face leaving a blank mask of pain.

"So the fight wasn't about hooking?"

I thought his face looked like a chameleon as it suddenly turned red again.

"What the hell does it matter what the fight was about? It was a family thing. What are you making such a big deal about anyway?"

"First, the cops are looking for a motive. Second, did it ever cross your mind that perhaps I wouldn't want to work for someone who played it like this?"

"Like what?"

"Like you feeding me what you think is important and making up half of that."

He flicked his wrist. "So resign, or whatever you guys do."

"You want to end our contract, say so. But that doesn't mean I'm gonna give up looking for the father."

"The hell it doesn't."

"The hell it does. A fellow can look into whatever a fellow wants. I just wouldn't be getting paid by you."

"Then why do it?"

"Cuz I've taken a liking to Marty. And if you end up in the slammer, it might be to her benefit if I found the father."

He pounded the table again. "Goddamn it! I told you I'm the only father she needs."

"Then why bother looking for the real one?"

He stood up and glared down at me. "I already answered that."

"I know. Cuz he's got more money than you. Is that the real reason?"

He stuck a large finger in my face. "Look. You want to find the father, fine. You don't, that's fine too. And I didn't do anything so how can I end up in the slammer?"

"Maybe I'll have you picked up for being a pain in the ass."

He turned and walked away.

"Am I fired?" I asked to the back of a white T-shirt. It didn't answer. I took that for a "No" and walked out into the heat.

Chapter 12

I waited for an opening in traffic and turned left off of Cicero and into Skyline Park, home of harness racing. Just to the south was Linden Racetrack where thoroughbred racing would start when the harness season was over. As I drove into the parking lot, I tried to envision myself walking over the rolling bluegrass of Kentucky. It didn't work. The din of traffic and the rotting factory smell and the brown sky full of pollution trapped in by the heat were too much to overcome. There were only a few cars in the lot and no one to stop me from parking. I locked up and walked between the grandstand and the dorms where the jockeys and hired help lived and made my way back to the stables.

I remembered coming here when I was small enough to have to hold Dad's hand while we waited in line to get in. Back then the place had an aura of magic that left me awed and enthralled. When Dad made chief he could afford the private boxes and prime rib. But I still chose to spend the day hanging over the rail at the finish line eating a hot dog with plenty of mustard. That's where the magic was.

I walked past the stables, casually watching old men go about their work and looking for the magic. I don't know if I had grown up or the real world had slowly encompassed me, but the magic was gone. I used to wander back here and daydream about the jockeys in their bright silks and the shiny, well-groomed horses. Now it was just another place—dirty and hot. And it didn't smell too good either.

Past the stables was the practice track where a driver was trotting his horse around the oval. Halfway down the straightaway a young kid was putting a fresh coat of white paint on the rails. Next to the track was a small corral where a girl who looked to be a little younger than me, stood in the center and, with a rope about twenty-foot long, guided a chestnut-colored horse around in circles. I put a foot up on the bottom rail, leaned on the top one, and watched as the horse pranced gracefully and rhythmically around just inside the fence.

Five minutes later she stopped the horse and, talking to him softly, gave him a hug around the neck. She had to stretch to do it. I had been admiring the horse but now I turned my attention to her. She had long auburn hair that was loosely pulled into a ponytail, was about five-foot-six, and looked to weigh about one-thirty. Her arms looked strong and I had no doubt she could handle the horse if he got out of hand. But the horse seemed to be reacting just fine to her soothing voice and gentle manner. Given the chance, I would too. Ignoring the sweat-stained shirt, there was a country-wholesome charm about her that made her very alluring. She was 100 percent woman without having to try at all. I walked around the corral to where she was letting the horse munch on apples.

"He's a beautiful horse," I said. "How old is he?"

She smiled. "Thanks. He's two. I was in the stall when he was born and have been with him ever since."

"He moves very well."

She laughed a laugh that was filled with bells and sunshine and made me decide that I wanted to come back and hear that laugh again. "He does just fine till he gets harnessed. Then he breaks stride and runs like hell. Daddy says he's trying to run away from the sulky and I should give up." Rubbing his nose, she said, "Maybe I will, but he hasn't beaten me yet."

"Good for you," I said. I watched as she fed him another apple and asked, "I wonder if you would help me?"

"If I can." She showed the horse she was all out of apples and rubbed his forehead.

"I'm looking for a Ronny Press. I wonder if you know where I might find him?"

Her light smile immediately turned into a scowl, and her jaw set hard and firm. "You a friend of his?" she asked with a look full of all the bad things you could get into one look.

"As of this moment, I'm neither friend nor enemy—just someone with some questions."

"Well then why don't you try the dark corners of hell? He'll be lurking in one of them."

I was too shocked to know what to say. This girl certainly didn't believe in beating around the bush. She must have noticed my stunned look because she immediately softened a little.

"I'm sorry," she said, without sounding sorry. "He's none of my business. He usually doesn't get here till mid-afternoon."

I smiled. "That's okay, you don't have to apologize. As a matter of fact, you've saved me the trouble of asking your opinion of him. Pretty much matches what I've heard before."

She returned the smile.

"Spence Manning," I said as I put out my hand.

"Kelly. Kelly Green. And no remarks about the name." She took my hand with the firm grip I would have expected of someone who worked with horses, but there was also a gentleness that came along with being a woman.

"Nice to meet you, Kelly. I think it's a pretty name." Her face was flushed red from the heat so I couldn't tell if she blushed or not. She clicked her tongue and led the horse along the fence to the gates, opened them, and walked back toward me.

When she reached me, I fell in beside her and asked, "Do you mind my asking why you're so down on Ronny?"

"No. And I might even answer if you tell me why you're asking."

We turned into a long barn with a double row of stalls. I thought for a few seconds before I decided that my gut feeling for this girl told me to tell her the truth. "I'm a private investigator working on a case, and my only lead seems to be Ronny Press." We passed several stalls in silence. Most were occupied and some had stablehands either spreading hay, filling water buckets, or sleeping against the dividers. "Do I get my answer?"

She looked up at me and made a decision of her own. "Yes, but not here. There's too many ears with tongues attached."

She stopped in front of stall number six, and I swung open the gate. The horse walked in by himself. Kelly took off the rope and hung it on a peg. Reaching into a bucket, she came up with a brush and a pick.

"This horse have a name?"

"Daddy named him City Slicker. He has a preference for the fast life—the horse, not Daddy," she said as she cleaned his shoes. "I call him Slick." She worked quickly and soon traded the pick for the brush and began combing his tail and mane. "He's probably not suited for harness racing, but so far I'm just as stubborn as he is."

I was wondering if I should ask her out when she solved the problem. "Do detectives eat lunch?"

"Only on Thursdays and Saturdays."

She raised her eyebrows and said, with a smile, "Well then this is your lucky day. I know a great Mexican restaurant just south of here. If you can wait till I'm done, we can talk there."

"Sounds great." I should have been glad to be getting some easy information about Ronny Press, but I found myself much more interested in Kelly Green. And the company would be nice for a change. I watched as she finished rubbing down Slick and got him some fresh hay and water. If I could get half the attention she gave to City Slicker, I would be a happy man.

All the while, she talked about her home in Kentucky where she had grown up on a horse farm and had developed a love for harness racing. She was twenty-seven, had a degree in Chemistry from Louisville, wasn't interested in basketball, and had gone to work right out of college for a research lab. After two years of missing horses, she quit, went back to the bluegrass state to train "Daddy's" horses, and hadn't thought of doing anything else since. Her father had two horses running at Skyline. Slick was just a hobby.

Kelly gave Slick a gentle hug around the neck. He snorted and lowered his head to nuzzle her shoulder. After slapping him on the rump, she closed the stall door.

"Give me a few minutes to clean up. I'll meet you where we came into the barn." She turned and walked out the near end of the barn.

I shuffled, hands in my pockets, back to the other end. I got a nod from a man pitching hay. Other than that, no one paid me any attention. I found a stool, parked it in a patch of shade, leaned against the barn, and waited for Kelly. She didn't take long. After twenty minutes, she reappeared in a flowery sundress, showing plenty of tan back despite the fan of thick hair that had been freed from the ponytail.

She offered to drive, and we headed for the back lot where the employees parked. We passed all the cars but one, a red Porsche sitting all by itself about twenty feet from the nearest car. No wonder she went home to Daddy. We got in, I oohed and aahed, she sluffed it off like it was just part of life in Kentucky, and, after turning the air on full blast, she pulled off the gravel and onto the blacktop drive.

Two minutes later we swung into a parking lot next to the El Pancho Restaurant. It was a dive if ever I saw one. Kelly chuckled and assured me that the food had no relation to the decor. It was going to take a lot of convincing.

Actually, it only took ten minutes and my first bite into the burrito that Kelly had insisted I order. She had ordered us the Giant Burrito Special, and it certainly lived up to the name. It was the largest burrito I'd ever seen and it was delicious.

While waiting for the food, I found out that Kelly's daddy raised harness horses and thoroughbreds, and she had been up here for almost a year racing at both Skyline and Linden. When the food came, both of us were too busy to talk.

I finished the last bite and decided, reluctantly, that I had had enough pleasure and should get down to business.

"So, what do you know about Ronny Press?"

After finishing her Modelo, dabbing her mouth with a napkin and settling back in the corner against the wall, she replied, "Not much, really. And then again, too much. He's the kind of guy you wish you didn't know at all. He makes my skin crawl just looking at him."

"What does he do there?"

She shrugged. "Not much that I can tell. About the only work I've seen him do is handling hay bales. I can't imagine the track pays him for just that, but he's always there. But then there are a lot of employees who don't do much, especially in this heat. The funny thing is he must have more money than most of the men because he doesn't live in the track housing. He's got an apartment a few blocks away." She fingered her glass.

"Nice place?"

She laughed. Her eyes sparkled. "It's not the Ritz, but it's more than the rest of them can afford."

"What's he done that turns you off so much?"

"Nothing really. It's just a feeling. Sometimes you just know when you look at someone. The police have hauled him and some of the others off for fighting, but that goes on. I don't know, maybe it's just me."

"Woman's intuition?"

"Something like that. I'm not usually wrong about people. What bothers me the most is he's got some kind of charm over one of the kids who works there. You saw him this morning. He was the kid painting the rail. Kid is the wrong word. I guess he's over twenty-one but he acts a lot younger. Bobby's not real smart but he's a good worker. Sometimes I get the impression he's a little slow. Unfortunately, he thinks the sun rises and sets in Ronny Press. And Ronny sure takes advantage of it. He orders Bobby around like he owns the track. And Bobby jumps when Ronny talks." She raised her eyebrows. "I wonder if that jerk has Bobby doing all his work for him?"

I swished an inch of beer in the bottom of my glass and said, "Could be, but that doesn't make him all bad. And it's not illegal."

She humphed. "Unfortunately. I'd love to see him behind bars."

"Are you afraid of him?"

She laughed. "No. Well, not face to face anyway. When I can't see him I worry. As a matter of fact, I think he's afraid of me."

I arched my eyebrows with unuttered surprise. "Intuition again?"

"No. Fact. A couple of weeks ago I turned a corner and came on him ordering Bobby to do some menial task he should have been doing. I was fed up and told him to leave Bobby alone and do his own dirty work. He took a step toward me and told me to mind my own business. I said it was my business, and when I raised my arms to fold them across my chest he actually jerked backward. I think he thought I was going to hit him!"

I smiled. "That sounds par for the course for a bully. You watch yourself, though. And, in the meantime, I'll have a talk with this Bobby. What's your feeling about him?"

"Bobby's okay. Like I said, not too smart. He hasn't been there too long, and he's fallen in with the wrong bunch. Easily influenced by the wrong kind of people. I've tried to drop some hints that he should stay away from Ronny but hinting hasn't worked."

"He had any law trouble?"

She sighed. "Yeah. We were talking one day and he told me about something that happened a little before he started working there. You probably read about it. He was the kid who..."

"Hey, Spence! I shoulda known I'd find you with a pretty lady."

Officer Miguel Hernandez slapped me on the back and winked at Kelly. I introduced them and slid over so Miguel could sit down.

He waved his hand. "No thanks. I'm picking up tacos to go. Stop in and say hi sometime."

"I was just there this morning, and I've got to go back this afternoon. Gonna do some shooting with Rosie."

His eyes got big and full of mischief. "Good luck. Nice seeing you, Spence. Pleasure, ma'am."

"See you, Miguel." I glanced at Kelly who was looking rather puzzled.

"I thought PIs didn't get along with the police," she said with a twinkle in her eye.

"I'm new at this. I haven't learned all the rules yet. But thanks for letting me know."

She smiled and raised her brows. I was pretty sure she wanted more information, but I, wanting to keep some mystery in our relationship, suggested we go.

We slid out of the booth. She insisted on paying for lunch, and I let her with the stipulation that she let me return the favor. She agreed.

Walking a half step behind her on the way back to the car, I had a wonderful view of that tanned back. I also wondered what was holding up the front of the dress. I figured there had to be some kind of physics law that worked it all out. On the way back to the track she was quiet, and I was busy changing my stereotyped view of girls who drove red Porsches. Kelly was a down-to-earth girl whom Mom would have liked a lot. And I always listened to Mom.

Chapter 13

I got to the station by two thirty. I wanted to ask Stosh about Ronny Press.

The front doors were open, and several large fans inside were blowing around hot air. Air conditioning is great when it works. A surly looking desk sergeant, whom I didn't know, looked up at me for a second. After seeing I didn't need him for anything, he wiped his neck with a handkerchief and turned his attention back to whoever was on the phone.

"Yes, ma'am. No, ma'am, there is no good reason why you have to be treated like that. But we can't do anything unless you file a complaint. We simply don't..."

I stopped at the fountain for a drink and then headed up the stairs. Stosh wasn't in his cubicle. As I was wondering where to look first, Rosie walked by.

"Hi, Spence. We still on?"

"Sure. I want to talk to Stosh first, but it should only take a minute. You seen him?"

"He was down the hall in the evidence room ten minutes ago. Don't be long. I'm not staying in this oven a minute more than I have to."

"Come on, how many jobs throw in a sauna as a benefit?"

"Yeah, I keep forgetting how great I've got it."

I've always loved surliness in a woman. But I couldn't blame her. I wasn't much thrilled about the heat myself. The last bank sign I saw read 102 degrees, and this old building was not far behind.

When I got to the end of the long hall, Stosh came out of the evidence room on my right.

"Let me guess," I said. "You guys figured you had it too easy so you turned off the air."

He humphed and dripped perspiration. "Damn thing's been off since ten. But it does put everyone on an even footing. Now my men are in just as bad a mood as the citizens we have sworn to protect."

"Men and women," I corrected.

I got a blank stare so I explained. "They're not just your men. In case you haven't noticed, there are women here also."

I was kidding. I knew he didn't mean anything by it. It was too hard to be sexually correct all the time. I knew Stosh well enough to know he judged his personnel only on the job they did. But I picked the wrong day to kid. It was just too damned hot. His response was to walk away.

"Hey, wait a minute, I got a question."

"Ask it while we're walking. I'm getting outta this hellhole."

"You know anything about a Ronny Press?"

With the reaction I got, the building might as well have exploded. He grabbed my arm, pulled me into the nearest empty room without caring whether or not my arm was still in its socket, and kicked the door shut with a bang.

I stood still, shocked by the suddenness and the angry look on his face. Before I could open my mouth, he opened his.

"Why is that name coming out of your mouth?" he spat.

"Just looking for some information. I didn't think—"

"And I'm waiting for an answer. And you're not leaving till I get one. Sit down."

I couldn't believe what I was hearing. I sat. He didn't.

"For chrissake, Stosh, I—"

"Spencer, right now. Where did that name come from?"

"He's the only lead I have in this case I'm working on. Why? Do you know him?"

"Yeah, I know him, and I'd rather you didn't. Tell me about it."

I filled him in and asked what he knew.

"You know how pond scum floats to the top? Well, if you scraped off the scum and threw it in a barrel, this guy would float to the top."

"I've heard that before. The guy seems to be somewhat short of a model citizen. But why the reaction? You about ripped my arm out."

He pulled out a chair and sat on it backward. I figured this was where he apologized for treating me so roughly. He didn't.

"This goes no farther than you. I don't give a shit who it is. That includes Rosie and Jesus should he pay us another visit."

He waited until I nodded. Then he checked the hall. No one was there.

"The name Jeffrey Grey ring a bell?"

"Of course. I may not give a damn about politics, but I know who the mayor of Chicago is." Jeffrey Grey had been mayor for about seven years, well-liked by the people, and respected by his opponents. He had earned the reputation of being fair, and he got the job done. His goal was to make the city a safer place to live. Stop the killing and stop the drugs, not necessarily in that order. "He has something to do with Ronny Press?"

"Unfortunately. They're half brothers."

I let out an appropriate whistle and asked why that fact led to my arm being twisted like a wet towel.

"We've been working with the feds on a drug connection for two years. It's led to Skyline Park. We know the end of the trail, and we're working our way back up." A tap on the window stopped the narrative.

I looked up to see Rosie pointing at her watch. I held up five fingers.

After waiting till she walked away, Stosh repeated his warning. "Not a word to her, Spence."

I didn't quite understand. "You mean she doesn't know about the investigation?"

"Of course she does." He stood up. "What she doesn't know is the connection between Press and the mayor. There are only three people in this department who do."

"Do you think the mayor is involved?"

I got another stare that meant shut up and listen. "Ronny Press has a record going back twenty years. In the beginning, mostly small stuff. But, as he spent more time in jail, he learned more and got better at his trades... burglary, theft, assault, breaking and entering. Pretty good at safecracking. Likes to play with knives."

"Drugs?"

"Not yet. But that's not to say a guy can't branch out. Most of his jail time has been in the south when he was younger. But he relocated and contacted his brother. The mayor met with your dad, told him the family story, and asked your dad to keep an eye on him."

"Looking for special treatment?"

Stosh straightened in his chair and wiped his forehead on his sleeve. "No. Just the opposite. He said where Ronny went trouble followed, and he wanted to be sure if trouble followed to Chicago that it got stopped before it started. He wanted us to know about the connection before we found out some other way and to let us know that he was behind us no matter what. What he asked for was, if there was trouble, that we let him hold the press conference if it came to that."

I shrugged. "Seems reasonable to me."

"Was to us too. Your dad was totally behind the man and agreed to keep it quiet unless something happened. He knew there are people who would try and make something out of the connection."

I nodded and looked at my watch. Five minutes were up.

Stosh continued. "Almost as soon as he was elected, the mayor started a big push against drugs. Extra manpower, overtime, special details. We've been making progress, and we're about to make some more. We've tracked a huge connection to Skyline and Linden and a few other places. We think Skyline is the key and we think Ronny Press is involved somehow, but we don't know how it's moving. The track is a pretty closed family. We've had two men working inside for six months, but nothing so far."

"Does the mayor know about the drug connection?"

"Sure. We keep him informed. And this is why we have to keep the connection quiet. If it comes out that they are related, the whole thing will be blown out of the water. I'm willing to bet the guys Ronny are working for don't know he's related to the mayor or they'd be pushing different buttons."

I didn't question Stosh's loyalty to the mayor, and I was inclined to join in myself, but a little nudging somewhere in my brain had to consider the possibility that it was a perfect situation for the mayor to protect his brother and to warn him before anything bad came down.

"What's the relationship between the two?" I asked.

Stosh shook his head. "I really don't know. The mayor didn't go into it and, as long as there's no trouble, I figure it's none of our business."

My eyebrows went up before I knew it.

"Don't give me that crap, kid. I've been at this game longer than you've been alive. I'm well aware that if they hated each other's guts we could have a different outcome than if they were pals. And if it becomes important, I'll find out. I've got a lot of faith in the mayor. All you have to remember is to keep your mouth shut and to stay away from Ronny Press."

"Are you telling me to drop the case?"

"I'd prefer it if you would sell encyclopedias door-to-door. You're less likely to end up in a box at an early age. But, since I know you're not going to give up that license, what I'm telling you is to come to me with anything. You got that? You see Ronny Press litter, you call me. Stay away from him. There's too much going on, most of which you know nothing about."

I pushed my chair back and stood up.

"Okay, kid?"

I nodded. "I have no desire to end up in a box, Stosh. If I need help, I'll call."

He shook his head. "Not good enough. You call before you stop to wonder if you need help."

I agreed, not because I really agreed, but because I knew I wouldn't get out if I didn't, and I knew Rosie was getting hotter every minute. I walked out, leaving Stosh feeling bad about twisting my arm.

I found Rosie at the end of the hall leaning on the railing at the top of the stairs. She fell in step with me and halfway down asked, "What was that all about?"

"He wanted my recipe for beef goulash. He's tired of eating frozen dinners. But don't tell the guys. He doesn't want anyone to know he's going in for gourmet cooking."

I got a one-word answer—"Shit."

Two hours later I was back in my air-conditioned mansion thinking about collecting some of my retainer. Shooting makes me hungry. I had torn the center out of several bullseyes. Times were when the tear would have been smaller, but I was satisfied. The gun had felt good in my hand.

I ate dinner, shot the bull with Beef, and asked Maria how Marty was. She was fine. She was upstairs with the sitter, Maria's niece, Linda. Maria invited me to stop by and see the spaceship Marty had made at camp. I said I would.

As I picked my way through the litter in the empty lot between the buildings, I heard a rumble in the distance. Six days in a row above one hundred and no relief in sight. The stalled air mass seemed to like it here.

I opened a bottle of IPA, sat on my antique, third-hand sofa, and thought about the case. There wasn't much to think about except that I had to talk to Ronny and Bobby. I did have one thing going for me—you knew you were getting somewhere if someone warned you to get off the case. Then I remembered it was supposed to be a bad guy who did the warning, and I hadn't met any bad guys yet—or had I?

Chapter 14

The early bird gets the worm. Luckily, I wasn't going fishing because, comfortable as I was in my air-conditioned bedroom, I didn't wake up until a brown-out stopped the steady hum of the window unit at 9:20. I had decided the night before that there was no urgency in getting to the track. Yesterday it had been late morning when Bobby was painting the fence. I figured today would be the same. I could talk to Bobby and still have plenty of time to get to Wrigley for the late-start Cubs–Cards game at three.

At 11:05, I was turning into the parking lot at Skyline. I made my way around back to the employee's lot, looking for a red Porsche. It wasn't there. I parked and walked through the stables to the rear practice track. Bobby was about fifty feet from where I had seen him yesterday.

With my hands in my pockets, I crossed the twenty-foot strip of grass to the gravel path which ran around the outside of the fence. Bobby was intent on his painting and had not seen me yet, so I stayed on the grass and moved to where I could get a better look.

He was wearing ragged blue jeans, a white T-shirt, and had a sweat-stained blue bandana tied around his neck. He was a skinny kid and, as good as I could figure from his sitting position on an old milk crate, not as tall as me. I guessed about five-foot-seven. Brown hair, bleached a little lighter than natural by the sun, covered up half of his ears. If I had to guess at an age, I would have said twenty. If he was older, he had that look of innocence that belies one's age. Kelly was right, it was a tough call. Strong shoulders and arms were evidence of the type of work one does at a racetrack. He wasn't working very fast, but, in this heat, I reserved judgment about his work ethic.

I watched for a few minutes and then stepped onto the gravel track and walked toward him. Not wanting to scare him, I figured the scrunching of gym shoes on gravel would let him know I was coming. I figured right. When I was about thirty feet away, he looked up with a smile on his face. But he must have been expecting someone else because, as soon as he saw me, his smile disappeared. And my warm, ingratiating grin didn't bring it back.

"Morning," I said, still smiling.

He nodded and wiped his forehead on a bare arm.

"You're doing a nice job on the fence."

No reaction, except for a stare that I couldn't read. It wasn't fear, but kind of a mild apprehension, a distrust that I had not yet earned. I put it down to the age-old motherly admonition of "beware of strangers." I made sure I was standing next to an unpainted section of fence and then leaned against it.

After trying to come up with an icebreaker, I said simply, "My name's Spence."

He dipped the paintbrush in the can and slowly covered another strip of board. He wasn't impressed by my name.

I tried another tact. "I'm looking for Kelly Green. You seen her?"

Without looking away from the fence, he said, "Sure, I see her all the time. She works horses here."

"I mean have you seen her this morning?"

Right then I got my first on-the-job-training lesson in being a detective. You're supposed to be able to sneak up on someone without their knowing it. And, even more importantly, you're supposed to know if someone is sneaking up on you. I realized I had flunked the second part when I heard a surly voice behind me say, "It's none of your business who he's seen and who he ain't."

I jerked my head around toward the voice and saw an equally surly person. He was standing at the edge of the gravel track in the grass.

"I don't recall asking you," I replied, trying to sound tough.

He crossed his arms on his chest. "I don't care what you recall. We all look after each other here."

I smiled. "One big happy family. How nice." Wondering what Bobby's reaction was, I glanced in his direction. The smile was back. Now I knew who he had been expecting. From what Kelly had said about these two, I guessed that the object of his admiration was Ronny Press. He pretty much fit what I had in mind. While I was matching my image to the real thing, I was trying to keep my stomach from turning. From his looks, tough, dirty, and dangerous, the word scum fit pretty well. But he must have had some charm under the surface because it was obvious he had worked it on Bobby and Marty.

Ronny dropped his arms to his sides and walked slowly toward me across the gravel. I wasn't impressed, mostly because I didn't see signs of a knife. We were the same height, but I was pretty sure my karate and judo training would serve me well. But, at the same time, I also knew that a knife could be thrown before you can get close enough to place your foot in a well-chosen spot.

"I suggest you move on, mister." he slurred.

I stood up straight and moved away from the fence. "Thanks for the suggestion, but I'm trying to find Kelly Green."

He nodded. "Sure. And, from a distance, the kid sitting on the crate looked like her so you thought you'd come over for a better look."

The kid laughed. Ronny didn't. There was a whole lot of tension in the air that had no reason being there. It had arrived with Ronny.

"No," I said slowly, "I thought maybe he could tell me where she was."

He had stopped about ten feet away. If he got any closer I knew I would have been able to smell the stench of stagnant pond water.

"He can't tell you nothin', and you're on private property. The public ain't allowed back here." He looked at Bobby and jerked his head toward the stables.

I was getting close to my limit for taking crap from somebody.

Bobby picked up the paint can and the crate and, giving us a wide berth, walked away.

I watched him walk tentatively around the track. Without taking my eyes off of him, I asked, "You Ronny Press?"

I snapped my head in his direction expecting to see a reaction. There was none. Either I had made my second mistake of the day or this was one cool fellow.

He stared back at me with eyes that showed absolutely nothing. I was surprised at the void behind those dark eyes sunk too deep into the eye sockets. It was as though his eyes were slowly being sucked back into nothingness. The skin was the same way—it was just too tight on his face. And his nose, a little off-center, had been broken at least once. How the hell could this Halloween specter have charmed that cute little girl? I tried to find some resemblance to Jeffrey Grey. There was none that I could see.

After five seconds that seemed like five minutes, he turned and followed Bobby. Ronny had gone but the tension stayed. It very slowly dissolved into the hot air. Maybe it had something to do with the humidity. Since the air was already full of water, the tension had nowhere to go. I didn't either. I wanted to find Kelly, and hanging around the track was my best bet.

A glance at my watch told me it was close to noon. The sweat rolling off my forehead told me the same. I'd have to find a cooler spot to wait. I found some shade at the end of the stable under an overhang at a spot where I could see cars coming into the lot. But I didn't wait long. It was too hot, and I was hungry.

Chapter 15

After lingering over a greasy-spoon Italian beef sandwich, I drove back to the track, which was still minus a red Porsche, and parked under a scrawny tree which at least gave a little shade. I rolled down the windows and tried to pretend I was on a beach in the Caribbean with nothing to do but sweat away the afternoon. It didn't work. But I didn't have to wait long. Ten minutes later, about one thirty, Kelly pulled into the park. I started the car and, following around to the employees lot, parked next to her. She was fooling with something on the seat next to her and didn't notice me get out of the car.

I walked around the rear of the Mustang and tapped on her window. She jumped a foot and then relaxed when she saw it was me. The window whirred down.

"I was hoping to see you again," she said with a smile. "But I imagined something a little less traumatic."

"Sorry," I said with my best look of apology. "Didn't mean to scare you."

"It's okay. I'm a little on edge with the crazy things that have been going on around here."

The car was still running, and I leaned on the door to take advantage of the cool air. "What crazy things would those be?"

"Oh, probably nothing, but if you'd really like to know, I'll tell you later. I'm in a hurry and getting more flustered by the minute. I have to deliver some papers for Dad and just discovered I don't have one. I've been here and to my hotel twice today, so I could have left it in the office here or at the hotel. I've got to go check the office."

"If I can help, let me know. And if you have a minute, there's something I'd like to run by you."

"How about later? I'm late already, and I'm keeping three people waiting."

"Sure. Check the office. I'll wait here."

"Great," she said with a smile. "Why don't you wait in the car? I'll leave it running."

That wasn't an offer that needed mulling over. I got in the passenger's side, picked her briefcase up off the seat, and sat down. The air was on full blast and it felt wonderful. The briefcase was a mess, evidence of her frantic search for the missing paper. I closed it, balanced it on my lap, and waited.

Activity at the track had picked up as employees showed up for work. A day like today couldn't be good for the horses. But, even with the heat, it was a pretty easy life—run a couple minutes a day and then back to nibbling hay.

Five minutes later, the driver's door opened, and Kelly got in as quickly as possible.

"This is nuts! I might as well be in the tropics."

"I agree. You find your paper?"

"No. I have to go back to the hotel. Can we talk tomorrow, Spence?"

There was something about this woman that made me decide I'd rather stay with her than go to the Cub's game.

"I'd rather talk today. Mind if I ride with you?"

"That'd be great, but it might take awhile."

I settled back in the seat. "I'm all yours."

She put the car into gear and roared off. I'm not much impressed by fancy cars but there was something about the deep throaty whine of the engine that was very impressive. We turned left onto Cicero Avenue and headed north up the four-lane highway.

Watching as she smoothly went through the gears, I tried to put my finger on why she made me feel so at ease. She was very pretty in a wholesome, country kind of way, had a good head on her shoulders, was strong without being pushy, and seemed to like me. But lots of women I met had those qualities. One of them was coming to town next week. There was something else, and I wanted to find out what it was. I didn't like things sneaking up on me. Whatever that something was, it made me trust her without thinking about it, and I decided I didn't like that either. I guess it was being brought up as a cop's kid, but I had long ago learned there were very few people you could trust all the time.

For instance, I'd trust Rosie with my life, but I wouldn't risk telling her about Ronny and the mayor. No, that wasn't true. I know she wouldn't tell if I asked her not to, but it would put her in a position that wouldn't be fair to her. Not that she would purposely tell someone, but it might interfere with her judgment or it might just slip out. And besides, Stosh had asked me not to. Now Kelly had no vested interest. Or did she? That was the problem with this business. Who do you trust? Dad had solved the problem. He trusted Mom and me and Stosh.

I now knew Stosh was closing in on some operation at the track. Kelly hung around the track. And bad people don't have signs around their necks advertising the fact that they're bad guys. In order to be good at being bad, it helps to look good. But my gut feeling about Kelly was that I could trust her. Maybe that was the extra something. But better guys than me have been set up. I guessed I'd have to put the wedding on hold till I got this straightened out.

I adjusted the air blower down a click. "Hey, are you aware someone committed mayhem in your briefcase?"

A light airy laugh followed. "No wonder you're a detective. You caught me, I'm guilty. I was trying to find that damned paper. I could swear I put it in there this morning."

I adjusted my legs. The cold air had tightened my muscles. "What is this paper?"

"It's a letter from Dad's lawyers in London. Gladstone and Veatch. He's buying some horses."

"Mind if I give it a try?" I offered.

She gestured with her hand as we slowed for a red light. "Be my guest, but I've been through it three times."

She turned right on Jackson and headed east. Traffic was light. The city seemed to have slowed to a crawl after a week of hell.

I opened the case and started to straighten the papers. First time through was fruitless. The second time I noticed one sheet seemed thicker than the rest. I wetted my finger and thumb, held the paper between them, and separated the two stuck sheets. Neither was from Gladstone and Veatch. But I figured if the humidity had stuck these two sheets together it could happen again, so I kept looking till I found the offender near the bottom of the stack.

"Got it, Kelly."

She glanced over the paper I was holding up. Without a word, she looked over her shoulder, slammed on the brake, downshifted, spun the wheel, and all of a sudden we were heading in the opposite direction.

As if nothing unusual had happened, she calmly said, "Thanks, now what do you want to talk about?"

"When I can talk again I'll let you know! You want to pull over and help me get my fingernails out of your briefcase?"

She laughed. This time it wasn't at all airy. It was full and hearty and very sexy.

"Sorry, just a reflex," she said with a concerned look.

"Sure, it's just a reflex if you're Richard Petty. Where the hell did you learn how to do that?"

"I have an uncle who runs a race car driving school back home. I've learned from the best, including Richard Petty, by the way."

"That's great. But next time give me some warning. Not that I don't trust you, but these are busy city streets. Give me a chance to let my life flash before my eyes first." I added race car driver to my Kelly list, and my hunch was the list would keep growing.

My heart had about recovered when a pat on the arm from the offending lady got it beating fast again. After walking away from Kathleen, I'd decided to keep my emotions under control, maybe let them out for a walk once in a while on a short leash. Kelly had snapped the leash.

"So, what's up?" she asked with no response from me. "Hey, Spencer!"

I jerked. "What?"

"I really am sorry. I really shook you, didn't I?"

"I was just thinking. What did you say?"

"I asked what you wanted to talk about."

"Well, to tell you the truth, there are several things. But the original one is I'd like you to put a name with a face."

"Any particular face?" She turned, slowly and legally, back onto Cicero and headed south, back toward the track.

"Yeah. Brown hair, ponytail, scraggly, broken pointy nose, and dark eyes that look like they're being sucked into a black hole."

Another laugh, one of those nice ones. "You do have a way with words. I wouldn't quite have described him that way, but it sounds like Ronny Press."

I nodded. "That's what I thought. I met him at the track. I asked him rather unexpectedly if that was his name and got no answer. Didn't even flinch. He should've blinked or twitched or something. It was like I was talking to a post."

"I'm not surprised, Spence. The guy is scary. I haven't found much human about him. I was so sure he just crawls under a rock at night, I followed him home once. That's how I found out where he lives. I wouldn't put anything past him, and that's why I worry about Bobby. Ronny is just using him and Bobby will do anything he says."

I told her about our morning conversation. Her response was unexpected.

"Great. Now I've got two men to worry about."

"Excuse me?"

A few blocks past the track, she turned onto the Stevenson Expressway and headed downtown. "Oh, I know, you're a big boy and can take care of yourself and can probably beat the crap out of Ronny Press. But I have a feeling he doesn't fight fair. And I have a feeling you do. And from what I've seen so far, I'd kinda like to keep you around for awhile."

Sure, drag that out. The reason I wasn't following in Dad's footsteps was he had had to fight fair, he had to stay within the system. I'd been hoping by doing it this way I could step outside the system once in a while. Maybe not. And now that I knew she cared about me, should I admit I cared about her?

She snuck a sideways glance in my direction. "This is where you're supposed to say, preferably with a Bogie drawl, 'Don't worry, Doll, I ain't goin' nowhere, and no tough guy's gonna change that.'"

I started to laugh, and by the time I stopped I had made a decision. I still wasn't sure what it was... that she could drive like Petty, did Bogart better than me, or had all the character traits of a Girl Scout. And it didn't hurt that she'd never fit into the uniform. I gave in. I realized that I already trusted her and admitted, to myself at least, that I cared about her a lot. But, for now anyway, I couldn't tell her that. But something about her made me want to take her up to meet Aunt Rose and sit and watch clouds and sailboats for a few years.

"Somewhere along the line, I'm going to have to talk to Ronny Press. Maybe I'll wait to tell you till after the fact."

"I'm not doubting your manhood. Just be careful. I've watched him and he's dangerous."

"Do I have a sign on my back like a new driver? Careful, new detective, stay clear, can't take care of himself." It was one of those statements you wish you could take back as soon as you said it.

We got off the expressway at Congress, and Kelly slowed to a stop at a red light. I knew my comment was out of line and was waiting for an angry return, but she glanced at me with only a questioning look.

As we pulled away from the light she asked, "*Are* you new at this?"

I fidgeted with the briefcase trying to think of some manly way out of this and couldn't. I didn't like the role of a rank amateur, but I had no choice. "This is my first case," I admitted. "But I've been taking care of myself for a long time."

"That really has nothing to do with it, Spence. People who can take care of themselves die every day. It's called life. Little kids who haven't even learned how to swing a bat yet are being gunned down in the streets. There's nothing certain about it. Just because you can take care of yourself doesn't mean some crazy won't take a shot at you while you're strolling down the street."

"I know. I apologize. It's just that I got the same lecture yesterday from my Polish baby-sitter."

"It wasn't a lecture. It was concern. And I'm glad to know I'm not the only one who is."

"Is what?"

"Concerned." She smiled. "If I was the only one who cared about you, I'd begin to wonder about my taste." She turned through traffic on south State Street into a semi-circular drive in front of an old, tall office building and stopped next to the walk. "Do me a favor? Stay with the car, and if anyone wants it moved, drive it around the block?"

I said I'd be glad to. She said she'd be back in ten minutes. She was. I asked her if she wanted to join me for a Cubs game and she gladly accepted. She asked who my Polish babysitter was. I told her about Stosh on the way to Wrigley. I explained he was a close friend of the family. I then asked why she hadn't asked about the case I was working on. She said it was none of her business, and if I wanted her to know, I'd tell her. I asked her to marry me. She said she would, but only if Buckner hit a game-winning home run in the ninth inning. I wondered if either of us was joking.

We sat in the bleachers, soaked up the sun, drank a few beers, and enjoyed the aura of Wrigley Field. To most Cubs fans it didn't matter if they won or not. They came to the park to watch baseball in one of the last old-time parks in the league. It was about sun and hot dogs and ivy on the walls.

The game was close, and I started to worry when it was 3-2 Cards going into the last of the ninth. Buckner was due up fourth. In little league the guy on deck would yell, "Hey, Tommy, save my raps!" Tommy would usually strike out. After two quick outs, DeJesus came up and on the first pitch lined a screamer down the third base line. He was standing on second when the left fielder fired the ball to third. And Buckner was up. He took two balls and then hit a long drive down the left field line. It left the park, foul by a hair. I let out a "whew" and got an elbow in the ribs.

"Want to call it off?" Kelly asked.

"Nope. I'm no welcher. I'm a man of my word. Are you aware of what is happening here?"

"Yup. I'm watching a great ballgame, and you're flopping around like a bass that's just realized it went after the wrong worm."

"Great. A fisherwoman too?"

"A sports enthusiast of all types," she said. "I grew up with four brothers and a gaggle of male cousins."

I didn't think I could have sweated any more than I already was, but I did. And I didn't stop after Buckner struck out. I had escaped, but not by a whole lot. And I wasn't sure if I wanted to.

I slid my beer cup under the seat and said, "Guess your bass slipped off the hook."

"Looks that way. But think of the story I'll have about the big one that got away." Her smile kinda made me wish I hadn't.

On the way back to the track, she filled me in on the strange goings-on there. There wasn't much, mostly just a feeling she had. Strange people hanging around the stables and something about too much hay and then not enough hay. I didn't quite understand and neither did she. But I had long ago learned to trust a woman's intuition.

She pulled up in back of my Mustang and wrote down her hotel number on the back of a card. I dreaded the thought of switching cars.

Someone should come up with a way of keeping your car cool while it's parked. Like maybe running the air conditioning off of solar power.

I opened the door and asked if a guy got a kiss on the second date. With a twinkle in her eye, she said she was quite a sportswoman but she never kissed a fish before, and she wasn't going to start now. After admitting that I deserved that, I asked her for dinner Saturday. She accepted, and I told her I'd pick her up at six.

I stepped out into the heat that the coming of evening hadn't done much about. As I opened my car door, I counted six times that my body had suffered through a thirty-degree swing in temperature today. That couldn't be doing me any good.

And, as far as Beef was concerned, I wasn't doing much good either. I'd found Marty's mysterious friend but that was it. Saturday I'd have to get to work.

When I got back to the office, the answering machine was flashing. The message was Aunt Rose reminding me that Kathleen was coming on Wednesday. Geez. Just what I needed.

Between the heat and the hot dogs I wasn't hungry. So I read a little and went to bed early with thoughts of Kelly Green making me absolutely crazy. But those thoughts soon turned to the dream I'd been having. It started with a long, dark, empty hallway. Then a few nights ago, my mom and dad were at the end of the hallway waving, and I ran toward them but never got any closer.

Chapter 16

What time does a hooker get out of bed? Yeah, I know, when the hour's up.

When I woke up Saturday morning, I was thinking of the normal wake up. I mean, they have to get some sleep sometime. If so, what time do they get up? I needed to talk to Elizabeth's neighbors, and it was something that was playing with my foggy mind.

I took half a grapefruit out of my mini-fridge and thought about it while cutting out all the little sections. I love grapefruit, but eating it is such a pain in the ass. I was spoiled; Mom always used to gut it for me. By the time I got to sprinkling on the sugar, I had decided early afternoon would be best. That would give me time to stop by the bakery where Elizabeth had worked.

Good news on the weather front. We were going to break the 100-degree string. Only a high of 98.

By ten thirty, I was trying to find a parking space anywhere within a block of the bakery. I settled for a block and a half and walked back through the weekend shoppers with arms full and children in tow.

A nicely browned loaf of bread was painted on a swinging sign on an arm extending out over the door of the Golden Loaf Bakery. Opening the door, I was greeted by the wonderful smell of artery-clogging delectables. Unfortunately, I hadn't considered the Saturday morning bakery rush and found myself surrounded by wall-to-wall people. From my vantage point I couldn't even see the counter.

I edged along the window and, standing at the corner of the glass showcase, waited for one of the girls to come within hearing range. A dark-haired teenager with her hair in a net, pimples on her face, and a white bag in her hand, came to within three feet of me and bent to reach the crescent rolls.

When she stood up, I struck. "Excuse me, I'd like to talk to someone who knew—"

"Hey! Wait till your number's called like the rest of us, or I'll break your arm!"

I looked to my right, ready to defend myself, and found a woman who looked as though she wouldn't have had any trouble breaking my arm and wouldn't have lost any sleep over it either. I apologized, found the number machine and took one. Fifty. They were on twenty-six. Keeping my spot at the edge of the counter, I leaned against it and tried to guess who would order what.

The crowd in front of me thinned out, and not many people came in after me. Finally, at 11:22, the dark-haired girl called number fifty. I waved my ticket, and she asked what I wanted on her way over to me, chomping on gum in cadence with her swaying hips.

"As I started to say about twenty minutes ago, I'd like to talk to someone who knew Elizabeth Williams."

"You don't want to buy anything?"

"No, I don't think so. My weight has gone up just standing in line. Did you know her?"

She glanced down the counter. Two young girls were filling orders, and a boy was exchanging full trays for empty ones. She looked back at me. "We're not supposed to be talking while we're working."

"If you can give me just a minute, I'd appreciate it."

She glanced away again. "It would help if you bought something."

I sighed. "Okay, give me a jelly donut."

"We're all out."

"Then put your hand inside the case, and give me the first thing you run into. Did you know Elizabeth?"

Crescent roll. "Well, we worked together, but I didn't know her very well. Not as good as Rita anyway."

"And Rita is?"

"They were best friends. That'll be twenty-eight cents."

I reached in my pocket and pulled out a buck. Handing it to her, I asked, "Is Rita here?"

"Sure, she's in the back." She rang up the sale and handed me the change. I was surprised it was all there.

"Would you ask her if I could talk to her, please?"

Just then a woman, late thirties, came out of the back with two trays of dinner rolls.

Tilting her head and snapping her gum, dark hair said, "That's her, ask her yourself."

Skipping the smart-ass comment that was on the tip of my tongue as well as the thank you, I moved down the counter.

Rita was busy balancing one tray on the edge of the case while she slid the other one in.

"Nice job," I said in my best ingratiating manner. "Didn't spill one roll."

The look I got would've frozen molten lava.

"If you want to buy something, you need to take a number, sir."

"No, no, I already paid my dues. See?" I held up my trophy bag. "What I'd like is to talk to you for a minute, if you could spare one."

"What about?"

"Elizabeth Williams. I understand you and she were friends."

She gave me a disgusted look. "I thought we were. What's it to you?"

"I'm a private investigator. I'd like to talk to people who knew her."

She wiped her hands on a powdery apron. "You trying to find who killed her?"

I wasn't sure what I was trying to find, so, at the risk of losing any credibility I had, that's what I told her.

A "Who the hell are you trying to fool" look slowly formed on her face. She asked who I was working for.

"My bills are being paid by her brother, but my efforts are guided by the best interests of her daughter, Marty."

Right answer. Her eyes softened, and she lost the attitude.

"Okay, give me five minutes and we can talk over lunch. You want a sandwich?"

"No thanks. I've got a roll."

Three little wrought iron tables with pink tablecloths stood against the wall. Each had two matching wrought iron chairs. I picked the table farthest from the door. Taking out my roll, I flattened the bag and used it as a plate. In a few minutes, Rita joined me.

Letting out a tired sigh, she said, "Saturdays are the worst. I'm running all day and these bones aren't getting any younger."

"They don't look that old."

"Thanks, but you'll have to take my word for how old they feel. You have a name?"

"I'm sorry. Spencer. Spencer Manning." I reached across the table and she shook my hand.

"Okay, Spencer Manning. I've got half an hour. Sure I can't get you something else?"

"No thanks, this'll do."

She bit into a tuna sandwich. I played with my roll. "You thought you were friends?"

Dabbing her mouth with a napkin, she said, "We *were* friends. We were very close. I guess I'm still angry at the... well, the turn her life took."

I was confused. "It wasn't her fault she was killed."

Shaking her head, she said, "That's not what I mean, but I'm not quite sure I believe that either. Sometimes the decisions we make lead us to things that are not, well, pleasant. Are you aware of her part-time job?"

"Oh, I see. Yes, I am."

"Well, we argued about that for days, but she kept saying she had no other alternative." She shook her head. "I will never believe that.

We lived in the same building, a nice place on Paulina, and then she just up and moved to that..." Tears welled up in her eyes. "It just kills me that she made Marty live in that hole with those goings-on." She dabbed her eyes with the napkin. "How is Marty?"

"She's fine, at least on the outside. Her uncle is taking good care of her."

She nodded. I felt sorry. Not for her, but with her. She obviously had cared a lot about Elizabeth and Marty.

Trying my best to sound wise, I said, "Sometimes people are driven by forces that the rest of us can't understand."

She shook her head. "Well, I'll never understand, that's for sure. She was a good person, and good people just don't end up like that. Or, if they do, life really stinks."

"Her brother also assured me she was a good person."

Fire burst out in her eyes. "Don't get me started on him. As far as I'm concerned, this was all his fault."

I raised my eyebrows. "Beef? How could it be his fault?"

She touched her sandwich and then pushed it away. "He could have given her money. He has to have plenty, he owns a business. If he had helped her she wouldn't have moved."

I was amazed at how quickly her face could change from sadness to anger. She looked like a different person.

"Did Elizabeth ask him for money?"

"No. She said she couldn't. He was always singing 'poor me' so she felt bad about asking. That's how people with money are—tell you how tough they have it so you won't ask for money."

"Do you know why she wanted money?"

Shaking her head, she answered softly. "I wish I did. I couldn't have helped her with money, but maybe I could have helped with the problem. I asked but she refused to talk about it. Just all of a sudden she didn't have enough money to live on. Once in a while she'd get a babysitter and we'd go to a show, and she never had any trouble paying her bills." She looked up at me. "She had enough to live nicely. Then all of a sudden she didn't." She looked away and stared into the distance. "I know I could have helped if only I could have gotten through to her. But she stopped listening to me and started listening to that damn Maxine."

I wanted to help Rita but I didn't know what to do. She obviously felt some responsibility for Elizabeth's death and still had a lot of anger left. So far I could use my psychiatry degree more than my PI license.

"Maxine?" I asked.

"Yeah. Maxine Brewer, her partner in crime, or rather the ringleader. Maxine's the one who talked her into moving and starting her new business. Maxine worked here, too, but was evidently doing so well on her back that she quit the bakery. We were all three talking one day, and Beth started talking about her money trouble. I had to go to the ladies room, and when I got back Beth was talking about the advantages of making money on her back. I knew Maxine had told her to move in with her and do that. I just couldn't believe it. I was so angry I couldn't even talk. Next thing I knew, Beth was moving. Didn't even tell me." Her eyes welled up with tears.

"You can never tell what's in somebody else's head Rita, or what they're willing to do when things get tough."

"But Beth just wasn't that kind of girl."

I guess we were dealing with two people here. A before and after Beth. But before and after what? If she wasn't that kind of girl, what would make a girl who wasn't that kind of girl do that kind of thing? Seemed like something worth learning.

"Do you know if she had any friends besides you at her old apartment?"

She was staring at something way outside of the room.

"Rita?"

Her eyes snapped back to me, and I repeated the question.

"No," she sighed. "I was the only one there she talked to. We were real close, kind of like sisters, you know?"

I nodded.

"There was something I always wondered about though. I was working two jobs to pay the rent. I could have lived somewhere cheaper but it was worth it for the safety and the clean place. But Beth just worked here at the bakery, and she had Marty to take care of." Her brow furrowed and she shook her head. "I still wonder how she paid the rent. She made about the same as me, and she sure didn't get any help from that no good brother of hers."

I ignored the slap at Beef. "There was no one else in her life? No men?"

"No. She went out by herself sometimes and I'd watch Marty, but usually she stayed home or the three of us would do something." Her eyes welled up again. "She really loved that little girl. That's why I can't understand..." Tears rolled down her cheeks. She wiped them away and apologized. "I'm sorry, I..."

I touched her arm. "No apology necessary. I'm sorry to have to bring this out."

"That's okay. If it helps Marty. You said you were working for her interests. How is that?"

"Well, I was hired to find her father. Maybe he can help somehow. Do you have any idea who it might be?"

Another sigh. "No. I asked several times, but Beth didn't want to talk about it. I had the feeling either he was dead or he didn't know."

As Rita took a bite of tuna, I asked if she ever heard Elizabeth mention the name Ronny Press. She finished chewing and said she hadn't. I described him. Nothing.

"Can you stand one more question?"

"Sure," she said with a little smile. "But then I have to get back to work."

"Sure. Did you and Elizabeth meet here at the bakery?"

"No. We were both volunteer workers for Mayor Grey's election campaign. We met during a coffee break and then started stuffing envelopes together. All we talked about was how wonderful he was. We were so happy when he was elected. He's done a great job for the people. I didn't like my job, and she said they needed someone here, and here I am. And she..." She just shook her head. The tears were back.

After again squeezing her arm, I thanked her for her help and gave her my card. She said to say hi to Marty. I said I would.

I sat at the table for a few more minutes and let the name Jeffrey Grey bounce around in my head to see if it would come out somewhere with an explanation I liked. It didn't. I left with it still bouncing around.

Chapter 17

A half hour later I pulled up in front of Elizabeth's apartment on Hunter. The neighborhood was struggling to keep some respectability but was losing the battle. Ten doors to the north there was a freshly painted picket fence with a bed of petunias on the inside. Several houses to the south started a row of dirt front yards, some with fences that were missing pickets and looking like a fighter's smile. The building had some new windows and some that were boarded up. The front doors were plywood. The sparse grass was being choked out by weeds which had completely taken over the vacant lot next door and ran all the way back to the el tracks behind the building.

There was a silent battle going on here between the north and the south with the decay of apathy slowly moving up the street. I had the feeling this was a war the south would win.

I pulled a U-turn and parked in front. After shutting off the air and the radio I got out and ran into a crowd of kids standing at the curb eyeing my Mustang. Feeling a bit nervous, I started across the walk.

"Hey, mister."

Turning toward the voice, I raised my eyebrows in response. I couldn't tell who had heyed me.

The tallest one nodded toward my car. "Nice wheels."

I guessed him somewhere between ten and fourteen. The youngest in the group may have been eight. It was hard to tell ages with kids. I wasn't around them enough. I knew one in junior high who was six-foot-eight who Bobby Knight would drool over. I answered, "Thanks," and started to turn away.

"Ten bucks to watch it."

"No thanks, I just had it washed yesterday." Again, I started to turn.

"Not wash. Do you see any of us holdin' buckets?"

That got a group laugh. I played along.

"Not wash?"

He slowly shook his head. "Watch. Ten bucks, and we make sure nobody does nothin' to it while you're inside."

An entrepreneur. We used to wash cars for two bucks. This kid just sits on the curb and looks at it and wants ten. Or I guess that's *gets* ten. I had no doubt that I was talking to the same guy who would "do somethin' to it" if I didn't pay.

Catching the drift of the situation, I bargained. I hate to be played for a complete sucker. I reached in my pocket and offered the kid a five. "Five now, five when I get back if you do a good job."

He looked at the five like it was an insult. "What? You don't think we'd do a good job? Ain't this an honest face?"

I kept my comments about his face to myself and stuck to my offer. I was perfectly willing to drive away and buy a junker for fifty bucks and come back and let him "do somethin' to it."

"I'm sure you'd do a fine job, but I just don't pay up front for anything. It's a policy."

He pursed his lips, squinted, and accepted my offer. Shaking his head slightly, he said, "Okay, you don't look like you're going to be too long anyway."

Another group laugh.

I handed him the five.

Shaking his head as I walked away, he said, "Sure is hard bein' in business these days."

I made my way up the sidewalk kicking at the weeds growing in the cracks. I wanted to check my car over my shoulder, but I didn't want to hurt his feelings by thinking I didn't trust him. He'd probably get just as much satisfaction out of putting a few dents in the fenders as getting the other five. I was halfway up the stairs when I realized what he thought I was there for. I didn't especially like him thinking that, but then I realized he was a businessman and business was business. Now I understood the comment about not being there too long. Kids sure can be cruel.

The front door creaked open and, after stepping inside, I gave my eyes a few minutes to adjust. I stood in a small entryway with stairs in front of me and doors marked 1A, B, and C on the left side of the hall. Narrow, vertical windows framed each side of the doors. On my left was a beat-up, brass-fronted mailbox unit recessed into the wall, the kind with little doors that open to get the mail. There were five slots on the top and four on the bottom. The extra spot on the bottom used to hold the doorbells. Now ten empty holes, a few with wires hanging out, gave the impression that there was no one here who wanted visitors. I squinted at the names below the mailboxes and found Brewer under 3A.

There was no carpet in the hallway or on the stairs, but there were tacks around the edges at the walls. The carpet had probably been stolen along with the doorbells, and no one here cared enough to replace it.

The stairs were worn and beat up, but they were solid oak and were trying to resist the decay eating away at the hundred-year-old craftsmanship. They reminded me of an old locomotive, standing on a siding somewhere, long ago stripped of its shiny brass parts, but still giving off an aura of strength and determination. I listened to the creak of the treads as I made my way up into the disparity of the building.

I stopped on the second floor landing, listening for some sign of humanity and barely picked up a faint TV set. From the outside came kids' scratchy voices. They sounded like we must have when the gang would get together and hang around. But I knew it was different. Gang meant something else to these kids.

A small window above my head let in a hopeful square of sunshine which lit up a graffiti-covered patch of green, flowered wallpaper. I sighed and continued up the stairs. My stomach turned as I climbed the last set, not because someone had been killed here but because this lonely, dead, apathetic building had once been Marty's home. This wasn't a place to live. It was a place to spend time while you waited to die.

The third floor was a twin of the second, without the patch of wallpaper. The first door I came to was 3A. Putting my ear to the door, all I heard was the chugging of the air conditioner. I knocked tentatively and waited. Nothing. My next knock was a little louder and longer. Still no response. The third try was my best "I really mean business" knock, and it did the trick.

From inside the unknown and unimaginable world behind the door came the gruff response, "Go away. I don't know what time it is, but it sure as hell isn't business hours."

I stopped humming the Tony Orlando song inspired by my third knock and replied, "It's not your business I'm interested in, it's mine, and for me it *is* business hours."

"Didn't you see the sign that says 'No Peddlers'?"

I hadn't and said so.

"Well, pretend you did and get lost. Whatever you're selling, I'm not interested."

"I'm not selling anything. My name is Spencer Manning. I'm a private detective and I'd like to talk to you about Elizabeth Williams."

A slight pause, just enough for her to lose the attitude.

A calmer and lower voice replied, "I told the police everything I know."

"I'm sure you did, but I'm not looking into her death. I'm trying to get some information for her daughter, Marty."

After a longer pause, the voice, much closer to the door, said, "If you've got some ID, slide it under the door."

I did and, a few seconds later, the sound of chains and bolts moving was followed by the door opening. I don't know what I expected, but my surprise must have been obvious.

"Not a pretty sight, am I," she said, running her hands through slept-on, shoulder-length, auburn hair. "What you see is the real thing. Come back tonight if you want the fancy edition."

I politely declined. She wasn't that hard to look at, but I knew what the fancy edition did for a living. My surprise wasn't because of the "just-out-of-bed" look, but rather that Maxine Brewer was just a plain, kind of pretty, normal girl who, under different circumstances, I might have been happy to see. I guess I had expected a floozy with long, painted nails and dyed hair. Her clear complexion, naturally wavy hair, lack of make-up, and long white T-shirt made me wonder why a nice girl like her was in a situation like this. She could have been the girl next door. The only clue to her late hours were dark lines under her eyes.

She led me to a brown, threadbare sofa, and we sat. The room was sparsely furnished. There was one other chair and a card table covered with papers. A kitchen was built into one of the walls and a hallway led to what I assumed was a bed and a bathroom. Dirty dishes decorated the kitchen. One picture on the wall showed a mutt dog standing up on its hind legs in a field.

"So, Spencer Manning, what do you want to know?"

"I'd like to know who killed Elizabeth Williams and why the Cubs can't win a pennant."

She smiled. "The first I can't help you with, but there is obviously at least one person who can. The second, I don't think anyone can help you with. And I thought you said you weren't looking into her death."

"Technically, I'm not. I'm trying to find out who Marty's father might be. Since I'm getting nowhere with that, I figure the two might be related. You don't have any idea who may have killed her?"

A shrug of her shoulders was followed by a soft no.

"Could it have been a client?"

"Could have been anybody, even you for all I know."

I let that pass. "Could she have had money lying around?"

That brought a chuckle. "If you live here, you don't have money lying around. But these days, five bucks is enough to kill for." She covered a yawn.

I had been trying not to lean back on the couch but my back was starting to hurt so I figured I'd brave the germs and got comfy. "You two were friends?"

"Yeah. I wasn't thrilled about the kid, but Beth and I were friends. Not bosom buddies, but close enough that she looked to me to help her with some problems."

"And the solution to one of those problems was to move in here and start hooking?"

Her back straightened, and the trusting look was replaced by an icy stare. "You want to judge me, you can get the hell out of here."

"Sorry. I plead guilty and promise not to do it again."

"Okay. Actually, it's kind of nice having someone in here who's not paying for something. Almost like company." Her body relaxed.

There was a whole lot of sadness hidden in that sentence that made me feel like charging in on my white horse and saving the fair maiden, but I resisted. You can't save everybody, and I'd already been pretty much told this was none of my business.

"Where did you meet Elizabeth?"

"We met at the bakery where we both worked. I had been there a couple of years when she came along."

"Had you ever been to her old apartment?"

"Yeah, a couple of times."

I leaned forward. "I'm wondering what happened to make her move here."

"Hey. I'm not stupid. I know this place isn't the Ritz. And if I had an alternative, I sure wouldn't be here. But it's better than starving or begging for nickels. Beth moved here because she couldn't make it anymore on her bakery salary. That guy is raking it in but he doesn't pay crap. Beth couldn't afford that apartment on her salary."

I didn't tell her I had heard that before. "But she was obviously doing okay for a while?"

"Yeah. She must have had money coming from somewhere else. The first time I was there I asked if she had a fund or something."

"And?"

"And nothing." She pulled her legs up under her, and the shirt slid up her thigh. It was a very nice thigh. "She just laughed and said she wished she did. It was none of my business, so I dropped it."

"So, what changed?"

Another shrug. "I have no idea. I asked, but she said she didn't want to talk about it. She said it was something she had to deal with alone."

"You'd think if a person had a problem they'd tell their friend."

"You must have plenty of friends, Spencer. Anything you wouldn't tell any of them?"

I shook my head. "No, that's what friends are for. There's nothing I..."

A smile crossed her face. "Thought of something, eh?"

"Okay, you win. But it's something very important that someone asked me to keep quiet." I had been wrestling with the Ronny–Jeffrey connection. I would have liked to have told someone. But I couldn't even tell Rosie and she's a cop.

Maxine slid her feet down to the floor and stood up. It was obvious she had nothing under her shirt but her, and all the *her* was in all the right places.

"So," she answered, "if you can have important stuff, so can Beth. Please excuse me for a minute. I gotta pee." She turned and walked away with a natural sway of hips that made a part of me wonder what the nighttime edition looked like. I was sure she would be hard to ignore.

I was back to the same square. What happened to Elizabeth Williams to make her move here and take up this kind of life and was so personal she couldn't share it with her brother or friends?

I stood and walked to the windows. Cheap, yellowed shades kept out most of the sunlight and some of the heat. The air conditioner was old and barely winning the battle. Dust flew off the shade as I pulled the string to get a peak outside. There was a larger crowd of kids around my car, and it was still in one piece.

Walking back across the room, I noticed the beam of sunshine from the exposed window spilling over the paper-strewn table and onto the couch.

The toilet flushed, water ran, the bathroom door opened, and Maxine padded back into the room. She was pulling her hair into a ponytail and feeding it through a rubber band.

She squinted at the little bit of light like a night animal suddenly discovered in its hole in the daytime. "Hey, close the blind. I've got enough trouble keeping it cool in here." She sat on the couch and puffed up a small cloud of dust that was transformed into hundreds of tiny golden beads momentarily suspended in the sunbeam. I pulled the shade back down and returned to the couch.

"Can I get you a drink of something?" she asked.

"No thanks, I'm fine," I lied. "Could we talk about the night it happened?"

"Sure, but I don't know much. I was out part of the time. Friday nights are busy."

"Tell me what you remember."

"In a minute."

"In a minute?"

She smiled. "Yeah. You can feel it before you hear it."

I was going to ask "Feel what" when I felt the vibration through my feet and, a few seconds later, heard the approaching el train. Steel wheels on steel rails suspended above the city like spiders crawling around on ceilings. Except much noisier. The tracks made a bend a few buildings to the north and headed south behind this building. The screech of cars sliding around the corner was deafening—certainly enough noise to cover a shot. My amazed look brought a laugh from Maxine, but I couldn't hear it. Then, just as quickly as it had come, it was gone and the air conditioner was the only sound in the room.

"How the hell do you sleep through that?"

"The human body is an amazing creation. It can get used to anything—even living here. So, where were we? Oh yeah, I—"

"Hang on. When's that going to happen again?"

Settling into the couch, she said, "You've got about forty minutes. Long enough?"

"I hope so. Talk fast."

"It was a Friday night. Both of us were working. I'm in the room here getting comfy with a john when I hear a racket from next door."

"What time was that?"

She shrugged. "Somewhere round ten maybe."

"Which apartment was hers?"

"B, right next to me. C is across the hall. I knew right away who it was and what she was in for."

"Who was it?"

"That brother of hers. She told me about him—said he had a helluva temper. She told him she worked nights at the bakery to make extra money, and he'd watch the kid on those nights, as well as others."

"Others?"

"Yeah. She farmed the kid out to her brother as much as possible. This is no place for a kid, so Beth would get her out of here as much as she could."

My view of Beth went up a little. But there was still the question as to why she was here.

"Beth would pick up the kid in the mornings at her brother's place and bring her to day care or camp or whatever. She was scared to death that her brother would find out some day and give her hell."

"How did you know it was him and not some dissatisfied customer?"

"He was yelling pretty loud and the door was open. Kept saying 'My sister this and my sister that.' I was worried that he might hurt her."

"Because he was yelling?"

"Partly. But she had said that if he ever found out it would be the end of her life."

"End of her life? Was she afraid he would kill her?"

She crossed her arms under her breasts and lifted them. It was a supreme lesson in self control—mine. "She never said, but I suppose she may have been. She was certainly afraid of his finding out." Her brow furrowed and she asked, "Do you think she could have killed herself?"

I shook my head. "I don't know if she could have but she didn't. Someone beat her to it." I leaned forward. "Could she have meant it some other way?"

"What do you mean?"

"Well, not necessarily death. But sometimes people think things are so bad they may as well be dead."

She gave me a look that I couldn't read, but I felt she was trying to figure out how safe she was with me.

After a deep breath, she said, "This isn't exactly what a girl would choose if she had other choices. But if it's what you choose you learn how to live with it. Beth really was a good kid at heart. It was one thing for her to live with it. It was something else if someone else found out, like her brother. I guess she would be disgraced or something. And it wasn't an easy choice."

I let that sit for a minute. "There are other choices, Maxine. How about the bakery?"

Her stare had been fixed on the wall across the room, and I thought I saw a softness in her eyes. When she looked back at me the hardness was back.

"There's all kinds of selling yourself. This is one kind I have control over. The kind at the bakery, I didn't. That bastard had strings tied to me and all the rest of them. He says jump, you jump, or you don't get your money. That's what it's all about, Mister PI. Those who have money control those who don't. Here I do the controlling. I have something someone else wants."

I couldn't help wanting to throw in my two cents, and I felt I had enough of her trust that she wouldn't throw me out. "But here is a bit more dangerous than the bakery."

"There's danger all over. You could get hit by a bus walking to church."

"Yup. But the difference is you don't purposely walk out in front of the bus. Here, the buses drive on the sidewalks. Any of these guys could break your neck, or give you any number of diseases you'd rather not have."

"Yeah, I've thought about that. As far as the diseases, they don't play without protection. And as far as the guys, I know most of them. So did Beth after a while. They're not going to hurt us. We serve a purpose. They're good customers, like Wee Willie."

I gave up being a philosopher. "Wee Willie?"

She nodded. "Wee Willie. They all have nicknames. Willie is a little lacking in a certain area. He was with Beth when her brother busted in on her."

"How do you know that?"

She started playing with the nap on the couch. "When I heard the yelling in the hall, I went out to see what the problem was. Like I told you, this big guy was yelling that his sister wasn't going to live in a dump like this, and he was going to take her home. He was crazy. Kept banging on the door demanding she open up. She must have been scared to death."

"She opened it?"

"No. He didn't give her the chance. He broke the lock."

I could see the fear in her eyes. And this time Beef wasn't leaving out information, he was lying. "Then what, Maxine?"

She looked at me. The fear had disappeared. It was replaced by the puzzled look kids get when they're trying to figure out something.

"It was as though everyone was frozen for a split second. The brother stood inside the room and then, all of a sudden, Wee Willie ran past him pulling up his pants. It's a good thing he got out or that guy would have killed him."

I didn't doubt that. "What did Beth do?"

"She told him to get out. Said she'd pick up the kid in the morning. But he wouldn't leave—said she was moving in with him. They yelled at each other for ten minutes or so. Finally he left after saying he'd be back in the morning to get her." She sighed. "Morning never came."

It was a matter-of-fact statement. That's how life is. "What time did he leave?"

"Probably a little before ten thirty."

"Did you hear anything else that night? More arguing or a shot?"

"No. I got rid of my john, talked with Beth for a few minutes and then went for a walk."

"What did you talk about?"

"Not much. I asked if I could do anything. She said no. I offered my place for the night since her lock was broken. She said that was okay, she'd be okay. I guess that was the wrong decision."

"What time was that?"

"Oh, probably a little before eleven."

"How long were you gone?"

"I got back around two."

"Did you hear anything after that?"

"No. I took some pills. They put me out cold."

"Do you know if her brother came back?"

She shook her head. "I suppose he could have. Anybody could have."

"You didn't check on her when you got back?"

"No. I went right to bed."

"Were you here when she was found?"

"Yeah. The cops woke me up Saturday morning. The brother was out in the hall. They asked me if I had seen him there the night before. I told them about the fight and the door. You know, he wasn't acting so tough anymore on Saturday morning. I wonder if he ever realized that if he hadn't broken the lock she might still be alive."

I had wondered that myself. I just let it hang in the air between us.

"Have you seen Wee Willie since?"

"No. The cops asked if I knew where to find him. I don't. I think he was scared enough to be long gone, especially after what happened to Beth."

"You okay, Maxine?"

A few blinks and a nod were followed by, "Sure. Nice of you to ask."

"Can you answer a few more questions?"

"Sure."

"Did Beth say anything to you about leaving town?"

I could see the answer. She was surprised.

"No. If she was leaving town it was news to me."

"You didn't see the brother again till they woke you up Saturday morning?"

"Right. The only person I saw was old Ethyl when I came back from my walk."

"Around two?"

"Right."

"Who is old Ethyl?"

She swiped at a fly that had landed in the middle of a pattern she was making on the couch cushion with her finger. "Ethyl is kind of the mother of the building. She's been here forever."

"Which apartment is hers?"

"At the time it was 3C, right across the hall. But she moved down to the second floor, 2B."

"Did she hear the fight?"

"You know, that's exactly what she asked me when I got back. I was opening my door, and she stuck her head out and asked me if I heard the fight. I said sure, how could you not? We laughed and I went into my apartment."

"When was that?"

"When I came in at two."

"That was all you said?"

"Yup. Well, about Beth anyway."

"There was something else?"

"Yeah. I wondered why she was there and asked her. See, she was supposed to be going to St. Louis with her brother. He was picking her up at nine, and they were going to drive at night when it was cooler. So I was surprised to see her when I got back."

"Why was she there?"

"She said they started off and then they had a flat. Her brother refused to drive without a spare, so he brought her back and said he'd get it fixed and pick her up at seven in the morning."

"Did he?"

"I guess. She was gone when the cops woke me up at nine."

"Would she be home now?"

"Probably. She won't go out in the heat. If you see her, tell her I'll bring down some lemonade later. She loves lemonade, as bitter as possible."

She puckered her lips and before they could unpucker I asked if the name Ronny Press sounded familiar. I thought she flinched, but if she did it was so tiny, and she recovered so quickly, it could have been my imagination. She replied "No" with no emotion at all and asked why I asked.

"Marty says an 'Uncle Ronny' used to come and bring her presents. Did you ever notice a skinny guy with brown hair pulled into a ponytail?"

"Nope. You know how kids are, making up imaginary friends."

I stood and put out my hand to help her up. She reached out and let me.

"Thanks, Maxine. I appreciate your help."

"Don't mention it. You're the first company I've had in—well, maybe ever."

"Try opening the shade a little more. Your hair takes on a pretty color in the sunlight."

I opened the door and let myself out. As I reached the stairs, the door opened behind me.

"Hey, PI."

I turned.

"I don't know who the father is."

"What?"

"I thought you said you were trying to find the kid's father. I have no clue."

Some detective. I totally forgot to ask. I guess I was more interested in the murder than I thought. "Thanks for reminding me. I got sidetracked by a pretty face."

I smiled. So did she. But hers included a blush, and her eyes had a warm sparkle. I had to pull hard on the reins to keep my horse headed down the stairs. This was a nice girl stuck in a rotten corner of life.

I'd also forgotten to give her my card. I handed it to her, pointing out that I had an answering machine at the office and a beeper on my belt. I asked her to call if she could add anything. We said goodbye again.

Standing on the edge of the landing, I kicked myself for forgetting about the father question. It wasn't the pretty face that made me forget... it was the murder. Stosh would not be happy. I wasn't either. Not only was I digging where he didn't want me digging, but I was screwing it up. Come on, Spence. Just because you're new at this doesn't mean you have to be stupid.

As I walked down the stairs, I checked my watch. The el would be here soon. I waited. In two minutes I felt the rumbling. A minute later the sound rose through the stairwell like a monster from the depths of hell.

Chapter 18

Standing outside Ethyl's door, I could hear the air conditioner and a TV set. I knocked. A high-pitched, crackly voice asked who it was. I told her. I also told her, in case she was nervous about strangers, that Maxine had said she might be able to help me with some questions about Beth. That probably wasn't necessary because she had the door open before I finished talking.

Another surprise. I was expecting a bag lady. Ethyl was someone's kindly, old grandmother complete with silver hair, a neat, old, flowered dress, and beautiful skin altered only by the wrinkles of time. She invited me in with a smile and an offer of homemade cookies. She went for the cookies while I surveyed the living room.

The apartment was the reverse image of Maxine's both in layout and decor. I felt as though I had stepped back in time. The room was immaculate, very homey, and looked like it had not changed in fifty years. The couch and chairs were worn and outdated, but clean and probably just as comfy as they had always been. Those little lace doily things covered the arms of the chairs. What do you call those? Something like Madagascar. Old pictures of a family and a house that I assumed was Ethyl's dotted the walls. The room was bright and cheery, warmed by sunshine diffused through lace curtains.

Ethyl returned, holding a plate of cookies in front of her. She sat me down on the couch and offered me one. Oatmeal. My favorite. It was good, and the couch was as comfy as I thought it would be. Ethyl was beaming with hospitality.

I assumed I was going to be here awhile. If Ethyl was as lonely as I thought, she'd talk my ear off before the afternoon was over. Not that she hadn't seen some choice history through those lace curtains, but I had other things to do, and I didn't figure she had anything new to tell me. I was wrong. Ethyl got right down to business.

"So, young man, you're looking into the murder of that poor girl."

"Yes, ma'am. I'm also trying to find Marty's father." I might screw up once but not twice.

A sad look added a few more wrinkles to Ethyl's face. It was the kind of look grandmothers save for kittens stuck in a tree or a kid's ice cream cone fallen on the sidewalk. "Oh yes, the poor little thing. She was always such a nice little girl."

"Did she or her mother ever say anything about a father?"

After a pause she shook her head and slowly said, "No, no I don't recall anything about a father."

She perked back up instantly with "Have another cookie" followed by an apology for not having lemonade.

I told her Maxine was going to bring some later. She rubbed her hands together, and her wide eyes sparkled. I guess that was her weak spot.

In between bites, I asked what she had seen or heard. She leaned forward and started in. I leaned back and listened.

"Well, I just shouldn't have been here at all. Robert and I were going to St. Louis for the weekend. Family get-together you know. Robert's my older brother. He refuses to drive in the heat, always has, even though he has one of those fancy new cars with all the buttons. So we were going to drive at night."

It was hard to hold back a chuckle at the thought of two eighty-some-year-old people driving to St. Louis in the middle of the night.

"Robert picked me up at nine and we were off. I fell asleep but it wasn't for long. There was a loud bang." Her arms flew up in the air. "Robert pulled off the road. He had a flat. He got out and looked and came back muttering something about paying a lot of money for a cheap... well, I can't say what he said next, you know."

I nodded and smiled.

"He changed the tire, and we turned around and came home. Robert refuses to drive without a spare tire. He said he'd get it fixed and we'd leave in the morning."

"What time did you get back?"

"It must have been sometime between ten and eleven. I'm sorry I can't be more precise."

"And Maxine says you heard the fight?"

"Heavens yes! Well, not the whole thing, you understand. By the time I got my hearing aid in there was just the yelling 'you can't have her she's mine' over and over."

If she had heard the fight, Ethyl must have been home before ten thirty when the fight occurred.

"Then what?" I asked, finishing my cookie.

Her hands spread out and then dropped back in her lap. "That's all. You see, that's when the train went by. I listened some more after the train, but it was quiet and I went to bed."

So whatever time the train passed was when Beef had left. And that was the last time anyone saw Beth alive. Except, of course, for whoever had killed her.

"You didn't hear anything like a gun shot?"

"No. Nothing like that."

"And nothing after that?"

"No, I took a tiny sleeping pill."

The place was a drugstore. "You told all this to the police?"

She looked surprised. "No, should I?"

Now I looked surprised. "Didn't they talk to you?"

"No, young man, they did not. Robert picked me up at seven and we left. He was not at all happy about driving in the heat. Said cars weren't made for that much heat. But we were fine."

"So you heard about the murder when you got back?"

"My, yes. Maxine told me all about it when I got back Monday. What a shame. And that poor little girl. Do you think I should call the police?"

I thought about it and told her no. Maxine had already told them about the fight between Beef and Beth. There was nothing new here. I started to get up and decided to try my Ronny question again.

"Just one more question, Ethyl. Did Marty or Beth ever mention an Uncle Ronny?"

"Oh my, yes. Marty just raved about him. You see, she and I talked quite a bit. He'd bring her dolls, and she'd bring them to my apartment to play and have tea parties."

I could feel my blood rushing. "Did Marty say anything else about him?"

"Nothing much. Oh, she was very excited one day because he had promised her a horsey ride, on a real horse. I thought she was making that up. The poor little thing."

"Did you ever see him?"

"No, not really."

"Pardon?"

"Well, I'm not sure. I think I saw him walking down the front walk once."

"Can you describe him?"

"The one I saw was one of those hippie fellows with his hair in a ponytail. Why men want to look like girls I don't know."

I assured her I didn't either. Thanking her and handing her my card, I asked her to call if she remembered anything else.

On the way out I commented on one of the pictures.

She replied, "Oh, yes, that was me when I was five. If you look close there to the left of the house you can see the old stable. We used to play in there a lot till prohibition years. Then we were told to stay out by my daddy. We finally figured out what he was doing in there." She winked.

"You sure do have a lot of pictures."

"Oh, this is nothing. I've got many more up in the attic in boxes along with old mementos. Don't know why I save them. They'll just be somebody's chore to throw out when I'm gone."

We said goodbye. I stopped in the hall as she closed and bolted the door, locking out the steady decay surrounding her. It might get the neighborhood but it wasn't going to get Ethyl.

Leaning against the banister, I congratulated myself for putting Ronny on the scene and thought about the mayor and Ronny and Elizabeth. I also thought about the possibility that Beef was a lot more involved in this than he let on. Maybe this was all about Marty. One thing I knew for sure was that Beef was pretty attached to that little girl. Beef would not have been happy that Marty was living here. And if Elizabeth was moving again he might be very worried. He had a temper, but was it enough temper to kill his own sister? He might kill in a sudden rage but it wouldn't be premeditated; at least not if it was his sister. If he killed her it was during the fight. But maybe there was another bullet waiting for Ronny if I found out he was the father. And maybe he deserved it.

Right now Beef had Marty and she was safe. But what might he have done to get her? One way or another, Ethyl was right—that was one poor little girl.

Chapter 19

When I reached the first floor, I peeked out the window to check on my car. It was hidden by a crowd of kids which had grown to about twenty. And there seemed to be a new ringleader. A kid about as big as Beef was shooing the little kids away from the car. I guessed his age at anywhere between fifteen and forty. Not wanting to show my money, I took a five out of my clip and tucked it into my shirt pocket. The situation had me a little on edge. Confronting a gang of kids trying to impress their leader all by my lonesome, especially in this heat, was going to take some finesse.

Wondering what was in store for me, I took a deep breath, puffed out my chest, and walked confidently toward the curb.

"There he is! That's the guy!" shouted one of the little kids jubilantly.

The crowd instantly shut up, and the big fellow sauntered around to the front of the car. The first fellow I'd done business with was leaning against the left rear door.

"Nice car," said the big fellow, showing crooked teeth through a plastered-on grin.

"It was when I drove up. I hope it still is."

"Of course. We aim to please."

I reached in my pocket, took out the five and handed it to him. Instead of taking it, I got a rather unpleasant look.

"That's ten short, mister."

"That was the deal, sonny. Five up front. Five now. Ask the kid shining up my fender with his rear end."

The smile returned. "Ah, I see the problem. That was the old deal. This is the new deal. Comes with new management."

Hmmm. "I made the deal with the old management. Ten bucks."

"Well the old management misjudged the amount of time you were going to be here. You're a better man than he thought." The laugh sign went on and the crowd reacted.

I waggled my finger at him to follow me and turned and walked away from the crowd. It wasn't the finger I would have preferred.

"I don't want to embarrass you in front of your little friends here, but a deal's a deal. Now I have one for you." I took out my ID and waved it at him just long enough to give him the impression I was official. "This is a quiet little piece of the world. We leave you alone and you run your little business here. Now, I can change all that or you can take the five, and I can perhaps throw some more money your way for some information." His eyebrows went up at the mention of more money.

"What kind of information?"

"Just comings and goings. Are you out here at night?"

"I'm out here all the time."

Right. I didn't point out that he wasn't here when I'd arrived.

"So you know who comes and goes?"

"Sure. Most are steady customers."

"Okay, I'll be back." I pushed the five into his hand.

As I walked toward the car, the sea of carwatchers slowly and reluctantly parted. My key was about in the lock when we all stopped dead in our tracks and looked to the north in absolute amazement. Until the reality of what had happened had set in, we stared open-mouthed at an unseen force which had just changed our lives. Looking back on it, I don't ever recall experiencing anything like it. In a split second, we were hit by a wall of cool, dry air and the temperature dropped thirty degrees.

One by one, the kids started to cheer and dance. They were all smiling. Those near me slapped me on the back and gave me high fives.

Mother Nature had diffused a tense situation and provided a common bond that we all would remember. I was pretty sure I wouldn't have any trouble if I ever had to come back here.

Opening the door, I caught sight of the big fellow. He managed an ever-so-slight Mona Lisa smile and gave me a thumbs up. I returned it, pulled away from the curb, and headed home to shower and get ready to pick up Kelly at six. With windows rolled down and the air conditioner off, I let the cool breeze mess up my hair.

As I drove away, I found myself feeling uneasy about Maxine's answers. If Beth had been her friend, I found it hard to believe she wouldn't have talked about her situation. Why was Beth there? And I was pretty sure I'd seen a slight reaction when I mentioned Ronny Press. If she hadn't seen him, she had probably heard about him, if not from Beth or Marty then from Ethyl. But why would she lie about it? But then again why should she trust me? I guess if I wore her shoes, I wouldn't trust too many people either.

Thinking about Maxine was only getting me frustrated. So I decided to put the case on hold for the evening and put all my efforts into enjoying Kelly Green.

Chapter 20

The cool front had blown in a definite change in my disposition. Pastel-tinted clouds in front of the setting sun in the west had taken the place of smog, and the world was bright and cheery again. Watching the city light up as darkness gradually fell had always been one of my favorite pastimes.

I turned onto Michigan Avenue at two minutes to six and pulled into the drive of Kelly's hotel right on the money. Her timing was likewise perfect as she was just walking out of the doorman-held glass door. I had kept our destination a secret, but when she'd asked how to dress for a secret, I had requested something breezy and light-hearted.

A beautiful, vivacious Kelly Green seemed to float down the steps. In an ankle-length, white sun dress, covered with patches of multicolored flowers, she was the picture of breezy and light-hearted and I told her so. Her musical laugh and warm smile made part of me wish I had lost the bet at the ballpark.

"So where are we going, Mr. Manning?" she asked, pulling the seat belt across her lap.

"North," I replied and pulled out into traffic.

"Good. That narrows it down. How did you manage the weather?"

I snapped my fingers. "I've got connections, and for a goddess such as yourself I called in some serious favors."

Turning in her seat to face me, she said, "I fall a bit short of a goddess but I do appreciate the effort. That heat was awful." She put her hand on my shoulder. "I'm looking forward to a mysterious evening and am at your command. I feel like I'm on a quest." She laid a green sweater in the back seat.

"Perhaps we are. We'll have to wait and see what we find. Personally, I'll settle for a quiet evening filled with good conversation, some witty remarks, a good steak, and perhaps the odd beer thrown in for flavor."

Another laugh. Very hard to resist. I could devote the rest of my life to making her laugh and have a fine life indeed.

Michigan Avenue ran into Lake Shore Drive. I swung onto the entrance ramp and drove north with the slightly choppy waters of Lake Michigan disappearing into the horizon to the east. If the north wind continued, the chop would build. I had seen twenty-foot waves on this lake.

A few hours ago, before I hopped into the shower, I had called my favorite hostess at my favorite restaurant and was assured that the table Dad had been reserving for as long as I could remember would be waiting for us.

The Drive ended at Hollywood. Turning right onto Sheridan Road, I wound my way through Evanston, Wilmette, Winnetka, and Kenilworth, one of the richest congressional districts in the country. Kelly watched with wide eyes and open mouth as we passed one palatial estate after another, sometimes catching a glimpse of the lake through openings in the dense tree cover. In several cases, gate houses large enough to comfortably house most people sat just inside high iron fences next to long, winding, blacktop drives leading to old stone mansions rising majestically on the bluff over the lake. The wealth here was beyond my comprehension.

It wasn't beyond Kelly's, but it was different. Where she came from, money went into horses and land that rolled off as far as you could see. Here, it was compacted into one lot after the other, large though some of them were.

"It's like a fairyland, not real somehow," Kelly said in amazement. "I can't imagine living in a house that big."

"Didn't you grow up in a big house?"

She laughed. "Not *that* big! Not half that big. Oh, we had money, but we didn't make a show of it. How could these people even use all those rooms?"

It was a rhetorical question, and we sat in silence and watched the homes roll by.

"It's not really the size of the houses that amazes me," Kelly said. "It's the amount of money these people must have. They can't have a worry in the world."

"Well, you know the old saying—money can't buy happiness."

"I know. And that's a shame. With all that money, you shouldn't let anything bother you. Our family would have been just as happy without the money. Dad always said money just buys relief from some of the burdens in life and gives you time to concentrate on what makes you happy."

"Well, I'll agree that if you're happy already it sure doesn't hurt to have money. But if you have to worry about money and paying bills then there isn't time to be happy. And there is something else these people's money can't buy."

She looked puzzled. "What?"

"A lot of these people have a big problem." I followed a bend in the road to the west and turned right onto Green Bay Road. I pointed out Ravinia on our right, the large outdoor bandshell that drew some of the biggest names from all types of music, and I told Kelly we were getting close.

"So, what's their problem?" she asked.

"Mother Nature. Those mansions were built with old money. Living on the lake was, and is, a status symbol, and obviously a location with a beautiful view. So you want to get as close as possible. But they didn't consider the fact that the lake is alive and constantly changing. Some ten thousand years ago, things were much different. In place of the lake there was a huge hunk of ice that would have made the Sears tower look like a needle in a haystack. The lake is the result of the melting of that glacier. Today, the land is wearing down. The bluffs are eroding so fast some of these homes no longer have a back yard. The bluff edge has eroded right up to the house and they're in danger of falling over the edge."

"Can't they do anything, like build a wall or something?"

"Oh, they're trying, but anything they do is only a short-term fix. Seems Mother Nature doesn't care how much money you have."

Kelly thought for a second. "They could move their houses."

"You can move some houses but these are a bit large. But they'd also like to keep their view. The problem is they just didn't think about eroding bluffs a hundred years ago. Everything changes. The lake is getting wider and shallower and some day will just be a big pond."

"I guess you don't fool with Mother Nature."

"No, I guess you don't. The problem is people don't think about her before they build. I've seen pictures of homes next to the mountains in California that were built in slide areas that show large trees with boulders lodged up in their branches. The people are surprised when a landslide wipes out their house. How do they think the boulders got up in the trees? If you're going to build there, fine, but don't be surprised when you lose your house, and don't yell for the government to pay for it."

"I must say, I'm impressed. Where did you learn all this?"

I waved my hand. "Just keep my ears open."

"A good quality in a PI, I would think. I'll have to watch what I say," she said with a laugh.

I laughed back, but her statement made me stop and think about the fact that I was going on all gut feelings here. I didn't really know Kelly Green or what was going on at the track or how much she really knew. But I just couldn't believe my gut feelings were wrong. She was so honest and open and carefree and beautiful and just about everything else that was good. Even so, I'd have to force myself to be a little wary.

After a few more minutes, we turned into a tree-lined, curving drive which wasn't marked by a sign. We followed the drive for a couple of hundred yards through a dense, forested area and finally came out into a clearing which served as a parking lot. It was almost full. But then it only held about twenty cars. To our left was the entrance to the restaurant. About thirty feet of old, gray, worn-out, cedar-sided building stood flanked by solid hedges and evergreen trees which completely blocked the views on the sides. There were no windows in the building, just a solid oak door. A small sign above it said "Stanton's."

As I opened Kelly's door, I said, "Well, this is it."

"Okay. But what is it?" she asked with a bewildered look.

I gave her my best mysterious look and told her she'd have to wait to find out. Her reaction was just what the Stantons had in mind for a first-time customer—kind of an "I'd rather go to McDonalds" attitude. I noted Kelly's apprehension with pleasure, knowing what awaited her on the other side of the wall.

Taking her hand, we walked down a stone path with the last sun rays of the day scattering through the trees and dabbling the plantings on either side with yellow. We reached the door where there was a small sign asking us to please knock. I did. A few seconds later the door was opened, and we stepped into another world. Kelly was holding tightly onto my hand. A smiling Nancy Stanton greeted us and invited us in.

"Hello, Spencer. How nice to see you."

"And the same to you, Nancy. You look wonderful as usual."

"Always the diplomat. But I'm sure I don't look half as marvelous as your companion."

I started to introduce Kelly but my companion wasn't listening. She was staring, with mouth and eyes wide open, at the view in front of her. Nancy and I laughed and let her take in the view.

What was hidden by the trees and hedges was the rest of the restaurant which flared out on both sides at forty-five degree angles. The building was built in the shape of a triangle. The door was at the peak of the two short, angled sides. We were looking out at the long side that faced the lake. The entire building was made of natural, hand-hewn timbers and a variety of wood paneling. From the foyer, the restaurant area was terraced in four steps down to the long wall which was all glass. There were only twenty tables in the whole place. Each one had its own waist-high nook and, because of the terracing, a perfect view to the east out over the lake. Just outside the glass wall was an outside eating area, beautifully landscaped. Beyond that, a winding path led down a sloped hill to a sand beach and Lake Michigan. The view was wide and nothing short of spectacular.

Nancy and Rod Stanton had bought an old, run-down house about fifteen years ago and had built the restaurant into the natural slope of the hillside. From the front, it still looked like the old house, dreary and boring. That was planned to contrast the change once you walked through the door. The restaurant was not advertised, and they frowned on publicity. Their customers had all learned of the place by word of mouth, and they tried to keep it as quiet as possible. If it were to become very popular, the old clientele would never be able to get in. Nancy and Rod were making a comfortable living and liked the fact that everyone who came was considered a part of their family.

"Thanks for getting us in on short notice, Nancy."

"My pleasure, Spencer." She lightly touched my arm and added, "Our sympathies about your folks. We were deeply saddened."

I covered her hand with mine and nodded. "Thanks for the card. That meant a lot to me." Theirs had been one of hundreds.

Giving my hand a squeeze, Nancy tilted her head sideways and said, "Maybe we should bring your friend back to the real world."

"I guess we should." I chuckled. Kelly was in what I called "Stanton shock," an experience she would never forget. I walked over to her, encircled her waist with my arm, and guided her back to Nancy.

Without taking her eyes off the view, she said, "I have died and gone to heaven."

The glow of pride on Nancy's face was wonderful to watch, and the look on Kelly's face was the same as a kid's at his first Christmas.

I made the introductions and Nancy led us to our table, third-tier center. It was just at the right height to see over the edge of the outside terrace and down the hill and still not have the sky cut off by the roof line. We sat.

"Enjoy," offered Nancy, and moved from table to table chatting with each of her friends along the way.

"This is amazing, Spencer. How did you ever find it?"

"I didn't. Dad did. The Stantons used to own a restaurant in the city. Dad helped them out with a problem they were having. They moved up here and, to show their gratitude, we had the honor of being their first customers. They invited us to their opening night. Dad and Mom and I were their only customers."

"Wow. That must have been some help your dad gave. When do I get to meet your parents?"

"Well, you're a little late. They died a while back."

The joy drained from her face and was replaced by sympathy as she tilted her head. "I'm so sorry, Spence. I don't know what to say. I would be devastated if I lost my folks."

"That's a fitting adjective." I reached out and she took my hand. "Mom and Dad would have liked you, and I feel close to them being here with you, so let's do as ordered and enjoy." Out of the corner of my eye I saw Barb, the only waitress I'd ever had, coming toward us.

I introduced Kelly, we talked for a minute, and Barb told us about the four entrees for the evening and took our drink order—Chablis and a bottle of LaBatt's. I asked Barb to bring the drinks out on the terrace where there were two other couples watching sailboats bob out on the lake. She was back in a couple of minutes, and we ordered dinner.

We sat in canvas chairs, and I immediately lost myself in a day-dream. It was a setting which invited silence. I thought about Mom and Dad and realized I didn't want to talk to Kelly about them. I didn't want to talk to anyone. Then I thought of Elizabeth and Maxine. What could be so personal that Elizabeth wouldn't tell anyone? When I came back to reality, I realized that Kelly had called my name several times. The drinks were on the table.

"Thinking about your folks?"

"A little."

"Can I ask what happened?"

"You just did. But, if you don't mind, I'd rather not talk about it now."

"Sure, Spence. If you ever want to..."

"Thanks, Kelly."

I pulled my chair closer to the table and took a long drink of beer.

I took a deep breath, exhaled slowly, and asked, "If you had something terrible happen to you that changed your whole life, would you tell someone about it?"

"Are we talking about your folks?"

I shook my head. "No, although I guess that would fit. It's easier for me to talk about other people's troubles."

"Not unlike everyone else. So what are we talking about?"

"The case I'm working on. Some things don't make sense."

"What's the terrible thing that happened?"

"That's one of the problems. I don't know. But it was bad enough to make a nice girl voluntarily fall to the bottom of the barrel."

She sipped her wine. "Care to tell me more about it?"

I suddenly decided to assume that the case had nothing to do with what Stosh was working on at the track, and it might help to get Kelly's opinion.

"I was hired to find the father of a little girl named Marty. She and her mother lived in a rather nice apartment building and life was rosy, or at least appeared to be. The mother worked at a bakery, a job that didn't pay enough to support the nice apartment, so there must have been some other source of income. Her two best friends say the mother, when asked, would not say what that source was. But then one day, evidently, the source dried up because she had to move. And the change was very dramatic. She moved in with a friend named Maxine in a run-down building in a neighborhood right on the edge of bad and joined her friend in making extra money as a lady of the evening."

I paused for another sip of beer and let that sink in.

"No relatives?" Kelly asked, with interest.

"That's part of the problem. Her brother hired me and I think he would have helped, but, according to him, she never asked."

"Won't she tell you who the father is?"

"That's another problem. She's dead. Killed in her apartment about a year ago."

Kelly sat up in her chair, and I filled her in on the events of that night.

"Police never got anyone?"

I shook my head. "The brother, Beef, is a suspect, but there wasn't enough evidence to charge him. And they lacked a motive. Elizabeth may have been planning on taking Marty away. If Beef knew about it, that would be a good one."

"Do you think he did it?"

I shrugged and spread out my hands, palms up. "I don't know what to think. He's not a fountain of information, and the information he does give is questionable. But if I had to bet, I'd say no."

"For Marty's sake, I hope not. Can you imagine? That little girl living with the man who killed her mother?"

"No, I'd rather not imagine. But I do have to figure it out and one of the things I can't figure out is why Elizabeth wouldn't tell her friends about whatever happened."

"Maybe she was ashamed. Or maybe she just couldn't talk about it, like you and your folks."

"I guess I can understand the last. But how could you be too ashamed to talk about it, but not too ashamed to become a hooker?"

"Maybe one has something to do with the other."

I squinted. "What do you mean?"

"I'm not sure. But something like a cause and effect thing. Maybe one caused the other."

"What would cause that?"

"I don't know. That's why you're the PI. Or maybe she was a hooker before, just a higher class one."

"Hmm. Interesting thought, but I don't think so. All involved have described her as a good Catholic girl, involved in civic affairs, and a good mother. She spent most of her time with Marty. And when she wasn't, she was helping with the mayor's reelection campaign. I think this is a story of a good girl gone bad. But what made that happen?"

I finished my beer. Kelly still had half her wine left.

"Another point," I continued. "Did she really not tell anyone or are the friends trying to protect her?"

"Good question. What's your guess?"

"I'm not sure about Rita. But my gut reaction is that Maxine knows something."

Just then a pigeon landed on the railing next to our table and cocked his head at us.

We both laughed. That laugh made me decide to trust her with more of the story.

"There's something else. My only lead on the case is someone Marty says visited them and brought her presents and promised her a ride on a horse. She calls him Uncle Ronny."

Kelly squirmed uneasily in her chair. "Oh my God. You don't mean Ronny Press?"

I nodded.

"This little girl gets dragged into this situation and then is befriended by Ronny Press? I hope this story doesn't get any worse."

"No. Not yet anyway. I asked Maxine if she knew Ronny. She said 'no' but I thought she flinched slightly when I said his name. I described him and got no response either, but one of the other neighbors said Marty had mentioned his name, and she was pretty sure she saw him leaving the building once."

"Do you want my opinion?"

"I would welcome it."

She swirled the little bit of wine left in the bottom of her glass. "If it was a man, I would say it was possible he wouldn't tell anyone. You guys have this tough guy thing you feel you have to live up to. We women don't have to keep up that image. My guess is Elizabeth would tell someone. And if it were bad enough, she probably wouldn't tell her brother. But her best woman friend? I would think so. And it has to be something other than just losing her other means of support. If you had a trust fund and it ran out, that's not a big deal and nothing to be ashamed of. I think you're right about Maxine."

"So, if Maxine is lying, why?"

"Maybe to protect Elizabeth."

"Elizabeth is dead. What's to protect?"

"How about Marty?"

"Maxine doesn't like the 'kid' as she lovingly calls her."

"Maybe she just pretends not to like Marty. Might ruin her image. If we knew the reason, it might make sense. And if it were simple you wouldn't be employed."

"I suppose." I jumped as a hand touched my shoulder.

Laughing, Barbara apologized. "I'm so sorry, Spencer. Your dinner is served."

I reached in my pocket, gave her my card, and said sarcastically, "If I ever need someone to do something sneaky, I'll call you."

"Deal. Now go eat before it gets cold."

We went and ate. At least I did. Kelly spent most of the time raving about her salmon. I preferred to eat my filet instead of talk about it.

After dinner we walked along the beach and watched an almost full, red moon rise out of the water looking twice as big as real and spilling a shimmering reflection across the gently rolling waves. We stopped at a pile of limestone boulders that looked too formidable to climb, and Kelly turned toward me. I didn't need an invitation to bend down and kiss her. When I pulled away she was smiling again, but this time just with her eyes. I kissed her again. This time she put her arms around my neck and snuggled close to me. The warmth of her lips and the pressure of her breasts against my chest were far more than I could resist, if I had wanted to resist, which I didn't. I was pretty sure she didn't either. I was also sure we could have both not resisted right there on the sand but for the fact that the romance of the situation was marred by the constant swatting of mosquitoes.

As I killed one on my neck, Kelly looked up and said in a voice I hadn't heard before, "There aren't any mosquitoes in my hotel room."

Not needing an explanation, I took her hand and we walked back up the hill and thanked our hosts. As we left, Nancy gave me a wink, and I realized what must have been written all over my face.

I took the expressway back instead of the slow route along the lake. Kelly was right. There were no mosquitoes in her hotel room.

Chapter 21

We woke up early but didn't get out of bed till ten. To say it was wonderful would not do the last ten hours justice. The strangest part was I felt like I could get up and walk out and never come back and not have to explain a thing. At the risk of ruining the moment, I asked Kelly about it.

"Kelly, I don't mean that I'm planning on doing this, but why do I feel as though I could kiss you one last time and never talk to you again and that would be all right?"

She laughed. "Because it *would* be all right. That's the best kind of love—one with no strings attached."

"If that happened, you wouldn't mind?"

"Ah, that's a different story. I would be disappointed and would miss you a lot. I feel closer to you than I have felt to anyone in a long time. But I don't worry about things I can't control. If, or when, the time comes when we part, we will have some wonderful memories, and I will have been able to share something I would otherwise have missed."

"That's an amazing outlook on things."

She curled her arm under a pillow and pulled it to her chest. "If given a choice between happy and not, I'd rather be happy. That's something I can control. So, if there is something that I can't control that makes me unhappy, I let it go."

"Can you teach me how to do that?"

"It's simple. You just decide." I shrugged. "And I'm not saying I'm always successful."

She started tracing designs on my chest which ended up keeping us in bed for another hour. After showering, we ordered in lunch and talked about Maxine some more. I decided to pay her another visit and, by two, I was once again parking in front of the building on Hunter. I was told there was no charge to "wash" my car.

This time Maxine answered on the first knock. She came to the door in jeans and a baby-blue T-shirt which would normally have been exciting but I was worn out.

"Working on a Sunday?" she asked.

"I took a day off last week, so my boss makes me work extra to make up for it. Mind if I come in?"

"Not at all," she said cheerfully, sweeping her arm into the room.

I immediately noticed a difference. The shades were up. "Wow! Sunshine!"

"It's part of my new outlook on life. I got up early today and fixed my hair a little too."

With hair curled at the ends and brushed, she looked lovely and I told her so. I was happy for her, but I felt bad. I hated to ruin her cheery outlook with more questions, but business was business. I think I would rather have taken her on a picnic. With my back to her and looking out the window, I casually asked, "Does the new outlook include telling the truth?" I slowly turned to face her.

The happy look was gone and it almost broke my heart. She looked like her best friend had stabbed her in the back. Maybe he had.

With a set jaw and a very controlled voice, she asked, "What does that mean?"

I had been holding my breath and now let it out and took a few steps toward her. "That means that Ethyl had heard the name Ronny Press and was pretty sure she saw him one day."

"And that means I was lying?"

"Not necessarily. But I find it hard to believe the name means nothing to you. If he was here someone would have mentioned him. He seems to have meant a lot to Marty." No reaction. "Also, I think you know something about why Elizabeth moved here. I think she would tell her friend." Still no reaction. "Maxine?" She was staring right through me.

After about twenty seconds, she opened her mouth and her lower lip began to tremble. Her shoulders sagged. She staggered to the couch blindly and almost fell onto it. "So what if I do? It doesn't make any difference now. She's dead."

"It might make a difference to Marty. And I don't like the idea that Ronny Press and a killer, if not one and the same, are still out there somewhere. Justice has not been served."

"Don't talk to me about justice. There is no justice in the world. Look at this building. Look at the people in it. Look at the neighborhood."

"Sometimes things are what you make them, Maxine. If you sit in Ethyl's apartment, you wouldn't think you were in this neighborhood." I sat down on the other end of the couch. "Okay. If not justice, maybe someday Marty will want to know who her father is."

"You think so, huh? You know it all. Maybe she's better off not knowing."

I gave her a few seconds before asking, "And why would that be, Maxine?"

Kneading her hands, she replied with choppy words like a machine gun spitting in slow motion. "The way the asinine judges rule these days, kids end up being taken from people who care about them and given to drug addicts and child beaters, the dregs of society, just because two derelicts got together and couldn't control their sex drive. They should make the judges go live with these... these..."

I happened to agree but I didn't say so. I just let her sit with her emotions and wondered what had sparked all this. Finally, she continued.

"So, what if you find the father and he wants the kid and the courts say she has to go live with some piece of garbage like..."

"Like who, Maxine?"

She looked down at her hands. "Nobody—like nobody. Then how would you feel? Is that the kind of justice you're looking for?"

"No, it's not. And I happen to agree with you. But the father hasn't come forward yet so what's to say he'd want Marty now?"

Still looking down, she half closed her eyes. "Maybe he doesn't know he's the father."

I knew she wasn't talking hypothetically here. But I couldn't force her to talk, and it was easy to see how strongly she felt about this. "Who are we talking about?"

She raised her head and looked straight at me, with no expression at all, and didn't say a word.

"Okay. Then let's try this. What happened to change her life, and why would you suggest a friend should move in here with a little girl?"

Leaping off the couch with fists clenched and her face twisted in anger, she screamed, "Goddamn you! I didn't suggest she move in here. It was all her idea. I did everything I could to talk her out of it!"

She walked to the table, leaned down with her hands on the edge, and stood there shaking.

I went over and put a hand on her shoulder.

She whirled, screamed "Don't touch me!" and turned away again, her head cradled in her hands.

I returned to the couch and waited.

A few minutes later, Maxine came back and sat on the couch. Tears were streaming down her cheeks, and she wiped them away with her hands. Staring off into space, she whispered, "It was my fault she died. I should have tried harder to keep her out of here." The tears started again.

I got a box of Kleenex from the bathroom and set it next to her.

She took two, wiped her eyes, and blew her nose.

"It wasn't your fault, Maxine. If you tried, you did all you could. If someone has their mind set on something, they're going to do it, no matter what. The fault lies with the guy who pulled the trigger. Period. It was simply an unfortunate chain of events that brought Elizabeth to that end. You've got to believe that, Maxine, and stop punishing yourself."

She simply shook her head.

I took a deep breath, not quite knowing how to continue. After listening to her sob for a few minutes, I said, "I think it would help if you told me what happened. You're just eating yourself up keeping all that inside."

In a few seconds, her face turned into the saddest picture I had ever seen. With lips pulled in, brow furrowed, eyes narrowed to slits, and tears flowing freely with no effort made to stop them, she sobbed, "He raped her."

She started to cry hard and her body shook with every sob. I slid over to her, pulled her head onto my shoulder, and put my arm around her. When she calmed down a little, I lifted her head by the chin and said soothingly, "You have to get it out. Who are we talking about?" I had a guess but I wanted her to say it.

In a very soft, tiny voice, she finally did. The name Ronny Press was barely audible.

"Can you tell me what happened, Maxine?"

She took a deep breath and let it out, closed her eyes, and nodded yes. "I need to use the little girl's room. I must look awful. I'll be right back."

Watching her walk away, still trembling, I realized I was exhausted. I was completely drained. I had never been that close to such powerful emotions. And the scary part was what might happen if I ever faced mine. I stood and walked to the window. Kids were playing soccer on the sidewalk completely unaware that Maxine's world had just drastically changed. It seemed as though they should have been able to feel the energy flowing from the building.

I listened to the water running in the bathroom and heard her blow her nose again. A cabinet closed, and a few seconds later Maxine came back into the room trying to look composed. She almost pulled it off. The tears were gone, but soap and water couldn't wash away the pain.

"You okay?" I asked, feeling kind of helpless.

"Sure. I'm a pretty tough broad." A faint smile touched her mouth. "Come here and sit. As long as I started I might as well finish."

When I was seated, she asked, "What are you going to do? If he's the father, I sure as hell don't want him or anyone else knowing it."

"Neither do I," I assured her. "You said 'if he's the father.' You're not sure?"

She shook her head. "No. Neither was Beth."

I looked at her, not understanding. "Pardon me, but how could the mother not know who the father was?"

"Because there are two possibilities. Within an hour of each other."

I let that sink in. "Two men? Was she raped by both?"

She shook her head. "No. One was her choice. The other wasn't."

"Do you have any idea who the one by choice was?"

"Kind of."

"Pardon?"

"I don't have a name, but she said the guy who raped her was the first guy's brother, so I guess his name is Press. No, wait. It was his half brother, so I guess his last name might be different. She didn't tell me."

I didn't tell her that I *did* know. And I wasn't liking it one bit.

"Would you like something to drink, Spence?"

"No thanks, I'm fine. Do you know any more, Maxine?"

She nodded and, pulling her legs up under her, got comfortable. "I know she was having an affair with a married man, had been for several years. They would usually meet somewhere where they could be alone, but sometimes he would come to her apartment. He did one Friday night and they made love. She said she was sure the guy loved her and didn't love his wife, but he was also very clear that he would never leave his wife. So she knew what she was getting into."

"Did you ask what his name was?"

"Yes, once. She said she wouldn't tell. If it ever got out he would be ruined."

I guess so.

She continued. "That night, the night she was raped, the guy left as usual and ten minutes later the doorbell rang. She figured he forgot something and opened the door without looking to see who it was. Ronny Press barged into the apartment. He told her he was the other guy's half brother and what was good enough for his brother was good enough for him too. Then he grabbed her and said if she cooperated she wouldn't be hurt and neither would her lover."

"Did he have a weapon?"

"Yes, he had a knife. Ronny told her he would tell everybody who she was sleeping with if she didn't sleep with him too. She tried to tell the guy she wasn't sleeping with the brother. He just laughed and made threats and flashed the knife. She said she let the guy... well, you know."

"Rape her?"

"She didn't call it rape. She said if she let him then it wasn't rape. And she let him to protect the lover. Helped her justify it." She shook her head. "I told her I couldn't imagine anybody being that important that I'd let some guy rape me. She said that was cuz I didn't know who the brother was. I still can't imagine Beth knew anybody that important. And what kind of guy would want her to go through that instead of facing the music? He could have helped her."

"I wish I could ask her that."

"I did."

"And?"

"She said she wasn't going to tell him. She knew what she was getting into. She knew he was married and would not leave his wife. But they loved each other, and she wanted whatever he would give her."

"When did she tell you all this?"

"Just before she moved. She came to me and asked a lot of questions about what I did. I thought she was just asking, but when I found out she was thinking about doing it herself I told her she was crazy. But she said what she did with Ronny was as much a whore as a real one so, as long as she needed money, she might as well get paid for it. That's when the story came out."

"She did this because she felt responsible for the rape?" I asked in disbelief.

"Oh, it was much more than that. She called herself a 'good Catholic girl'—before, anyway. She had somehow decided it was all right to sleep with a married man but the thing with Ronny was unforgivable. So, if she was willing to give up her body for one thing, why not give it up for another. She was a failure to herself and her family and to her religion."

"So moving in here was the only option she had? What about her brother?"

Maxine smiled slightly and said, "You're doing the same thing I did. I thought a lot about it, trying to figure it out. But I was thinking like I think, not like Beth thought. It wasn't the only option she had. To her, it was the only option she deserved. It was like wearing a hair shirt to atone for her sins. And when I asked about her brother, she said he had troubles of his own."

"My God." I couldn't at all comprehend this. "I can't believe Beef would have turned her out. He's crazy about Marty."

Maxine shook her head. "She wouldn't ask him. She had disgraced her family and her God. As far as she was concerned, she didn't deserve anything more than..." She looked around the room. "This."

I tried to let it all sink in. "What about Marty? Surely this wasn't good for her?"

"She knew that too. And it only made her feel worse about herself. She sent her to stay at her brother's as much as she could, but she couldn't do without her completely. Marty was all she had left that was any good. Without Marty, I think she might have killed herself."

I didn't even try to understand. Back to facts where I felt safe.

"She was sure she got pregnant that night?"

"That's what *I* asked. That was the last time she slept with anyone— well, till here. The married guy called her, and she kept avoiding him with one excuse or another. When she found out she was pregnant she finally broke it off."

The fact that she got pregnant at all was bothering me. "Did she say how long she was seeing this guy?"

"A few years."

"And she had gone all that time without getting pregnant? She must have been using some kind of birth control, so why not that night?"

"Exactly. They had started using a condom but that's such a pain. You know, takes the spontaneity out of it. So she went on the pill. But sometimes she forgot or stopped. That was one of the times. But that had happened before and she didn't get pregnant, so she figured her luck would continue."

"What rotten luck."

"Very," she agreed.

I stared at the wall for a minute, letting it all sink in. As Maxine crossed her legs, I asked the obvious question. "So she had no idea which was the father?"

Maxine frowned. "No."

"How did she know Ronny was really the half brother? She just took his word for that?"

"She said she knew. They looked like brothers even though there were many differences. She said Ronny was like the evil twin."

"Whew. So that explains the father problem. But what happened to make her move?"

"I don't know. And that's the truth. I do know that before Marty was born, she quit her night job. She worked doing cleaning in a library. But she didn't move out of the apartment, and I know she needed both jobs to make ends meet, even without a kid. I asked her how she could afford it. She wouldn't say. Just kind of laughed it off. I didn't bring it up again."

"Do you have a guess?"

"At the time I figured she was getting money from whoever the father was but, when I found out the rest of the story, and that she wasn't sure who the father was, I wasn't sure anymore."

I wasn't either. A quick glance at my watch confirmed what my stomach was beginning to tell me. Almost dinner time.

"One more question?"

"Sure."

"I assume you did know Ronny Press was hanging around here?"

"Yeah. Marty said something to me one day about Uncle Ronny and I had seen the guy with the ponytail. I asked Beth if it was the same guy who raped her. She got very defensive and angry and asked how I could think such a thing. But I was pretty sure it was. Pretty strange, huh?"

I agreed.

"Some things just make no sense," she said with a sigh.

"Everything makes sense, Maxine, once you look at it from the right angle. It all depends on your point of view. You and I just haven't found the right angle yet."

"Well, do me a favor. If you find it, let me know."

"Be glad to. But only if you'll do me a favor."

Cocking her head, she asked, "And what would that be?"

"Have dinner with me. I'm starved, and it's no fun eating alone."

"You're telling me, but now who's lying? I can't believe you ever have to eat alone. But if you're serious, I'd love to."

"Serious is my middle name."

"Give me a minute to change." She headed for the bedroom and, over her shoulder, said, "Don't disappear on me."

I assured her I wouldn't.

"And do me another favor. Call me Max."

We went out for a burger and a coke, talked about nothing, laughed, and pretended all was right with the world. And when I dropped her off I got a kiss on the cheek.

One message was waiting for me at the office. I predicted who it was from. I was right. I called Aunt Rose and we talked for a few minutes. She told me business was good and she needed help, but finding someone good was hard. She asked when I was coming up. I said soon. And she reminded me that Kathleen was coming on Wednesday.

Hanging up the phone, I rolled my eyes toward Wisconsin and called Stosh. I needed an appointment with the mayor. At first he laughed, but as I got into the story, the other end of the line got pretty quiet. I kept it short. He said he'd talk to the captain and would reach me in the morning.

Last call of the day to Kelly. I felt like a teenager as I laid on the bed and we filled each other in on our respective days. She asked question after question, right up to the kiss on the cheek. She assured me she wasn't jealous. I was hoping she would be, a little anyway. I told her I'd see her in the morning. I was going to the track to try talking to Bobby and was hoping I could catch him without his shadow. She said she had a meeting and wouldn't be there till the afternoon.

We said goodnight five or six times. Finally, I pressed down the button and hung up the phone. Ah, young love.

I thought about the case and wondered what, if anything, I should tell Beef. I wasn't sure. But, since I was making progress, I *was* sure I should start collecting my fee.

I fell asleep watching replays of the Cubs losing. They were going into the all-star break with the worst record in baseball. The Sox, just finishing a weekend sweep, were tied for first. I wouldn't be able to show my face in the diner.

Chapter 22

Monday morning dawned as a normal Chicago summer day. A breeze off the lake, clear skies, and just a hint that it would get hot as the day went on. The overbearing heat and humidity was, thankfully, gone.

I got to the track at ten and, knowing Bobby hadn't finished his painting job, made my way around back to the practice track. I went slowly, trying to keep in the shadows, watching for Ronny Press.

I got lucky. Bobby was sitting on a pail painting the bottom rail, and Ronny was nowhere in sight. I watched for a few minutes and then made my way toward him, coming from the side. I didn't want to scare him. He saw me coming and, except for a few quick, nervous glances, ignored me.

"Hi, Bobby."

No answer, but quicker brush strokes.

"Sure is nicer weather, isn't it?" That usually works. Not this time.

"Mind if I sit down?" I sat down on the grass. "Do you like horses, Bobby?"

Another quick glance. Staring at the fence, he said, "I'm not supposed to talk to you."

"Why not?"

"Please go away."

"Why?"

"I'll get into trouble if I talk to you."

"With who?" I kept my eyes on the stables. This time I wasn't going to be surprised.

"Ronny."

"Do you always do what Ronny says?"

He shrugged his shoulders.

"Ronny isn't here so could we talk for a few minutes?"

"He doesn't have to be here to see. I'll get in trouble if I don't do what he says."

I thought I could see the kid shaking. "Well I don't want to get you into trouble. Is there someplace else we could talk?"

"I don't have anything to talk about. Ronny says not to talk to you."

One of the trainers came out of the stables leading a horse and walked him toward us. "Have you worked here long, Bobby?"

"A couple of years."

"Has Ronny worked here all that time?"

No answer.

I started to try again when I saw someone else move between the stables and then disappear into the shadows. I kept watching. Less than a minute later Ronny came out of the shadows and headed toward us. I stood up and started to walk away.

As he came within hearing distance he yelled, "I thought I told you to stay away from here." And looking at Bobby, "And I thought I told you not to talk to him."

I came to Bobby's rescue. "He was doing a very good job of that even without your help."

He spun and took a few steps toward me. "You're on your way out. Keep going."

"Did you buy the track?"

Looking at me, he snarled, "Come on, Bobby, you're done painting for awhile." Ronny grabbed Bobby's arm, pulled him up and led him toward the stables. The paint can and pail didn't follow. The brush would be useless in about five minutes.

I watched them walk away. Ronny didn't let go of Bobby's arm. The weather hadn't done much for his temperment. I felt sorry for the kid. And I knew if Ronny didn't want me talking to Bobby that badly, then I needed to talk to Bobby. There must be a way. Maybe Kelly would have an idea.

I drove back to the office and caught Kelly at her hotel.

"Kelly, do you have any ideas how I could catch Bobby alone? Does he do anything but hang around the track?"

"Doesn't sound like he'll talk to you anyway, Spence."

"Maybe not, but I'd like to try."

"Well, the only time he leaves is to go over to a bar after the races. But he goes with Ronny and a bunch of the stablehands and trainers."

"It's worth a try. What's the bar?"

"It's called Mean Spirits. It's over on 34th Street, a few blocks east of Cicero. Just a block from the apartment building Ronny lives in."

"Nice name. Maybe I'll pay a visit."

"Be careful, Spence."

"Sure. Thanks. Talk to you later."

I had barely hung up when Stosh called. He asked if I could be there at eleven and told me to wear my best jeans.

I had an extra half hour and drove over to 34th Street. Mean Spirits didn't look like the dive I had expected, but I didn't like the idea of walking in on Ronny and friends after they were filled with alcohol. I parked at the curb and looked around the neighborhood. On either side of the bar were stores of various sorts, some with second-floor apartments. Next to the bar to the east was a short alley that led to the alley behind the bar. Three storefronts past the alley was a parking lot with a sign that said "free parking" for patrons of the bar. I headed for the station.

Chapter 23

Thad been wondering what was keeping Stosh. I've always found it hard to wait for other people. I had guessed that Stosh had to talk to the other two people who knew of the mayor's link to Ronny and I was right. He had said the meeting would include the chief. He also requested that I refrain from any smart-ass comments. I agreed. I worked on accepting the fact that I would be grilled and then told to butt out and go home. I supposed I would have to agree to that too, but it wouldn't be quite so easy.

I parked next to Rosie's Ford in the police vehicle lot and walked around to the front door of the station. The air conditioning was whirring and there were far fewer surly looking government employees. For some the air conditioning didn't matter.

As I walked in, Stosh was coming down the stairs from the second floor offices. He turned around and waited for me and then led me up. I followed him into an empty interrogation room where he briefed me on the meeting.

"As soon as Chief Ranek gets here, we'll start. He and Captain Daniels have already decided how they are gonna handle this, so you've got no say in the matter."

He gave me a questioning look. I shrugged back. I assumed Stosh's look was asking if that was okay. My shrug was answering "What the hell can I do?" He continued.

"I don't know what that decision is, but whatever it is, they will probably want to hear all this from your mouth. Just report the facts, and only speak if you are spoken to."

"Gee, I'll do my best, Mrs. Roamer."

"Who's Mrs. Roamer?"

"My third grade teacher."

Stosh nodded several times and then asked, "Is that your last smart-ass comment? Cuz if there are more in there dying to get out, let's have 'em now."

I smiled. He didn't. "No, that's it, sorry. Just felt like a little kid. I can be serious if I need to, and I certainly realize how serious this is. I'm just not too happy about bringing the bone to you guys and then fading into the sunset."

"At the moment your happiness is not my main concern. But, if it helps any, you did some nice work."

"Thanks, Stosh. I'll behave."

One of the detectives poked his head into the room. "Captain's looking for you, Lieutenant."

Stosh wagged his finger. I followed.

Captain Daniels' office was in the far corner of a room cluttered with a maze of old wooden desks, some occupied by Chicago's finest. I shook hands with Chief Ranek who offered his sympathies about Dad and Mom and introduced me to Captain Daniels who echoed the chief. He stood a head taller than I and was dressed in a neatly pressed tan suit. As we shook hands, I glanced down at his yellow tie and what appeared to be the top of Fred Flintstone's head peeking out above the vee of his coat.

Noticing my slightly quizzical look, he laughed and unbuttoned his coat, exposing the rest of Fred dressed in standard orange leopard-skin. "Birthday present from my kids yesterday. Promised them I'd wear it. I thought it was tied low enough so Fred wasn't visible."

I glanced at Stosh and got a warning look back.

"Looks fine to me, although I was kind of partial to Wilma."

Everyone laughed. It was the last laugh of the meeting.

The chief pointed to a chair and we all sat, Captain Daniels behind his desk. The chief spoke first.

"Spencer, Lieutenant Powolski repeated your findings to Captain Daniels and he to me. We'd like to hear the story from you directly so we can be sure we're all on the same page."

I told them everything I knew that had to do with the mayor's involvement. They all asked questions just to make sure they understood what I was saying. The chief stood up, walked around to the front of the desk, and sat on the edge.

He stared at me for a good ten seconds and then asked, "Spencer, how sure are you of your source?"

"I'd say very sure," returning his serious look.

He shook his head and crossed his arms over his chest. "We're talking about the mayor here, and a mayor everyone likes. Well almost everyone. We're raising these questions based on the word of a... a..."

"Hooker." I was always a very helpful fellow.

"Yes, hearsay evidence of a hooker. You're positive?"

"Yes. I'm positive. She had nothing to lose or gain by telling me, and she didn't and doesn't know that the mayor is the brother. Maybe if she did, she would be playing a different angle, but I don't think so. Even if she knew, I'd still trust her."

Silence from the crowd. A detective walked up and sat on the desk outside the office, obviously waiting to see Stosh or the captain. Stosh waved him away. After a deep breath, the chief continued.

"Okay. Captain Daniels and I decided how we would handle this if your information held up. This may be something which is entirely the personal business of the mayor and therefore none of ours. We are not here to question morals, one way or the other. But because of the murder investigation, we have to look into it. And that has to be done carefully."

I could sense an impending request to butt out.

"Captain, would you like to continue?"

Captain Daniels sat back down, folded his hands on top of the desk and looked at me. I glanced quickly at the chief and Stosh and saw I was the center of attention. Captain Daniels started to fill me in on the plan.

"Spencer, I will tell you what we have decided our first choice of action is and you can respond. We all feel that this should be handled as unofficially and carefully as possible. We aren't here to judge anything if it is none of our business, and we don't want the mayor to think we are making this a police issue. But it is obviously something that needs looking into." He glanced at Stosh and continued. "What we suggest is that you meet with the mayor and explain what you have found. He and your father had a good relationship, and I think he would likewise respect you. We will set up the meeting and simply tell the mayor there is an urgent matter you need to speak with him about. You will then brief us concerning the results, if it is pertinent to the investigation." He paused. No one spoke.

"Are you willing, Spencer?"

I took a deep breath and let it out. This wasn't what I was expecting. "Certainly. But are you sure you want me to go alone? No one from your department?"

"We're sure," answered Chief Ranek. "Stosh says you have a good head on your shoulders and will handle this tactfully. We think that if this is private it should stay private, and this is the best way to do that. I'll let the mayor know that's the case. Also, we realize that you didn't have to come to us with this information. There is no question of not trusting you."

I squirmed in my chair. "Well, thank you, gentlemen. When do you want to set up the meeting?"

"We're going to try for this evening," said the chief. "Mrs. Grey will be out at a fundraiser for one of her kids' groups so, if the mayor is willing, you can meet at his house and have some privacy. Are you available?"

"Sure." I wanted to be at the bar to see if I could talk to Bobby but that wasn't till after midnight.

"Good. I'll make a call right now."

Stosh offered to buy Cokes, and he and I and the captain walked around the corner to the break room.

Ten minutes later the chief joined us and told me it was set up for seven thirty. I asked if the mayor had asked what it was about. He hadn't. I got the address and said I would be in touch. Stosh said to call him in the morning and walked me to the front door.

"See, kid, you shouldn't be so cynical."

"No I shouldn't. Thanks for the support, Stosh."

"No need, Spence. All three of us agreed. Your going through the academy helped, and your coming to us first helped even more. You're as close to a cop as you can get without pinning on the badge. Just do me one favor."

"And that is?"

"This is the mayor, for chrissake. Wear something nice."

Laughing, I replied, "I'll see what I can do."

I climbed in the car and headed for the Blue Note. I needed to talk to Johnny.

Chapter 24

At 7:20, I pulled up in front of Mayor Grey's two-story brownstone. I sat in the car for five minutes trying to calm down. My nerves were shot. After rehearsing what I was going to say all afternoon, I still wasn't sure how to begin. At 7:25, I and my best slacks and polo shirt got out and walked up to the wrought iron gate. I was sure there must be surveillance on the mayor's house, but I couldn't spot anyone. Maybe one of the houses across the street. There was an intercom system built into the fence, and I pressed the buzzer. Ten seconds later I got an answer.

"Yes?"

"Good evening, sir. I'm Spencer Manning. I was told you would be expecting me."

"Yes, Mr. Manning, please come in."

He buzzed the gate. I opened it and made my way up the walk as it closed behind me. I was surprised that he would let me in without asking for ID but then decided that whoever was watching the house would have my picture. If they thought anything was wrong the gate would not have opened.

As I walked up the flagstone steps, one half of the double oak doors opened, and Jeffrey Grey invited me in. He was dressed much nicer than I.

We shook hands, I told him to call me Spence, and he led me down a carpeted hallway. As we walked, I glanced into rooms on either side.

The first was a library, dark shelves from floor to ceiling and uncomfortable-looking chairs scattered about the room. The second was a toy room but not like any toy room I'd ever seen. The room was immaculate. A toy horse, blocks, cars and trucks, dolls, and other toys were arranged as if they were being showcased rather than played with. Their children were very well trained. I guessed the third room was a den. I caught a glance of a large maple desk, a globe, more books, and chairs that *did* look comfortable. A couple of paintings that looked like they'd be more at home in the Art Institute hung on the far wall.

The hallway opened into a large, bright room that I would call a media center. More hallways led out of either side. The hallway on the left side was flanked by a wall of stereo equipment on the left and a bar on the right. The north wall was almost all glass and looked out on a garden and a high brick wall. The mayor motioned me to the sofa. He sat opposite me. Classical music was just barely audible.

"Would you like a drink, Spence?"

"No thank you, Mr. Mayor. I have a long evening ahead of me."

"Okay. Let me know if you change your mind. And please call me Jeffrey. Your father did. I was so sorry to hear about the accident. He was very valuable to me."

"Thank you. He was pretty valuable to me too." I was perched on the edge of the sofa. I didn't think I should get too comfortable.

He sat forward in his chair and put his hands on his knees. Strong hands, well-manicured nails. He was a good-looking man. "So, Chief Ranek told me you had something to talk to me about that he wanted kept private. What can I do for you?"

I had been thinking about this moment for hours and rehearsing different approaches. I still had no clue how to start. Basic facts seemed the best idea.

"I am a private investigator and have been working on a case that seems to involve you." I assumed he already knew the first part. But the second was probably a surprise. I assumed he thought I was there to ask a favor. But he showed no sign of surprise.

"Tell me about the case."

Very cool. Of course he didn't know what I knew. I was trying to keep myself from shaking.

"I am working on a case involving Elizabeth Williams."

Still no surprise. But there was something that changed in his face. A little sadder maybe.

"Yes, the poor girl. I heard about her death. But isn't that police business?"

"Yes, sir, it is. I'm not working on the murder." The word death didn't seem quite serious enough for what had happened.

He sat back, folded his hands on his stomach, and didn't make it easy on me by asking what I was working on. This interview was going to be even tougher than I thought.

"I was hired to find the father of Elizabeth's daughter, Marty."

That got a very small reaction. Raised eyebrows. "And you think that has something to do with me?"

"Well, yes. Indirectly."

"And that means?"

"That means your name was not mentioned, but it was not hard to make the connection."

"Would you like to explain?" The friendly manner was gone.

What was the easy way to do this? I decided there wasn't any. "The father is one of two people. One of the possibilities appears to be you."

He got up and walked to the bar and poured himself a straight whiskey. With his back to me, he carefully said, "Chief Ranek told me you would be talking to me in absolute confidence and that I could trust you to keep your information to yourself. I had no idea what you wanted. Now that I know, I would like to know where you got your information."

"Yes, sir, I can understand that. But, at the moment, I can't tell you. You just have to trust me that the information is reliable."

He turned to face me. "I do? You are telling me something that could ruin my career and my marriage and you can't tell me where you got your information?"

I took a deep breath. I tried not to think about who I was talking to. "I am not out to ruin your career or your marriage."

He took a sip of the whiskey. "Then what are you out for?"

"I am trying to find Marty's father. She's a wonderful little kid. Be good if she had a dad."

"And you are trying to tie the father to the murder?"

"Not at all. The two don't have to be connected. As a matter of fact, I don't think they are."

We stared at each other for a good minute. Then he returned to the chair and sat.

"Do Chief Ranek and Captain Daniels know what you came here for?"

I nodded. "Yes."

"And they are interested in my answer?"

"Not necessarily. If there is a tie to the murder, then yes. But if it is a personal problem it is not their concern. I think that's why they sent me."

He swirled the whiskey in the glass and stared out the window. His eyes returned to me. "I appreciate the way this is being handled. Others would not have been as discreet. What do you want from me?"

"Would you mind answering some questions?"

"No, if I can. But I feel like a bad host, drinking by myself. Sure I can't get you a drink?"

Thinking that would somehow make things a little easier, I answered, "Sure, whiskey on the rocks would be fine." He got up, poured, handed me a short glass, and walked to the window.

"I love looking out here when the sun is setting," he said. "There are so many shades of green and they change from moment to moment as the angle of the sun changes. Inside this garden wall I can pretend the rest of the world doesn't exist."

I was surprised. I would never have thought that a mayor would want to get away from the world. I thought the reason for taking the job was love of the limelight.

He returned to the chair and sat with an air of resignation. "Ask your questions, Spence."

I looked at him and our eyes met. I sensed sadness and felt sorry for him, but I didn't know why. I sipped the whiskey. It was very smooth and I assumed very expensive.

"The obvious question is, are you Marty's father?"

He shook his head and said "No" without hesitation.

"Did you know Elizabeth Williams?"

"Yes, I did."

I wasn't going to get any extra information. First rule of question answering—don't give away anything that isn't asked that the questioner might not have in the first place. I had a feeling I wasn't going to get anything that would help.

"How did you know her?"

"She worked on my campaign. She was one of the most valuable volunteers I had."

"Was that all there was to it?"

"Meaning?"

"Meaning did it go beyond a working relationship?"

He emptied his glass. "Spencer, I do not mean to be evasive, but if I tell you I am not the father, then shouldn't that be the end of it?"

Seemed logical to me. "Yes, sir, I guess it should."

"Good. Then, if you don't mind, I have work to do."

"Don't mind at all. Thank you for your time."

"Certainly. And, again, I am sorry about your parents."

He showed me to the door and closed it softly behind me. Expensive doors always close quietly. I opened the wrought iron gate, and it closed behind me with a clang. I looked around again for surveillance and saw none.

Pulling away from the curb, I wondered where that had gotten me. Nowhere. Which is about what I had expected. The only progress would have been if the mayor had answered "yes." Now I was still left with two possibilities. Just because he *said* he wasn't the father didn't mean he wasn't. And he had evaded my last question instead of answering it. I was leaning toward believing him about not being the father, but you never know. I was also wondering if I should have mentioned that the other possibility was his half brother. No. I needed to do some more digging and withholding information worked both ways. I needed something concrete to link him to Elizabeth. The word of Maxine wasn't going to get me too far.

Chapter 25

It was a little after eight when I left the mayor's house. I had two more stops to make before the night was over. A couple miles to the west the neighborhoods started to change, for the worse. Twenty minutes later I was back at the track. The sun had set.

I drove to Ronny's apartment and parked across the street, as far from the streetlight as I could get. A light was on in his unit, number 205, and the front door was open. I was guessing that, if they went to the bar, it would be around ten. And I had no idea how long they would stay. It could be a long night, and I was fighting the urge to close my eyes. Whiskey made me sleepy.

The building was early ramshackle and struggling to maintain that. Ripped screens, cracked and peeling paint, missing shingles, and a front lawn that was mostly dirt were the outward signs of neglect, the collect-the-rent-and-mind-your-own-business school of ownership.

People came and went. Every so often I caught a shadow moving across the inside wall of 205. A gentle breeze blew in off the lake, moving around scraps of paper in the street. At a quarter to ten, the light in Ronny's apartment went out. He came out, slammed the door, and ran down the steps, skipping several. The door of a beat-up yellow Chevy creaked as he pulled it open and slid in. It had been a long time since those hinges lined up. After lighting a cigarette, he put the car into reverse, banged into the car behind him, pulled out, screeched to the corner, and turned left. Away from the bar but toward the track.

I watched for another twenty minutes. Five minutes later Jesse appeared out of nowhere and slid into the passenger seat of the Mustang. I tried to look like I wasn't surprised.

"Hi, kid. I can disappear just as easily!"

"Good. You may have to."

"The mark gone?"

"About a half hour ago. You get somebody to cover for you at the Blue Note?"

"Sure, my nephew is filling in till I get back."

I twisted toward him and gave him my best serious look. "You sure you want to do this? Not too late to change your mind. It's for a good cause but it is nonetheless illegal."

"Sure. What's the worst? You say this guy's not likely to call the cops, right?"

"Right."

"And we're not stealin' nothin', right?"

"Right."

"So maybe the guy comes back and tells us to get the hell out. Unless he's got help. Then maybe we get hurt a little."

"That doesn't sound like fun, Jesse."

"Been hurt before," followed a shrug of his shoulders. "And I can do a little hurtin' myself."

"Well, I don't think he's coming back for quite awhile. We should be alone."

"What is it we're looking for?"

I sighed. "That's one of the problems. I'm not sure. I want you to just get me in and then be a lookout. I'll do the searching. Maybe I'll know what it is when I see it. You make your way around the back and get in. The lock should be a piece of cake for a man of your talents." I smiled. "Give me a wave and I'll come up."

He smiled too. "You're the boss. Ready?"

"Sure. When we get in, blend in by the front window and watch for company. The guy is skinny, about my height, and drives an old, beat-up yellow Chevy."

"Got it. See you in a couple minutes."

"Take you that long?"

"It's not the doin', it's the gettin' there without lookin' out of place. And you never know what might be waitin' on the back porch. If there's a crowd I'll be back."

"Jesse, I still would rather you show me how to do this. The lock on that door can't be that tricky. You don't need to stick your neck out."

"I know. You're not twistin' this old arm. I'm glad to help after what your old man did for me."

"That's history, Jesse. You don't owe him or me anything."

"I know that too, son. But you see the real reason is I don't have that much faith in your learning ability. So, if you don't mind, I'll just take care of this and we'll get the hell outta here."

I ignored the insult and nodded.

Jesse left as quietly as he had come. He had done time for what he was about to do, so I knew he had thought about it. I watched my mirrors for trouble, keeping one eye on the front window. After five minutes I started to worry. After ten I decided to go and see what the problem was. As I walked across the street, trying to keep my heart from racing, I saw him wave in the window.

I let out a breath and casually climbed the rear stairs. The second door to the left of the stairs was 205. There was no one in sight. Music was blaring from one of the units down on the end. Normally I wouldn't be happy about someone else's noise. This time it was a present that would cover any noise I might make. The latch was broken on the screen. I pulled it open and quickly slid into the apartment.

I couldn't see anything, but my nose was working fine. There was a sour smell that I knew didn't come in with me or Jesse. I closed the door and let my eyes adapt.

I found Jesse next to some heavy, orange drapes at the corner of the front window. "What took you so long?" I asked.

"I had to wait for Romeo trying to convince Juliet to come out for an evening on the town. She finally told him to come back when hell freezes over."

"Nice smell."

"Sure, if you live at the dump."

The room was a mess. Clothes, dirty plates, racing forms, and open bags of chips. I didn't want to see if they were empty. If there was something to find it probably wouldn't be lying out in plain sight, and I really didn't want to touch anything. I couldn't remember when I'd had my last tetanus shot.

"Do your thing, kid. I'll watch the front. And watch out for the—"

I jumped three feet as a crack came from the next room. As I moved toward the front door Jesse grabbed my arm.

"Calm down, Spencer. Mr. Clean has a bug zapper in the kitchen. Must have a thing about flying insects. Now crawlers is another matter."

"Who the hell has a bug zapper in the house? I knew the guy was strange, but Jesus."

Jesse went back to the window. "Get goin'. I'd like to get the hell outta here."

I walked down a center hall that led to the kitchen in the back right. Bedroom and bathroom on the left. Bedroom first. The smell was worse in the kitchen. I had smelled garbage before but this was distinctive. Garbage and sweat and who knows what else. I had never smelled anything quite like it. I assumed it was coming from the garbage, but there was garbage everywhere. There was a can in the corner. It was almost empty. The sink was full of dirty dishes. Looked like he had used them all up and then given up eating. Or maybe he just picked the least dirty plate for his next meal. A rickety card table was piled with dishes and racing forms. A cup of coffee had spilled and soaked one of the forms. It was still wet. I was finding it real hard to believe this guy was from the same family as the mayor whose house seemed a universe away. There were hand-written lists of horses' names lying with the forms.

The bedroom probably was the place he would hide something, but I hesitated. If this was how he kept the spaces company could see, what would the private bedroom be like? And I had absolutely no intention of combing through the bathroom. Ordinarily I would have taken a deep breath and walked in. But I didn't want to do any deep breathing. I didn't want whatever was in there too deep in my lungs. The door was open. I peeked in. Not much to see in the dark, so I got my flashlight out of my back pocket.

The room was a mess, but the garbage seemed to be confined to the rest of the place. Clothes strewn all over and a bed that looked like it had never been made. The only other furniture was a nightstand and a four-drawer dresser. One picture in a frame with broken glass lay flat on top of the dresser. It was of Ronny standing next to a good-looking horse. I shined the light over the surfaces and saw nothing interesting. I kicked at some of the stuff on the floor and decided the drawers were the obvious target for a search. Rifling through Ronny's underwear didn't seem too appealing either. I should have brought gloves. The bug zapper cracked again.

The bottom drawer was almost empty. Just a pair of jeans and a grungy baseball cap. Cardinals. The second drawer was filled with old racing forms, some dating back three years. They were covered with numbers, horses' names were checked or circled, and dollar amounts were written in the margins. I assumed this was Ronny's ledger of bets. Looked like he hadn't done too badly for himself. Some entries were in the thousands. What did he do with it? There was nothing else in the drawer. The third drawer held shirts and cotton tops. I pushed them around enough to see if anything else was there and got lucky. A white, business-sized envelope was at the back of the drawer. I took it out. Nothing on the outside but it wasn't sealed so I opened it.

Inside was a picture of Marty and several canceled checks. They were all for $500 and were all dated within a few days of the first of the month and were made out to Elizabeth. There were nine checks, and the dates spanned three years. I took out my notepad and jotted down the dates. The checks were imprinted Mr. and Mrs. Jeffrey Grey, signed by the mayor and endorsed by Beth. The picture looked fairly recent. On the back was written "Birthday, three years old." Looked like a woman's writing. I guessed it was Beth's. I also guessed that she wanted the father to have a picture of his daughter. Maybe she knew who the father was after all. I put the picture back in the envelope along with all but one of the checks. I considered taking them all, copying them, and bringing them back, but decided the less time spent here the better. I kept one and closed the drawer. I figured if Ronny ever bothered to check he probably wouldn't remember if he'd had eight or nine.

The top drawer was the underwear drawer. Gotta have one of those. But I really didn't want to go there. Besides, I already had what I was looking for—a physical connection to Beth and Marty. But it wasn't exactly what I was expecting. After making sure the drawers were all closed, I made my way back to Jesse. One thing I didn't have to worry about—Ronny would never notice if anything had been disturbed.

"All done, kid?" Jesse asked without taking his eyes off the street.

"Yup. Let's get outta here."

"You find what you were lookin' for?"

"I think so. Thanks, Jesse. I'll let you know if it helps."

"I don't wanna know nothin', Spencer. I was never here. And if anybody asks, I don't even know you."

"Deal. Thanks nevertheless."

"You're welcome nevertheless. Now get your butt out. I'll lock up and leave after you."

"You want me to wait in the car and make sure you get out okay?"

"I already got out okay. What you see now is just your imagination. Move."

I moved. I pulled the door closed and shut the screen as quietly as I could. Still nobody around. I drove a mile away, pulled into a strip mall and parked. Squirming in the seat, I got out my notepad. The dates were all between Marty's birth and Beth's death. I made an assumption. Since Marty's picture was in the envelope, the checks were sent to Beth for support of Marty. So, could be the mayor was living up to his responsibilities. Or could be he was paying for his brother's. But, if the notes on the forms were winnings, Ronny could afford to pay his own way. But then he would not be the type to own up to responsibility. Another question was if Ronny had that kind of money, why live in that dump? And why work a menial labor job at the track? As I thought of the questions, I jotted them on a new page in my pad.

My last appointment of the day was at eleven. I planned to stake out Mean Spirits in hopes that Bobby was there and would come out alone. But with the way Ronny babysat the kid, that wasn't likely. Actually, I didn't have much of a plan. I figured I'd play it by ear.

I had figured out one thing. I had often wondered how anyone could stand working stables at the track. In Ronny's case the answer was easy—it smelled better than his apartment.

Chapter 26

Sometimes you do stupid things out of frustration. Showing up at Mean Spirits was probably one of those things, but I was willing to do it anyway. Ronny was so determined to keep Bobby from talking to me that I figured Bobby must have something to say. And since I didn't know where Bobby lived, I figured I'd take a shot at the only place besides the track I knew he'd be. And I had backup, so I thought I was hot stuff. I parked on the street and waited for Johnny to find me. He didn't take long.

At five after eleven, Johnny leaned down, and that took a good deal of leaning, and stuck his head in the passenger window. I told him to get in. That was easier said than done, even with the seat back all the way.

"Spencer, you want me on your payroll you gotta get a bigger vehicle."

"Johnny, when I am able to afford a payroll, I'll add a Cadillac to my fleet."

"Now you're talkin'," he said with a big grin. "You figured out how we're gonna do this yet?"

"Well, there's still a few things I haven't worked out," I said hesitantly.

"A simple no will do."

"Okay, no. The goal is to get this kid alone so I can talk to him. He's led around by this Ronny Press who's not hard to spot. Skinny, brown ponytail, rat-like face, bad teeth, about my height. The kid looks like a clean-cut kid you'd introduce to your sister."

"Not *my* sister, pal."

"Okay, not mine either. Let's play this by ear. If Bobby comes out alone it's easy. I grab him and we talk. There's an alley a few doors away I thought would make a good spot. You cover me. If they're together, I suggest that Bobby and I take a walk. Ronny will suggest otherwise. You convince him he's wrong."

"You sure they're here?"

"I'm sure Ronny is here. His yellow Chevy is in the lot across the street." I pointed. "And I am told that where Ronny goes, Bobby follows."

"You just expectin' the two of them?"

"I'm hoping so. But if there is a crowd, we use some common sense. Did you bring along some help?"

"Sure. I got two more."

"They as big as you?"

He laughed and stretched his arm out the window. "Nobody's as big as me. I figure they're gonna be drunk and not thinkin' too straight. So once you isolate the kid, I can handle this Ronny and three more. After that I don't like the odds, drunk or not."

"Okay. But let's even it up. If they've got more than us we wait. Okay?"

"Fine with me. I got nothin' against better odds."

"Where are you going to be?" I asked. The driver of a passing car honked and yelled something out the window. I looked around and didn't see anyone.

"I'll be around. Don't worry. We'll be close. Now I gotta get outta this tin can before I cramp up."

He opened the door and had as much trouble getting out as he had getting in. Some disadvantages to being big. However, tonight the advantages tipped the scale in my favor.

The traffic was moderate. There weren't many cars in the lot across the street. A wooden sign on a post let everyone know the parking was just for the bar and where they could expect to have their cars towed. I wondered who checked and if any cars had ever been towed. I had considered going in to see how many people were in the Ronny party but if the crowd was sparse I would be noticed. So I stayed put. But as I watched I decided the crowd wasn't that sparse. More were going in than coming out; it was just a walking crowd, not a driving crowd. This was a typical neighborhood bar, and they called them neighborhood bars because people from the neighborhood went there to drink.

Who goes to a bar on Monday night? I would think you'd need some time to recover from the weekend. I guessed the same people who went to bars any other night. After awhile they all blended together. Why should Monday night be any different? But there were basically two types that went in. There was what I would think were the regular customers, the neighborhood guy who was stopping after the late shift to wind down or was getting away from his wife, sitting with a glass till he knew she was asleep and he could go home to quiet. Rather come here than fall asleep in front of the television. He was forty or older. Then there were the young couples, early twenties; guys hoping to get lucky, dressed in gaudy slacks and loud shirts, hair slicked back, and towing giggling girls done up in their Monday-night best. Usually they came in two couples at a time. The guys would have liked it that way. More courage if a pal is around. Someone to give knowing looks to and wink at with a nod toward the lucky girl. The couples were the kind that the older guys would shake their heads at and order another beer.

There were single girls but not very many; ages between the older guys and the younger couples. And they didn't look like they would take any crap from anybody. They were going in for a drink, not to look for love; but maybe if love found them that would be a bonus. Judging by the walk-in crowd, the place was doing a decent business. I rethought going in for a look but decided against it. I didn't want to take a chance on alerting Ronny. He was a jerk, but he was a wary jerk. If he saw me, he'd get out fast. If I waited outside I would have surprise on my side and that counted for something, even if I still lacked a concrete plan. I hoped the surprise would be his and not mine.

The evening was comfortably cool. I was not at all sleepy anymore. The stink in Ronny's apartment had jarred me awake. At twelve thirty more people were coming out than going in. I hoped that one was closing time. I should have checked. At a quarter to one, Bobby came out.

He looked around like he was expecting somebody, stretched, and yawned. I started out of the car, feeling pretty lucky. But that didn't last. By the time I closed the door, Ronny was at his side along with two more fellows I didn't recognize. They all looked around like they couldn't remember where the car was parked. Then I got lucky again. Ronny reached in his pocket, pulled out his keys, and tossed them to Bobby. Mr. Bigshot figured he deserved a chauffeur. All of a sudden I had a plan. The bar was two doors away from the alley which was another couple of doors away from the lot where the yellow heap was parked. At the rear of the lot was another alley that ran parallel to the street and connected to the first alley with a tee. I was on the other side of the street another couple of doors down. It would be easy to meet Bobby in the parking lot without Ronny knowing.

Keeping close to the buildings, I walked slowly to the edge of the lot and waited in a doorfront. A television was playing in the apartment above. Ronny got delayed by a single girl leaving the bar. She was pretty, almost as tall as me, and tough-looking. He tried to convince her she should give him the time of day. Maybe he was taking one last shot after getting turned down inside. He didn't get any farther outside. She gave him a look that shut him up and turned in my direction. Bobby followed a few steps behind. She crossed the street before she got to the lot. Bobby turned in and headed for the yellow car parked against the rear wall. In the dim light of the parking lot the yellow looked like vomit. I followed and caught up to Bobby as he reached the car. He saw me without recognizing me at first. As he unlocked the door he turned his head and squinted. It took a few seconds but it finally sunk in. When it did, confusion turned to fear.

"What are you doing here?" he sputtered.

"I figured we could talk for a few minutes," I said calmly.

"I can't talk to you." His fingers fumbled with the keys as he struggled to get in the car.

"We're safe here, Bobby." I looked around and swept my arm over the lot. "See, no Ronny."

"Ronny is right out on the street waiting for me. I'm getting the car." His eyes darted to the street where raised voices carried from the bar.

"It's okay, Bobby. Sounds like Ronny is busy. Let's take a walk." I took his arm and started toward the alley. I was expecting him to give in if Ronny wasn't in sight. I was wrong.

"Ronny!" the kid yelled as loud as he could. "Ronny, help!"

I led him back toward the alley, almost dragging him along. I thought if I could get him in the dark he might be scared enough to shut up. He kept yelling. As we reached the alley, Ronny and friends came running around the front. One more yell from Bobby brought Ronny running toward the alley.

"You again! Let go of him. What the hell do you think you're doing?" He pulled Bobby away from me. "I think I've taken as much of you as I care to. If you don't listen to being asked nicely I guess we'll have to try something else. Bobby, get the car started and be ready to take off."

Ronny moved to my left and his pals moved to my right. They moved slowly and looked like they meant business. They looked like wolves circling for the kill.

"Not exactly a fair fight," I said with more control than I felt. I was hoping the odds would even up but you never know. Johnny may have slipped on a banana peel.

"Fair was asking you to butt out, twice. I'm done with fair. I'm not putting up with your crap anymore."

The car started. Bobby pulled out of the space and turned to face the street.

They were only three feet away from me when Johnny stepped out of the shadows behind me.

"How about my crap? Ready to try some?"

They all stopped. My eyes didn't leave Ronny. He was startled at first by Johnny; anyone would be. His eyes widened just a bit. But then he got cocky again as he got some guts from his friends and the gun he had just pulled out of his back pocket.

"Big don't impress me." he said with a snarl. The shadows on his crooked teeth made it look like several were missing, and his eyes had narrowed to little beads of black. "Just means more bullets. And we still got numbers. You're not too smart after all. Why don't you just walk away from your big buddy." He motioned to my left with his gun.

I started to move slowly. I had the advantage of being able to see what was happening behind Ronny.

"Ronny, you should never leave your back uncovered," I said.

"Nice try. How stupid do you think I am?"

I didn't have to answer. The car shutting off made him look over his shoulder. One of Johnny's friends had turned off the engine and taken the keys. Ronny took in the man moving up on him from behind and another by the car. He still didn't look too concerned. After all, he was holding the equalizer. But in the few seconds that glance took, Johnny had pulled his gun and it was bigger than Ronny's.

"What a nice little party this is," said Johnny with a big smile. Even in the darkness of the alley those white teeth shone. "Seems like we got more up our sleeves than you do. Or maybe we just got more sleeves."

Ronny looked at me with intense hatred which slowly faded. "Okay. We were just kiddin'." He put the gun back in his pants. "Somethin' you want?" he spat.

"Nice of you to ask," I said. "First you can drop that gun on the ground and kick it over this way." He did. I picked it up. "Next you can all move over against the garage, hands at your sides." They moved, Ronny kicking the side of a trash can on the way. "Now, I would like to have a talk with Bobby without you around."

He sneered at me. "Why don't you leave the kid alone? What the hell do you want?"

"Maybe nothing. But I won't know that till I talk to him, and you've been getting in the way."

"I don't think he wants to talk to you."

"And I'm getting tired of what you think. Let's see if Bobby can think for himself." I kept the gun out just in case they had any more surprises. A slight smell of garbage drifted by on a gust of wind.

"He doesn't do much thinking. He's not too smart."

"I'll remember that. Thanks."

Johnny was at my side, gun pointed at Ronny.

"Okay, here's what's going to happen. You three will climb in the car and go home. Bobby will stay here, and we'll find out if he can think for himself."

"And how's Bobby getting home?" Ronny asked.

"I'd be glad to drive him," I answered.

"I don't like that answer," said Ronny.

"What you like doesn't matter anymore. Now let's all walk slowly over to the car."

"You don't know what you're getting into here." Sounded like a try at cocky but it was laced with hesitation.

"Then I guess I'll be surprised. Now move." I pointed toward the car with the gun.

They led the way. I motioned for Johnny to wait in the alley and told Johnny's friend to get Bobby out of the car. The trio got in, Ronny behind the wheel. I thought about what I wanted to ask Bobby and realized I didn't really know. But if Ronny was being this protective, there must be something he didn't want the kid talking about.

I pushed the door closed and said, "Drive away and keep driving. I don't want to see you back here."

He started the engine and snarled at Bobby, "You don't have to tell him nothin'." They drove off, tires screeching when they hit the street. Dust billowed behind the car.

I asked the two friends to watch the street and walked back toward the alley with Bobby. This time I didn't have to drag him.

"Ronny says I don't have to tell you nothin'," he said with a quiver in his voice.

"You don't, but maybe you'll want to."

He looked confused. "Why would I want to?"

I had no idea and shrugged my shoulders. "Never know, Bobby."

We reached the alley. Johnny had faded back into the shadows. We stood on the edge of the spilled light from the lot and the dark of the alley.

"So what would you like to tell me, Bobby?"

"Nothin'. I don't have to tell you nothin'."

"Does that mean there is something to tell? You just don't want to?"

The confused look returned. It didn't take much. He didn't know if that was something he could answer. A door slammed somewhere down the alley. Bobby jumped.

"Bobby, who are you more scared of, me or Ronny?"

"I'm not scared of Ronny. He's my friend."

I didn't want to hang around too long. I was pretty sure Ronny would be back, with more help. I put my arm around Bobby's shoulder. "What would he do to you if he thought you talked?"

"He knows I wouldn't."

"Sure. He trusts you. But sometimes people have ways of making other people talk even if they don't want to."

His eyes filled with fear. I continued.

"And Ronny knows we have those ways."

He stood with his arms crossed in front of him, shaking.

"What do you mean? What ways?"

I pulled him a little deeper into the shadows. "Why do you think Ronny drove off without a fight? And how do you think I got Ronny's gun?" I showed it to him. "Do you think he's scared of me?"

"N... no," he stammered. "He said he's not scared of you."

"Right. So if he's not scared of me then there must be something else he is scared of, right? Cuz I got his gun and he left you here without a fight."

I could see him trying to figure it out. He looked around. "I don't see nothin' besides you."

As he said that, Johnny walked out of the deep shadows. The gun was out of sight, but he didn't need the gun to be intimidating. Even I was a little afraid.

Bobby's eyes bulged in his head and he gasped.

"You see, Bobby. There is something Ronny is scared of. So scared that he left you here. He's not such a tough guy, and he's not such a good friend either. Now, I'll just have my friend here take you off into the dark part of the alley, and we'll see if you want to talk after that."

I waved. Johnny took one step toward Bobby, and the kid cracked.

"Okay! Okay! I didn't mean to do it. Just keep him away from me. Please!"

Johnny stopped.

I was puzzled. "Didn't mean to do what, Bobby?"

"To kill those people. It was just supposed to be an accident. I was supposed to run them off the road as a warning, but there was a curve and I lost control. I really didn't mean it." He put his face in his hands and started to cry, shoulders shaking.

I looked at Johnny. He looked as shocked as I felt.

"Bobby, what are you talking about?" I asked carefully.

He wiped his eyes on his sleeve. "Don't you know? Isn't that what you wanted me to tell you?" he stammered between sniffs.

"That's one of the things. I just want to make sure. Which two people are you talking about?" I really didn't want to know.

"That police guy. But I didn't know his wife was in the car too. Honest. I didn't mean to hurt them. It was just a warning."

Somewhere during his explanation I had stopped listening. I was having trouble believing that the guy who killed my parents was standing in front of me. Robert Dayton—Bobby. I felt Johnny's hand on my shoulder. I'm sure he put it there to keep me from doing something stupid, but it wasn't necessary. I didn't feel as angry as I thought I would if I ever met who did it. I didn't feel anything. Maybe after the shock wore off. For the moment, I figured I'd better start thinking again. Ronny was sure to come back, and I didn't want to be there.

I tried to talk calmly. I was sure Bobby wouldn't notice the shake in my voice. "Bobby, what do you think Ronny will do to you once he knows you told us?"

He shook his head, viciously. "He won't like it. No, he sure won't."

"I know that. But do you think he will hurt you?"

"I've seen him hurt people."

Bobby didn't like to think; maybe because he wasn't very good at it.

"Do you think we would hurt you?"

He hesitated and then shook his head no.

"That's right. Now that you told us, we're your friends. And Johnny here protects his friends. Do you think he can protect you from Ronny?"

Bobby looked Johnny up and down and was duly impressed. "Yes, I think he'd be a good protector."

"Then would you like to go with Johnny till we take care of Ronny?"

He nodded yes.

I couldn't hate this kid. He was just the errand boy doing what he was told. And if Ronny was so concerned about keeping him quiet, Ronny must have been the guy who did the telling. Him I could get around to hating. In fact, I already did.

"Johnny, we gotta get outta here. Would you take Bobby with you and keep him somewhere safe?"

"Sure thing, Spencer. You okay?"

"Yep, for now. Don't know about later. Don't tell me where he is. I'll call Stosh and see how he wants to handle this. I'll call you."

"You got it." He squeezed my shoulder and motioned the kid to start walking. "Let's go, kid."

Frozen to that spot in the alley, I watched them walk toward the street. About halfway through the lot, Johnny yelled over his shoulder, "Get the hell outta here, Spencer. You don't want what's comin', at least not by yourself."

I barely heard him and couldn't move.

"Spencer, do I gotta come and carry you?"

After a deep breath I got my feet moving, but I really don't remember walking to the car. And I barely remember driving back to the office.

Fumbling with the keys, I let myself into the office and sat down at the desk. I needed to think about what had happened and see if there was anything I was missing. I didn't think so, but what I'd gotten certainly wasn't what I had been expecting. But then I wasn't expecting anything in particular. I needed to call Stosh and glanced at the phone. After a moment of thought, I realized I didn't know what I should tell him, if anything. I also realized that the red light on my answering machine was flashing. Probably Aunt Rose reminding me that Kathleen was coming on Wednesday. Not what I needed to hear at the moment. But thinking about Stosh wasn't getting me anywhere. Maybe a friendly voice would help me see straight. I pushed the button.

The tape rewound and a voice that was not Aunt Rose said, "Okay, you got the kid. We want him back. We tried warning you nicely, like we tried warning your old man. He didn't listen and look what happened to him. Last warning. And no cops. How is your friend Miss Green? Let him go and there's no trouble."

Like I hadn't had enough surprises for one night. I replayed it several times. Didn't change. I was being warned. But for what? I'd never even told Bobby or Ronny what I wanted. And obviously it wasn't just me they were threatening. And who was "we"? Ronny evidently had friends.

It was late, a little past one. I knew she would be asleep, at least I hoped she would, but I had to know if Kelly was safe. I picked up the phone and dialed her number. A groggy, sleepy voice answered. It was the most beautiful voice I'd ever heard.

"Kelly, it's Spencer."

"Thank goodness. I don't take well to strange calls in the middle of the night."

"Well just because it's me doesn't mean it isn't strange. And this is. I need you to listen to me. Are you awake?"

"As much as I will be, which isn't much. Is something wrong?" she asked hesitantly.

"No. And I want to keep it that way. Do you trust me enough to do what I say without explanation till later?"

She paused. "There is something wrong, isn't there?"

"There is that chance. I need you to get out of that hotel right now and check in somewhere else without telling anyone where."

Silence.

"Kelly?"

"Sorry. Are you serious?"

"Very. I will explain later. It involves Ronny."

"Oh, Spencer, I knew there was trouble. What happened? You okay?"

"Yes, and I will tell you later. Will you do as I ask?"

"Okay, if you think it's necessary."

"I do. Pack light. Try and get out in ten minutes. Five would be better. Take your car and drive around. Make sure you're not being followed. If you are, try and lose them."

"Try? How short is your memory?"

"Okay. Sorry. Lose them. Check in and get some sleep. In the morning call Stosh at police headquarters." I gave her the number. "Either he or I will talk to you then."

"Spencer, I have to be at the track for a workout in the morning."

"Don't till you talk to us. Don't even call. Don't talk to anyone or go outside of your room till you talk to me or Stosh. Okay?"

"Okay. Spencer, should I be afraid?"

"Not if you follow directions. Now hurry. Wait, I've got a better idea. I'm heading to Stosh's house. Meet me there. He's got a spare room. I'll explain then."

"Okay. I'm a bit scared."

"Good. That will keep you on your toes. Now hurry and keep your eyes open."

"What am I watching for?"

"His yellow Chevy, but any car following you."

I gave her the address and directions to Stosh's house, and we hung up.

I called Stosh and briefly explained the situation. He suggested I move quickly and said he'd get the spare room ready. He asked me to bring the tape for the lab to listen to. After warning me to watch for a tail, we hung up. I popped the tape out of the answering machine and replaced it. This case had come a long way from a little girl eating chocolate cake.

Chapter 27

I beat Kelly to Stosh's and gave him the gun. It was a little after two and I was getting worried. But I was glad I had a chance to give him the story without her there. I didn't want to worry her any more than I already had.

Stosh walked into the living room and handed me a cup of coffee. He sat in his recliner. After taking a sip, I put down the cup on the glass-topped table. As I did, I heard a car pull into the driveway.

We both got up. It was Kelly.

Stosh whistled at the car. "Nice crowd you're running with, kid."

"That's nothin', wait till you meet her."

I answered the door and put my arms around her. Sleepy and no makeup and she looked beautiful. I took her bag and her hand and led her into the living room where Stosh was waiting. After introductions, we all sat, she on the sofa next to me. She turned to me.

"Now that you've got me scared to death, can I get an explanation?"

"Sure."

"Would you like some coffee, Miss Green?" asked Stosh.

"That would be great. Thank you. And please call me Kelly."

He got up and headed for the kitchen. "Spencer, hold that explanation till I get back. I'd like another run at it. Why don't you two put your cars in the garage? Spencer, put mine in the drive." He tossed me his keys.

I reached out and touched Kelly's hair and told her I was getting worried because it had taken her longer than expected.

"Well that's your fault. You got me so paranoid I thought every car I saw was following me. I took several detours."

"Do you think anyone was?"

"Probably not. But there was one yellow car that was behind me for a couple of turns in a row."

"Ronny's?"

She laughed. "No. I'd know his beater anywhere. This was a real car. Anyway, whoever it was finally turned off."

"I'm glad you're okay, Kelly. I was worried."

"I'm okay. But I'd feel better if I knew what was going on."

"Wait for Stosh and I'll tell you everything." Almost. We moved the cars.

When we sat back down, Kelly put her head back and closed her eyes. The world is full of all kinds of things, some wonderful, some nasty. I was going to do my darndest to keep her from running into the nasty.

Stosh came in and set the coffee cup on the table, returned to his chair, and pulled up the footrest. He stretched and yawned. "Okay, kid. Once more. But if the young lady wants to hear, you'd better wake her up."

"I'm awake," she said. "Just resting my eyes." She opened them and sipped the coffee, grimacing a bit.

"Sorry," said Stosh. "I don't make it much."

She shook her head. "No, it's fine. Thank you."

I repeated the story, leaving out the threat to Kelly and some of the window dressing. By the time I was done, she had moved close to me and was holding onto my arm. I expected her first words to be concern for her plight. I was wrong.

"Spencer, I am so sorry about your parents. Manning. You know I didn't remember what their names were. Why didn't you mention it before?"

"It's not the kind of thing that comes up in conversation."

"Well it did. Remember when we were having lunch and you asked me if Bobby had any trouble with the police? I was about to tell you that when we were interrupted by your friend." She shuddered. "You would have known then." Her voice was soft and caring and tired.

"But if you had maybe we wouldn't have Bobby. And I think there are other things he knows."

"I think you're playing with dynamite."

"I think so too," Stosh chimed in. He put down the footrest and sat forward in the chair. "Lets see what we've got here, I mean besides the laws you've broken. Should we count those first?"

"Broken?" I asked. "Maybe bent, but not broken."

"No? How about kidnapping."

"Geez. Whose side are you on?"

"The law's side, kid."

I rolled my eyes. "Yeah, the law that handcuffs the cops while the bad guys roll out their cannons and stand there laughing."

"We've been down this road before, Spencer. We know where we stand and it ain't gonna change. It's the way I have to do it."

"Yup. We both have our ways. I'll just continue with mine."

"It's a free country. Till you break the law. Then I come after you, my way of course." He leaned back. "I'd rather not see you behind bars."

"Me too. In the meantime, my way turned accidental death into murder. And maybe got you a witness for whatever the hell is going on at the track that you are scratching your butt about and who knows what else. And, by the way, I even got some info on my own case while I was out solving yours."

"Let's not get too cocky. I agree you opened some doors. But you are also here because you're hiding from the bad guys that you're so proud of bringing to the surface. And may I point out that you are not the only person you placed in the line of fire?"

I looked down at Kelly. Her head had slumped against my shoulder and this time she was asleep. Her breathing was deep and her breath was warm on my arm.

"Yeah okay. I'm not a big shot. But we got something, didn't we?"

"We?"

"Yes, we. I was coming to you anyway, even if I didn't need a place to hide."

"Yeah we got something. Probably a lawsuit. Even a half-assed lawyer could make kidnapping stick."

"It wasn't kidnapping, Stosh. I gave him a choice. He decided to come with us."

"Sure. After you scared him to death."

"I don't see it that way. And I don't think Bobby will either. I think he's on our side."

"I hope so. It's done. We'll just have to see where it falls. But these aren't amateurs you're playing with, Spencer. They mean business. I don't think they meant to kill your folks. It probably was just supposed to be a warning. But I guarantee you they don't care much that they did. Where's the kid?"

"I'm not sure. I figured I didn't want to know in case they grabbed me and tried to torture it out of me."

He pointed his finger at me. "Spencer, this is not a TV show. It's not a game. These guys are real, and they won't care if you happen to die."

"So I guess we better catch them first."

"Not we. Me, and my friends with the badges. I'll get some protection for you and Kelly. Nice lady by the way. And you butt out. Got it?"

"Got it. I don't have a death wish."

"I know. But you do have this streak of justice. Sometimes the bad guys win."

"Not if I can help it."

He stood up, ran his hand through his hair, and frowned. "I won't always be there to help, Spencer."

"I know. I'll be careful. And you do have Bobby and a confession."

"To you."

"And Johnny."

"To me would be better. I'll go have a chat with him and see if the story stays the same."

I nodded and twisted on the sofa. The arm Kelly was leaning against had fallen asleep. "You haven't said thank you."

He laughed. "Sorry, so far all I see is trouble."

"Well if that's how you feel, next time I won't call," I said with a smile.

"Sure you will. You're not stupid, just too brave for your own good."

As he picked up the coffee cups he asked, "Now what's this about *your* case?"

"I talked with the mayor last night."

Stosh raised his eyebrows but said nothing.

"He knows Elizabeth but says he's not Marty's father. Wasn't too talkative."

"What did he say about Ronny?"

"I didn't mention Ronny. The mayor had pretty much told me that since he wasn't the father, he was done talking. And I figured he wouldn't be too impressed with my source of information about Ronny. So I decided to wait till I had some proof that tied Ronny to Elizabeth."

He nodded. "Probably a good idea. But how are you going to get proof?"

"I already got some. I have a picture of Marty and canceled checks made out to Elizabeth that tie in Ronny."

"Ronny's checks?"

"No. The checks were signed by the mayor."

Stosh set the cups back down and sat on the edge of the table. "So how do they tie in Ronny?"

"They were found in Ronny's possession."

"By you?"

"Yes."

"They just happen to fall out of his pocket while you were waltzing in the alley?"

"Not exactly."

"Then?"

I decided I was in enough trouble. So far my infractions were just bending the rules; breaking and entering was a different story. "Let's just say I know where they are."

"Okay, but if your ass gets caught in the wringer, I can't help. Your doing something illegal is just as illegal as their doing something illegal."

"Yes, sir." I glanced at the clock on the wall. A little after three.

He gathered the cups and shook his head. "Kids. I suppose you're going to talk to the mayor again?"

"I'd like to. You want another group meeting first?"

"No, I don't think so. As long as it's still personal, you handle it. Don't accuse him of something you can't back up. Best to show him what you've got and let him do the talking."

"Sure. You want to set it up?"

"No, you call him. I'll get you his private number before you leave. And please remember there is a murder case there too."

I promised. "You thinking he could have done it?"

"I try not to think without facts. How many checks are there?"

"Nine."

"Over what time span?"

"A few years."

He pursed his lips and left the room with the cups. A clink in the kitchen was followed by footsteps back into the living room. "Why would the mayor write checks to Elizabeth if he wasn't the father? And if he was willing to pay her for that long, why would he suddenly kill her?"

"Two good questions."

"See if you can get an answer to the first. Don't go near the second. Understand?"

I did.

"Okay, let's get a little sleep. I put sheets on the bed in the guest room for your lady friend. You can have the couch."

I woke Kelly enough to make it down the hall and into bed. I returned to the sofa and put off doing any more thinking till morning.

After kicking off my shoes, I sat on the sofa and don't remember lying down.

Chapter 28

I woke up to birds chirping, a room filled with sunshine, and the smell of coffee. But the smell of this morning's coffee was more enticing than that of last night's. I soon found out why—Kelly had made it. I stretched and fought the urge to stay on the sofa. It was only a little past seven and I wasn't trying very hard. I wanted to stay and listen to the birds; they sounded so carefree. Nobody was threatening them. The cats must have slept in. But then I got another incentive to get up; the sizzle and pop and aroma of frying bacon pulled me into the kitchen feeling a little self-conscious in my slept-in clothes. I must have looked awful. My face felt like the skin was sagging downward. But I took some solace in the fact that Kelly was in the same boat. The only good-looker this morning would be Stosh and that was a stretch at best.

Turning the corner of the kitchen, I found I was wrong about Kelly. Somehow she looked like a fresh breeze feels on a hot day.

I kissed the back of her neck and asked, "How do you do that?"

She turned the bacon and answered, "Do what?"

"Not look like I feel."

She laughed. "It's magic we women learn at an early age. Hair pulled back and up and add a ribbon and you have something far different than the scraggly mess I'd have with it down. And I have the benefit of a shower and makeup and fresh clothes, casual as they may be. I didn't take much time to pick out an outfit. You probably just ran out and didn't think of clothes. Right?"

"Guilty." I put my hands on her shoulders. "Can I help?"

"You can go wash up. I think your friend is done in the shower. If you hurry you can crack some eggs."

I hurried and met Stosh coming out of the bathroom.

"All yours, kid. You look like hell."

"Good morning to you too."

"Nothing personal. We can't all be Greek gods." He slapped me on the back and took a deep breath. "Something smells good."

"The cook is busy."

He lost his bluster and whispered quietly, "God, I miss that smell."

I patted his shoulder.

"You'd better hurry or I might steal your woman. There's a spare toothbrush in the vanity."

"I'm hurrying." Everybody was in a hurry this morning. My woman. Happy and scared at the same time. As I washed my face, I thought about Kelly. She was certainly "a keeper" as Dad would have said. But I wasn't sure if I was in the market for keeping. And I didn't know if she was either. But what if she was and I walked away and never found another? Too much to think about. I had other problems, like whether or not I'd be a statistic tomorrow. I toweled off, brushed the taste of Ronny's filthy apartment out of my mouth and headed for the feast.

The back door was open. Birds were singing as they waited for their turn at the feeder by the porch, and a breeze was blowing the yellow and green curtains on the window over the sink. Stosh was brushing eggshells into the garbage, and Kelly was turning the eggs. Bacon and orange juice were already on the table. A police radio crackled softly in the background. We ate like people who planned on living another day.

Between bites, Stosh said, "Kelly, I wish you didn't have to be here under these circumstances, but this is wonderful. I usually run off to work with a bowl of cereal."

That pretty smile filled the room with everything nice. "Glad you like it. But give me your opinion, Mr. Powolski. Do I need to be here?"

He soaked up some runny egg with his toast and ate it before answering, "I really don't think so. But your white knight here thinks so. So better safe than sorry. And please call me Stosh."

I knew he was saying that to make her feel better. He thought she needed to be there too.

"Do you think I can go back to the hotel, at least to get some more clothes?"

I let him do the talking. She'd probably listen to him more than me. "Well if you want to keep Mr. Big Deal PI happy, maybe you'd better stay here for a couple of days. If you want to give me your key, I'll send an officer to your room to pick up some clothes. Same for you, Spence."

There was an ongoing chatter on the radio.

"Let me see if I understand," I said slowly. "You want me to spend the day here alone with Kelly?"

He washed the last of the toast and eggs down with orange juice. "Think you can handle that?"

"I'll give it a try," I said and wiped my mouth on my paper napkin. "So what's the plan?"

"The plan?" he asked.

"Yeah. What about Bobby and my appointment?"

Stosh quickly glanced at Kelly and raised his eyebrows.

I put my hand on Kelly's arm. "Don't worry, Stosh. She already knows most of my case and the accident is public news."

"Yeah, but if it's murder, I don't want that public. And I'd rather—"

Kelly put up her hand and butted in. "I understand. I'll go make the bed. Spencer can clean up while you guys talk."

"No offense, Kelly. I don't mean that you would—"

"No offense taken." She touched his arm lightly.

He looked like a neglected puppy. Kelly's kiss on his cheek perked him up again. We both watched her go. As she did, the room lost some of its brightness.

"Whew. Spencer, where did you find that one?"

I explained.

"So the track taketh away and the track giveth. I don't know if she makes up for threats on your life, but she's a big step in that direction."

"I agree." I pushed back my chair and started to clear the plates. "So what's the plan?"

"The plan is you stay here and let me do my job. Let's let things calm down and see what's what. I'll pay a visit to the Blue Note."

"Okay. Tell Johnny what you want to do with Bobby. But what about my call to the mayor?"

"I'd rather you lay low for a couple of days. The mayor isn't going anywhere. And I'd rather no one else knew about him." He carried his plate and glass to the sink.

I caught his meaning. "I'm sure she's okay, Stosh, but I'll keep it to myself." I ran the water till it was hot and rinsed the dried yellow egg off the plates. "I'd like to talk to the mayor though. I hate sitting on a lead."

He looked at me and winced. "You've got to sit on it for awhile anyway. I know you're not much on fashion, but slept-in clothes are out this year. Give me your key and make a list, and I'll have someone run over and grab some fresh clothes. We'll talk about the mayor when I get home tonight."

"What time do you get home?"

"Usually around six. Stay put till then. Watch the Cubs game. Get some sleep. Now make me a list of what you want. Make it enough for a couple of days. I'll call during the day. I'm going to say goodbye to Kelly."

I found a piece of paper and tried to make a list of things I needed. It wasn't very long. The hardest part was trying to remember if I had anything halfway decent besides the clothes the mayor had already seen me in.

A door slammed next door, and a deep voice yelled something back at his wife. He started his car and revved the engine before backing out of the drive. Road rage. It starts at home, at least in this case. Stosh grabbed the list out of my hand and waved as he went by.

"So long, kid. Behave."

I waved to his back. At the moment I was too tired to not behave. But by afternoon I would be rested and couldn't make any promises.

Chapter 29

I don't like sitting and doing nothing, even if I get to take it easy and watch a ballgame. If there was something going on, I wanted to be in on it. So if it weren't for Kelly, I would have taken my chances. But she did change things. I was responsible. I put her in this situation. And I wanted to have a serious talk with the guys that would threaten an innocent bystander.

I was reading the sports page in the den when Kelly reappeared looking like flowers after a spring rain. She sat on the other end of the couch and crossed her legs under her.

"So we've got the day off?"

"Yes, ma'am. Doctor's orders."

"Can I call the track and tell them I am going to miss the workout?"

"Sure. Make it short."

"What should I tell them?"

"Just tell them something came up, and you might be gone a couple of days."

Taking a deep breath, she stretched her arms out in front of her and then folded them across her chest. With a furrowed brow, she asked, "Do you really think it could be days? I need someone to take care of the horses."

I tried to sound unconcerned. "Is that such a terrible fate?"

She leaned over and kissed me on the cheek. "No, if it were planned. But somehow this lacks the carefree vacation atmosphere."

I nodded. "Guess so. But no, I don't think it will be long. Stosh is just being careful. He needs some time to get a handle on this. Once he talks to Bobby he can move on these other idiots."

She nodded but didn't seem all that convinced.

"You tired?" I asked.

"I could probably use a nap. How about you?"

"Yeah, me too. Think I'll finish reading the paper."

She snuggled down into a pillow against the arm of the couch and closed her eyes. As I glanced at the standings, my eyes started to close. I gave up, arranged the pillows on the opposite end of the couch from Kelly, and joined her. The phone ringing woke me up at one p.m. I ran to the kitchen and answered on what I think was the sixth ring.

"Hi, kid. Not interrupting anything, am I?"

"Yeah, sleep."

"Sure. Whatever you say."

"You call for anything important or just to annoy me?"

"Couple of things. We have Bobby in the station. He doesn't know a lot but gave us enough to look at Ronny a little harder. We picked up clothes for you and Kelly. I'll have an officer drop them by—someone you know."

"Thanks, I could use a change."

"And you've got another appointment with the mayor tonight. Around eight."

I was surprised. "I thought we were leaving that alone for a bit."

"I did too. But the chief thinks he should know about the checks."

"You involved?"

"Not yet. Still personal. If he wants us to look into anything where Ronny is concerned he can let us know. But if it is still personal, it's between him and you."

I thought for a second. "How did he sound?"

"A little fed up at first. I told him you had found something that he should know about. He still sounded like I was bothering him. But when I told him about the picture and the checks he was quiet for a good ten seconds and then quietly agreed to see you. I think you will find a little less hostile atmosphere."

"Did you tell him where I found them?"

"No."

"Good. Are we still quarantined?"

"Yeah, but don't act like it's hard on you. Any guy would pay hard money to switch places."

"Yes they would. I guess what I'm asking is, after talking to Bobby, you still think we should lay low."

"It would be nice if Bobby gave us enough to run out and arrest the gang, but he hardly knows his name."

"Tell me about it."

"If he did know something he'd probably spill it. He's scared to death of going to jail because of the accident. I told him we're after the guys who put him up to it and asked him to try and remember anything about the track or Ronny. I'll have a few more talks with him. And luckily for you he confirms going off with Johnny of his own accord. Strictly his own decision."

"I wasn't worried."

"You should have been. Hey!" he yelled away from the phone. "I told you I wanted that report yesterday. Get your ass in gear. You got ten minutes. Sorry, Spencer."

I readjusted the phone on my ear after having dropped it when he'd yelled. "So will you be home for dinner?"

"Yeah, about six."

"Kelly wants to cook. Mind if I run out for some food?"

"Yeah. Stay put. I'll get some steaks."

"Come on, Stosh. You're overreacting. These are two-bit punks."

"They're two-bit punks who trashed your office and Kelly's room and don't mind running people off the road, if you've forgotten about that. Stay put. I'll get you an escort to the mayor's tonight. Rosie okay?"

"Rosie is more than okay. You were going to leave out that little detail about the trashing?"

"I was thinking about it."

"I'm a big boy, Stosh."

"Big boys need help too, Spencer."

"Did they break the locks?"

"Nope, picked them nice and clean. And locked up behind themselves. Now don't get any ideas. Get some rest and figure out how you want to deal with tonight."

"Will do. I'll see you. Hey, Stosh, how many kids does the mayor have?"

"The mayor? He doesn't have any. Why do you ask?"

"Just curious, thanks."

We hung up. Kelly was glancing through the paper when I got back to the couch.

The expression on her face asked the question. I filled her in, telling her about my office but not her room.

"This is sounding serious, Spencer." She was a tough cookie but there was a tremble in her voice.

"I guess it is, Kelly. But you're safe here. Don't worry."

"I'm worried about you too. You're staying here with me aren't you?"

I sat down on the table in front of her and took her hands. "Sure. I'm going out tonight but Stosh will be here."

"It doesn't make any sense. What do they think I know?"

"It's not what they think you know, it's what they think I know. They're after you to get to me. I won't let them have you."

"Do you know something?"

I shook my head. "Not a thing. Stosh may have learned something from Bobby. If he did, he's not talking. And if there is something going on at the track it's not my problem." I picked up the remote and turned on channel nine to catch the Cubs pre-game show.

"What about the little girl?"

"That *is* my problem. I'm making some progress. I'm having a chat tonight with someone who may be involved."

Again her expression asked the question.

"Don't worry. I will have an escort. One of Chicago's finest."

"Okay." She smiled and touched my arm. "Spence, I can't tell you how sorry I am about your folks. I can't imagine losing mine."

"Thanks. Sometimes life's no fun—especially the dreams."

"I know you want to get whoever is responsible. But these are not nice people. Please be careful."

"I promise."

"Good. Now let's take the afternoon off and watch the ballgame. We can make a few bets if you'd like." One eyebrow raised, and a little smile curled up her mouth.

I pulled away and said, "Unless it's for cold, hard cash, I think I'm done betting with you. No offense."

She laughed. "Well then how about if I see what Stosh has in the fridge and see if I can scare up some sandwiches?"

"Sounds like a plan. Let's go see." I got up, took her hand, and pulled her up to me. After a long kiss, I said, "I'm sorry I got you into this, Kelly."

She rested her head on my chest. "I'll be okay. I don't think Stosh will let anything happen to either one of us. If I can help, let me know."

I felt a little hurt that she was looking to Stosh for protection instead of me, but that was probably the smart thing to do. "Okay. Let's go eat."

On the way to the kitchen the doorbell rang. I headed for the front door and peeked out the window. It was Rosie with a suitcase. I invited her in for lunch. She said she was running but would be back at six and would want to know why a nice guy like me was mixed up with hoodlums. She also asked if I had a gun. I told her I didn't think I needed one. She gave me a look and waved as she walked back to the unmarked car.

The afternoon sun had filled the kitchen with a bright light. It had been much darker at breakfast. It was readily apparent that Stosh was not big on cooking. The fridge was about empty. The crisper was empty. The meat drawer had one unopened, pre-wrapped package of assorted meats. The bottom shelf held twelve cans of Old Milwaukee. The top shelf had what was left of the milk and orange juice from breakfast. One egg was in the side tray along with a small jar of mayonnaise and a bottle of ketchup. I closed the fridge and pulled open the freezer. It was full—of jelly-filled donuts. Wish I would have known that at breakfast.

Kelly shook her head. "Men." She had found rolls and paper plates and napkins. "You go back and watch the game. I'll make lunch." She gave me a hug and pushed me out of the room. Five minutes later she joined me and set two plates on the table. One more trip brought two beers.

"Thank you, ma'am. I'll have to give you a good tip."

"If I can drag you away from this game, I'll take you up on that."

"You may not have to drag too hard."

We ate and watched. In the third the Cubs were losing eight to two. Tip time.

Stosh called around five to say he'd be late. Rosie would get me at six and I could eat with her. He'd bring steaks for him and Kelly.

Chapter 30

Rosie and I stopped for dinner and then headed south on Lake Shore Drive. The windows were open and the pungent smell of alewives wafted through the car. She asked if I could tell her what was going on. I had already decided I couldn't. Trying to keep the mayor anonymous was kind of like a puzzle. You could know one piece of the puzzle but not the other. Kelly knew I was looking for Marty's father. So I couldn't tell her I was going to see the mayor. Rosie knew I was going to see the mayor so she couldn't know the story. Not hard to put two and two together.

We laughed and chatted about old times. To our right, the sun was setting through banks of layered clouds, leaving behind a trail of pastel colors as it sank toward the horizon. Before I knew it, Rosie was parallel parking in front of the mayor's house.

I got out and leaned back in the window. "Thanks for the ride. You waiting?"

"Yup."

"It shouldn't be too long."

"No hurry. But I'd hurry if I were you."

I was confused. "Why?"

"Because Stosh is back on his home turf with your girlfriend."

"Aah. Somehow I don't think I have anything to worry about, but thanks for your concern. See ya."

As before, the mayor made me look like a slob. I knew the way. I glanced in the same rooms. The toy room looked the same. None of those toys had been played with.

I sat in the same chair. This time I asked for a beer. He took one out of a small fridge built into the wall and mixed himself a drink. He handed me a bottle of Heineken's and a fluted glass and set a napkin on the glass table. The room was much darker than it had been the last night. The sun was peeking in and out of the clouds.

"Mrs. Grey is not at home?" I asked.

"No, Mrs. Grey is up at our home in Wisconsin. It's been in her family for years. She enjoys the peacefulness. Actually we both do, but it's a bit harder for me to get away." He smiled. So did I. "I understand you found something and have some questions concerning our last discussion." He sat opposite from me, legs crossed casually.

I knew that Stosh had told him about the picture and the checks. I hadn't said anything to Stosh, but I wished he hadn't told the mayor what it was I'd found. That had given the mayor plenty of time to come up with a story. I wondered how much truth I would get.

"Well, it's not something I have, it's something I saw," I said as I poured the beer. Perfect. The head just started to flow over the edge of the glass.

"And that is?"

"That is a picture of Marty, Elizabeth's daughter and canceled checks made out to Elizabeth signed by you." I watched. There was no surprise, but, of course there wouldn't be... he already knew that.

"And what are you assuming from that?"

Not quite as friendly an atmosphere as Stosh had expected. "I'm not assuming anything. But I am wondering why you would be writing Elizabeth checks and hoped maybe you could explain."

"Where did you find these checks?" he asked in an icy tone. I guess he didn't feel like explaining.

We looked each other in the eye for a good ten seconds. "I'd rather not say," I answered.

He finished off his drink. "Then I'd rather not explain."

I had thought that would be a stumbling block. And I couldn't blame him. I would have reacted the same way.

"How about this," I offered. "I tell you who has them, but not how I saw them." This was getting too much like *Let's Make a Deal.*

He thought for a minute and then agreed. I took a long drink of beer.

"They are in the possession of Ronny Press, who, as I understand it, is your half brother." Then I realized that was not public information and that he knew exactly who was supposed to be privy to it. I hoped he would let it pass. He didn't.

"That is not public information. How did you find out?"

"I didn't find out, I figured it out. I got some information from one source and some from another and put two and two together. This time it came up four." That was a lie. Stosh had first told me, but I could have figured it out later from the information I'd gotten from Maxine. So I figured it wasn't really a lie.

"Was one of your sources the police department?"

"No, it wasn't." At least not in the Maxine scenario.

While we were staring each other down again the phone rang. He answered it at his desk. I was glad for the distraction. I felt like a lion fighting for territory. We were doing a slow dance around each other trying to figure out what we could believe and where the trust level was. It was draining. I relaxed back in the chair, finished my beer and eavesdropped. He didn't make any attempt to be private.

"...yes, dear, that would be fine. No, but I don't have time to go into it now, I'm in the middle of a meeting... no, dear, it isn't... yes, it is business. I am a busy man, I can't get everything done during the day. Yes, I will try and come up for the weekend. Goodnight."

By the "dear" I assumed he was talking to Mrs. Grey. But his manner was succinct, and his tone was polite at best. He mixed another drink and sat with a tight, drawn, almost angry look on his face. To break the tension I asked for another beer. When he handed it to me, he had relaxed a bit.

"Sorry for the interruption," he said.

I poured and talked at the same time. "That's fine. I'm in no hurry." The sun had dropped behind the wall in the garden, but the room hadn't gotten much darker. I looked around and noticed two lamps glowing dimly. He hadn't turned them on. They must be on a sensor.

He crossed his legs and said, "I'm not either. But this is a rather awkward situation that perhaps we could bring to a close if we stop the fencing match and get to the point."

"I agree."

"So, you have told me what you found. What is it you want?"

I drew patterns in the moisture on the outside of the glass with my index finger and answered, "I realize you said you were not Marty's father. But the checks made out to Elizabeth would suggest that you had..." I paused and thought about the right way to say it. "...that you had... accepted responsibility for something and were sending her regular payments for that responsibility. The question then becomes what is, or was, that responsibility?"

I was looking straight at him. His eyes first met mine, then he lowered them to his hands that he was slowly rubbing together in his lap. I continued. "The obvious answer is that you were paying her child support for Marty, which would make you the father." His eyes narrowed a bit, and his lips pursed and his hands kept rubbing. Other than that, he looked frozen.

Then he took a breath and said carefully. "I think I would agree with you. That is indeed the logical conclusion. However, it is the wrong conclusion. I am not Marty's father."

He was so calm that I believed him, but it didn't make sense and I like things to make sense. I was about to ask him what the checks were for when he reached for his glass and asked me, "May I ask why you are so intent on finding the father?"

"Sure. The easy answer is that my client wants to know. But, to tell you the truth, if you ask why my client wants to know, I'm not quite sure."

"I assume you would not tell me who your client is?"

I nodded. "Right." Lights in the garden had come on, and the lamps in the room were at full brightness. Nice touch.

"As the mayor of this city, I could probably find out. But I have a pretty good idea. Let's assume your client is Elizabeth's brother. I don't remember his name. It really doesn't matter."

"No it doesn't," I agreed. "There's still the matter of the checks and why the logical conclusion is the wrong one." I spread my hands, palms up. "I'm open to other possibilities." He didn't offer any and I was becoming exasperated. "Mr. Mayor, I would really like to believe you, but I need some logical explanation."

He leaned forward and sighed. "I would like to give you one, and I do have one. But you have to understand my position as mayor. I am trying to walk a thin line between obscurity and scandal. I am not Marty's father. If you are assuming that I am, then you are also suggesting that I had an affair with Elizabeth. That is something I would like to avoid if at all possible."

"No one has suggested that."

He nodded. "Not in so many words. But that is the result if I am the father. And if the papers or my adversaries heard the questions you are asking there would be a scandal no matter what the truth is."

"I understand that. And they will not hear it from me. That I hope you understand."

"Yes, I think so."

I tried a different approach that I hoped would be less personal and threatening. "Do you have any idea who the father is?"

A look passed over his face that I took for exhaustion. Later I realized that it was sadness and helplessness. "I don't know, no."

I felt sorry for him, but didn't know why. There was something there that I could feel but not explain. "Would it surprise you that Elizabeth didn't know who the father was?"

"She thought it was me."

He offered another beer. I declined.

"That is not quite true," I offered. "Elizabeth knew the father was one of two possibilities, but she didn't know for sure."

He was silent.

When asking questions, it was always helpful to know whether or not someone was lying. It could help when deciding when to trust someone's answers to questions you didn't know the answers to. I knew the answer to my next question. "I don't know how to make this easy, and I suppose if it is none of my business you will tell me that, but were you having an affair with Elizabeth?"

He straightened in the chair like I had jabbed him in the back, looked straight at me and said, "No, I was not."

So much for trust. But I had to admit he was good at lying. If I hadn't known the truth, I would have believed him.

Then he quickly added, "I was having a relationship and a friendship." He slumped back down in the chair and stared out into the garden. "We talked often about the word 'affair.' We both hated it. It sounds so sordid and what we had was not sordid." He looked back into the room. The sad look was back. He looked like a kid whose balloons had just floated away, not quite believing that it had happened.

I felt helpless, like when I was talking to Marty that day amongst her toys. I also thought that maybe he wanted someone to talk to.

"Spencer, you said there were two possibilities. Was the other just some guy off the street?"

"It was just some guy off the street, but not just any guy. It was your brother Ronny."

I expected surprise but there was none. He closed his eyes, gently covered his face with his hands and said very softly, "Half brother." When he looked back up at me there were tears in his eyes. "Ronny is Marty's father. My God—how?"

"He raped her."

His face lost its color, and he was shaking.

There was no way he could fake that emotion. I wanted to leave him alone, but I had to know how he knew he wasn't the father. After all, she had slept with him that night too. "I want you to know I believe you. But why couldn't it have been you?"

Before answering he looked at me for bit. Then his face changed and I could tell he had made a decision.

"Spencer, can you stay a bit? I'd like to answer that question, and it may take awhile."

"Sure. But there is an unmarked car and one of your employees waiting for me outside. Let me go tell her."

"Sure. Do you mind letting yourself out? I need to freshen up a bit."

"No problem. I'll have to make a stop also. Those beers have caught up with me."

"Sure. The bathroom is through that door and then on your left." He pointed.

We got up at the same time, and he invited me out with a sweep of his arm. Walking alone down the hallway, the big house seemed awfully empty. I left the front door ajar and walked to the dark-blue Ford. I expected to see the moon but clouds had rolled in from the west. The night was warm and muggy, and there was a warm breeze out of the south. As I reached the car, the passenger's window glided down. Rosie had the car running with the air on.

"You get lost in there?" she asked with a smile.

"I wouldn't mind. All the comforts of home."

"Several more from what I saw of your place."

"Sure. Easy to take cheap shots when you're sitting here wasting the taxpayer's money on gasoline to run the air."

"Hey, I gotta get some perks for ferrying around the likes of you."

"Thanks, friend. Just for that I'm gonna make you wait some more. I just came out to let you know it might be awhile. Do you want to wait?"

"Those are my orders."

"I'm really sorry, Rosie. You must have other things to do."

"No problem. I was just—"

"Goddamn!" I had felt something wet on the back of my right leg and had turned around to see a schnauzer running away.

Looking concerned, Rosie asked, "What's the matter, Spencer?"

I pointed to the rear of the car where the dog was standing about twenty feet away. "That damned dog just peed on my leg." I took off running after the dog and chased it halfway down the block before I gave up. I kept thinking I was catching up and then realized it was staying five feet away just to keep me running. If I slowed, it would too. So I finally conceded defeat and walked back to the unmarked car. I expected some sympathy and maybe I would have gotten some if Rosie wasn't so busy laughing. And I'd been feeling bad because she had to wait for me. The hell with her; she could wait all night.

Wondering what to do about my pants leg, I returned to the house and let myself in. I was pretty sure that walking into the mayor's house smelling of dog pee would not fall under Stosh's idea of behaving myself. I tried to wash it out in the bathroom.

The mayor was waiting for me. I sat carefully, keeping my pants leg away from the chair. He started to ask me something and then stopped and sniffed. I hoped he would think he was imagining it.

"Spencer, I was wondering something. You said Elizabeth knew it was one of two people. If she is dead, how do you know she knew that?"

It was a question I really didn't want to answer. I was hoping it wouldn't come up because I didn't want to bring Maxine into it. Even though I trusted her I knew there would be a credibility problem.

"Well, I..."

He took a deeper breath and, before I could finish, asked. "What the hell is that smell?"

I had to own up. "I'm sorry, sir. It's me. While I was talking to my driver I'm afraid one of your neighborhood canines decided to use my leg for a fireplug. I tried to wash it out."

He thought it was funny, too, but at least offered to help. We were about the same size. He offered to loan me a pair of pants and throw mine in the wash. I was going to take him up on it when the doorbell rang.

He walked to a monitor set in the wall by the bar. "It's a woman holding up a badge. Someone you know?"

I got up and joined him. It was Rosie. "Yes, that's my ride. Would you buzz her in?"

He did. I beat him to the front door.

Before I could justly reproach her for belittling me in front of the dog, she said, "Spencer, I just got a call from Stosh. Kelly is gone. He wants to talk to you. Call him at home."

I asked the mayor if I could use the phone. I called Stosh and he explained.

"She wasn't here when I got home. We have a car at the track and her hotel. Did she say anything to you about leaving, Spencer?" Stosh asked.

"No. I told her to stay put. Is the car gone?"

"Yes."

"Good." I felt a little better. "She likes to drive. Probably got tired of being cooped up and went out to get some air."

"Yeah, and if by chance somebody spots her?"

"Unless they shoot out her tires, they'll never stop her. She's good with the wheel."

"Any idea where she might go?"

"Anywhere I guess. Specifically the track or her hotel room."

"She that dumb?"

"No she's not. She wouldn't go to the track, but maybe she needed something from her room."

"Then we'd get it like last time. You did tell her about the room, didn't you?"

"Well—"

"Holy shit, Spencer! When did you stop thinking?" I could tell he was trying hard not to explode.

"Can I help?"

"Nope, are you done with the mayor?"

"No, we were just getting started."

"Then stay there. The only safer spot for you would be in a cell, and I'm thinking about that."

I couldn't blame him. "Okay. Let me know as soon as you find her."

"Sure, kid." He hung up.

I found Rosie by the front door.

She looked concerned. "We'll find her, Spencer."

I nodded and walked her back to the car.

Chapter 31

We sat in the car and said nothing for several minutes.

As it started to rain, Rosie asked, "So, we staying or going?"

"Staying." I watched a few big drops splatter on the windshield and tried to guess where the next one would fall. Not even close. "Stosh doesn't need my help, and I have some more to discuss with the mayor." I let out a big breath. "And I guess I should get back in before it starts to pour." After opening the door, I said, "Come and get me if you hear anything."

She nodded.

I closed the door, buzzed the gate, and walked slowly back to the house letting the warm rain splatter against my face. The mayor met me at the door and led the way back to the family room.

He gave me a quizzical look. "You don't look so good, Spencer. Something wrong?"

"Yeah, a friend of mine is missing," I said with concern.

"I'm sorry. I'd offer you the aid of my police department, but I guess you already have it. I can offer a drink. Would you like something stronger?"

I shook my head. "No thanks. I need to think straight. If I want to get wasted I'll let you know."

"Fair enough. You up to continuing?"

"Sure."

"Well why don't you change into a pair of my slacks and rinse out yours." He pointed to a chair where a pair of khaki slacks were draped over the back.

I changed in the washroom, rinsed out my pant leg, and returned to my chair in the family room. I had wondered how I would keep my mind off Kelly. Maybe best to just keep asking questions.

"We may get interrupted again," I explained. "But when we were interrupted last time I believe I had wondered how you were so sure you are not the father. Are you denying you had relations with Elizabeth?" I knew he did. Elizabeth had told Maxine as much.

He hesitated and looked past me at something that wasn't there. When he returned his eyes to me he had made a decision.

"No, I am not denying that. As a matter of fact, my relations, including going out for ice cream with Beth, were the happiest times of my life."

I didn't try to hide the shocked look on my face. "So this wasn't just a fling? You actually cared about her?"

He nodded with a lost look on his face. "Yes. We were very much in love."

I couldn't believe I was sitting here with the mayor of Chicago, listening to him tell me about his affair. "You don't have to tell me about that. That is none of my business."

"I'd like to, though. I need to tell somebody and I think I can trust you."

"Why do you think that? You don't even know me."

A tiny smile flicked briefly across his face. "Sometimes you just have to go with a gut feeling."

"Pardon my asking, but if you did have relations with her, how—?"

He held up his hand and interrupted before I could finish. "I had a vasectomy."

"After you met Beth?"

"No, way before. Before I was married as a matter of fact."

I didn't know much about vasectomies. I did know that sometimes they didn't work. So I asked, "How do you know it worked? Could you still have gotten her pregnant?"

"No," he responded adamantly. "I had also had relations with my wife for many years. We have no children. It worked."

Okay. He wasn't the father. That meant Ronny was. That was not a pleasant thought. I realized my job was over. But I still had a lot of questions. I told him so.

He simply said, "Ask."

I did. "You had it before you got married. Was it for some medical reason?"

"No. I didn't want to have children."

That wasn't what I was expecting. "That is surprising. You don't find many women who don't want to have kids."

He shifted on the couch. "I didn't say Mrs. Grey didn't want to have kids. I said I didn't."

"That must have made for a tough situation. She obviously married you anyway."

He took a deep breath and let it out slowly. "I didn't tell her."

My look was enough without any verbal response to get him to answer.

"I know. Not very fair. I'm not proud of that. But she wouldn't have married me if I had told her. And at the time I was in love with her."

"Can I ask why you didn't want kids?" I didn't point out that perhaps he shouldn't have married a woman he didn't think he could confide in.

"It goes back a ways." He looked past me again and then continued. "I had a father who was a tyrant. He would get drunk and then take it out on us kids. There were five of us including a half sister and Ronny my half brother. I was the oldest and felt responsible for the younger ones. For some reason he usually picked on Ronny. I would try to get in his way so he would hit me or I would push the others out of the way and take the beatings for them. I learned how to duck and move so it didn't hurt so bad."

I stared in amazement. "What about your mother? Didn't she help?"

"She did what she could, which included getting her share of the abuse. But she died when I was ten. Things went downhill after that."

I told him I was sorry. He said that was just something he had to deal with by himself.

But I didn't understand. "So you didn't want kids because you had a bad childhood?"

"Not exactly. I did a lot of research. I found that in a lot of cases kids who are beaten go on to beat their own kids. I didn't want that to happen."

"Well, certainly that is something you could control. You don't look like a child beater."

"Thank you. But what does a child beater look like? And the control is the problem. In a lot of cases, it seems to be something you can't control. It's learned behavior."

I knew there was a lot of controversy about this and let it drop. Whether it was true or not, he believed it. I listened to the rain pattering against the windows and saw a streak of lightning flash to the west. It was ten fifteen. I wondered if Stosh had found Kelly.

"Mrs. Grey want kids?"

"Oh yes, very much. Her doctor told her there was nothing wrong with her so she tried to get me to go to a doctor to see if it was me. I, of course, have refused for various reasons."

"How about adoption?" I asked.

"A kid is a kid. I wasn't willing to take the risk."

"Has your wife accepted that you're not going to have children?"

He lowered his head and pursed his lips. "Not really. It has been a problem. She gets very angry. Louise has been in and out of therapy at various times. One therapist suggested working with kids and that has helped. She has started kids programs and volunteers at various day care centers. She seems to be fulfilled by that. She even goes with me to the hospitals and makes balloon animals for the kids."

"Do you love her?" I realized that was none of my business but neither was the rest, and he could tell me to butt out if he wanted.

He answered quickly. "No. No I don't. Not anymore."

"Does she love you?"

He slowly shook his head. "No. I don't think she ever did. She liked the politics. We met at a fundraising dinner. I came up the hard way, through the ranks. Her family has money and supported my candidacy through the years. One thing led to another." He looked out at the rain and sighed. "Oh, we were in love for awhile, but that wears off if you don't have much in common. We never talked much. Not like..."

He picked up his glass and swirled what was left of his drink in the bottom.

"So you stayed together because it was convenient?"

He shrugged. "I guess. But she did want a family, and I have always felt guilty about that."

The phone rang. He didn't react.

"Do you want to get that?"

"No. The machine will pick it up."

He looked drained, like he wouldn't have had the energy to get up anyway.

"So what happened with Elizabeth?"

It took him what seemed like a long time to answer.

"We met working on my campaign for mayor. There was just some, well, chemistry, I guess. She would stay late and we would sit and talk. One night we discovered we were closer than we had thought. We didn't plan anything. It just happened. But I never led her on. We got together sometimes outside of the office. But I told her I would not leave my wife, and she understood that. It was all her decision. She decided to stay."

I wondered if that decision had somehow gotten her killed, but kept it to myself. I had been letting him talk to get it off his chest. I needed to concentrate on Beth. The phone rang again. Again he ignored it.

"Can we get back to Elizabeth?" I asked.

"Sure. What would you like to know?"

"How did you find out she was pregnant?"

"She told me."

"When was that?"

"It was a couple of weeks after the night she said she got pregnant. That night I had gone to her apartment. It was a Friday night. My wife had gone to Wisconsin for the weekend." His brow furrowed. "You know, I was late because Ronny had shown up here."

"What did he want?"

"Money. That was all he ever wanted. Had some great plan to make money down south somewhere, but he needed a stake. I gave him a couple thousand just to get rid of him. I also told him I didn't want to see him in Chicago again. He promised. I figured it didn't mean much, but I knew it would buy time and hoped he would actually find something to keep him busy."

"So you went to Beth's and I assume you, uh..."

"Yes, we did."

"But this had been going on for awhile, and she didn't know about the vasectomy. Was she using some kind of birth control?"

"Yes. She never told me what. But we had to make arrangements to get together so she always knew and could prepare. Of course it didn't matter because of the vasectomy. But I didn't want anyone to know, not even Beth. That night she said she forgot her birth control. I said I thought it would be okay and not to worry about it. She was very nervous but went ahead."

"What did you say when she told you she was pregnant?"

He let out a big sigh. "I didn't know what to say. I felt betrayed. I knew it wasn't me so she must be sleeping with someone else. I was very surprised and hurt. I asked if she was sure it was me. She got mad and started to cry." He leaned his head back and looked at the ceiling. "She asked what I was suggesting. If she didn't want to admit there was someone else, I didn't have the heart to tell her I knew there was. I decided after what I had put her through, I couldn't push it. I had no right to feel hurt, but I was. I asked if she wanted to have the baby. She again got angry and said of course. So I told her I would give her money for the baby. I sent a check for baby things and then sent five hundred a month. I—"

The phone rang again. This time he excused himself saying he'd better get it. I got up and stood by the glass doors and watched the storm. The rain had stopped but there was still lightning. But the electricity in the room was greater than outside. I thought how amazing it is that someone with an image like the mayor's could have such a story in his closet. You never know what is going on with the people you meet from day to day.

He came back into the room.

"Everything okay?"

"Yes. It was my wife. She's going to come home Thursday for a meeting and then go back to Wisconsin for the weekend." We both sat.

"How do you think Ronny got the checks?"

"I think he stole them."

"Hmmm. Here's another question that's maybe not so easy. Why did you write checks? Why not send a money order or something without your name on it?"

"I guess that was stupid. But I wanted some evidence that I had supported Marty in case everything hit the fan."

"But you weren't the father. Rather easy to prove."

"I know. It doesn't make much sense. I guess I would have liked to be the father. I can't really explain it."

"So where were the checks?"

"I kept them up in the house in Wisconsin, along with cash and a yearly picture of Marty that Elizabeth sent, in a safe no one knew about. It was hidden in a paneled wall."

"How did Ronny find out about it?"

"I've been thinking about that since you said he had them. All I can figure is he saw me open it one night and came back. Louise and I were up there for a few days, and one night Ronny showed up. Hadn't seen him for about three years. He had some trouble down in Georgia. Spent some time in jail, but less than he should have because of me. I should have let him rot."

"Why didn't you?"

"I felt responsible for him. And sorry for him I guess. He had a tough life. He got it the worst from my father. But he was out on probation, and I made it clear that if he screwed up again, I wasn't helping."

He got up and mixed another drink and talked as he did. "He asked for more money. I told him I would give him a thousand dollars, but it was the last time. I said that if he asked again I would have him looked at with a microscope and find something that would put him back in jail. He must have seen me open the safe."

"When were the checks missing?"

"About a week later, Louise was up at the house alone. She called one night. Said she had been out shopping. When she came back she thought she heard some noise in the house. She went to the back door and found it open and thought she saw someone running away. It was dark and she didn't get a good look. Then when she walked back into the house she went in the den and found the safe open."

He took a drink and continued. "She was very surprised—asked why I didn't tell her there was a safe there and asked what was in it. I just said I used it to keep extra cash and asked if there was anything left. She said it was empty. Thank God. That's all I needed would be for her to ask questions about the pictures and the checks."

"You're sure she didn't find some? Ronny did not have a full set and there was only one picture."

"How do you know that?"

"I saw them."

"Where?"

Back to a question I didn't want to answer. But he deserved to know, for credibility if nothing else. I decided what the hell. "They are in his dresser drawer."

He looked confused. "He had you in his apartment?"

"No. I broke in."

Confusion turned to surprise. "You pick locks?"

"No. But I know someone who does."

"Ronny does too. And I guess he's good with safes."

"I guess." I repeated my question. "Why do you think your wife didn't get anything from the safe?"

"I guess I'm just hopeful, but she never said anything."

"Does she own a gun?"

"What kind of question is that?"

"Simple one. Just wondering. Should have an easy answer."

"It does. Yes, she does."

"Know what kind?"

"Yes, a twenty-two."

I nodded. Lots of those around.

"How did Ronny get in? I assume you have security like you do here."

"No we didn't. I hate the security here. Like living in a bubble. I wanted a place I could get away from all this. But Louise refused to stay there alone. She came back that night. Wouldn't go up by herself till I had an alarm system put in and yard lights."

"Anything happen after that?"

"Like what?"

"Like anything."

"Well a few months later Louise's emotional stability got worse. Her psychiatrist suggested she be put into a care center—used to be called asylums or institutions. It was all very hush-hush and very expensive. She was in and out for a year."

"Why?"

"The same old thing. Wanted me to go to the doctor. I refused. It was then that she turned the front room into a toy room. It hasn't changed in three years. Not one toy has ever been moved. She has nieces that come over, and she won't let them play in there."

"Did the care center help?"

"I guess. When she got out she got involved with the kids' programs and that seemed to satisfy her."

"You kept sending checks to Beth?"

"Yes. Five hundred dollars. But at some point she called and asked to meet. We did." He looked wistful. "She looked so lovely. She asked for more money. Said with Marty getting older she needed another five hundred."

"How did you feel about that?"

"I was angry and almost told her the truth. I realized I was paying her the money to assuage my guilt at not being man enough to marry her. But another five hundred was beyond my guilt. Besides, I didn't have it. The bills from Louise's care were huge. I told Beth as much."

"How did she react?"

"She just seemed sad. Resigned. I never saw her again. I kept sending checks. Then I got a letter from her giving me a new address."

"Did you ever go there?"

"I drove by once." A look of despair came over him. "I felt so awful. I wondered what had happened to her. I realized that whatever it was, it wasn't my fault, except that I had refused her money. I just couldn't do anything different. She always knew that."

He was trying hard to talk away his guilt. But he never would.

"Rather ironic," I said.

"What?"

"You gave Ronny money but refused Elizabeth."

"Are you saying I got her killed?"

"No. Are you?"

"I don't know. Maybe I am. I've certainly been thinking it for quite awhile."

"Have you heard any more from Ronny?"

"No. He knows I've had enough. Chief Ranek told me he was back and working at Skyline and maybe mixed up in something. He asked if I wanted any special treatment for him if he was involved. I said no, lock him up and throw away the key."

I glanced at my watch—11:20. Nothing from Stosh.

"Spencer, you have me wondering about my wife and those checks. I wonder if she did take them."

"Most likely Ronny took everything in there and then only saved what he thought he needed."

"Why would he save the picture and the checks?"

The gate buzzer went off. We both looked at the monitor. It was Rosie. He buzzed open the gate, and I excused myself and let her in.

"Spencer, Stosh has Kelly. He's bringing her to his house and wants you to meet there. She's okay. Are you done here?"

"I am now. I'll be back in a minute."

I told the mayor they had found my friend, and I needed to go. I told him I would get back to him.

"Spencer, can you spare one more minute?"

I was anxious to go, but said sure.

"I'd like to hire you."

"For?"

"I'm worried about the checks. I'd like you to search the Wisconsin house and see if she has them hidden anywhere." He handed me a map. "We use this for our friends. It's fairly easy to find. Just a little north of Algoma along the shore. Here's a spare key and the security code. The safe is empty, so you needn't check it. My wife will be back Thursday morning for a meeting and then is going back on Friday and then will be there for a week. So if you can get up there Thursday I'd really appreciate it."

I said I would.

"Let me know what I owe you."

I waved him off.

We walked to the door.

"And thanks for listening, Spencer."

"Sure."

I opened the door and had taken a few steps when he called me.

"Spencer, do you have any idea why Ronny would keep the picture and the checks?"

I did. "Blackmail."

"But I never heard from him."

"Not you. Beth. I'd be willing to bet that's why she had to move. She didn't need the money for her. She needed it to pay Ronny."

"Why would she give in to blackmail?"

"To protect you. Gotta go." That wasn't quite true but I figured he deserved it. I had also thought about telling him that Ronny had probably followed him to Beth's the night he gave him the money, but he could probably figure that out for himself.

There was little traffic and Rosie drove fast. On the way, she filled me in. Whoever grabbed Kelly had drugged her and dumped her in a field. When she came to, she walked to a gas station and called the cops. They found her car a couple blocks away.

There were three unmarked cars in front of Stosh's house. Stosh's cruiser was in the driveway. Rosie pulled in behind it.

Chapter 32

I walked in in the middle of the conversation.

Kelly was saying, "My eyes were taped shut, and they put sunglasses on me. They took me up a flight of stairs, probably concrete. Then a screen door screeched open, and I was pushed inside. Someone took my arm and led me through another doorway and pushed me down on the floor and warned me about what would happen if I made any noise. The place smelled awful."

I stopped in the foyer and listened. I didn't want to interrupt her.

"Were there any noises you can remember?" Stosh asked.

"No. Oh yes. Every once in a while there was this electrical noise, kind of a zap like a short circuit."

"Was the smell pretty much what you smell like?"

"I smell like that? I can't smell much. I think my nose was deadened."

"I assume you could identify the smell if we can find the place."

"Sure, but I'd rather not have to go back there."

I butted in. "She doesn't have to go back there. I know where it is."

Kelly jumped up and put her arms around my neck. I held her tight, trying to ignore the odor. Stosh was sitting in his chair. Two other detectives stood against the far wall.

"I am so sorry, Kelly. Are you okay?"

She pulled away but did not let go. "I'm fine, Spence. Could use a shower though. But I'm the one who should be sorry. I should have stayed put."

"That's past. From now on I don't take my eyes off of you."

She rested her head on my chest.

Stosh piped up. "What do you mean you know where she was?"

"Cuz I spent some time in a place that smelled like that. Can't be two of them."

"Care to share?" Stosh asked.

"Yeah, my buddy Ronny." I stroked Kelly's head. She looked up at me. "That sound you heard was a bug zapper in the kitchen."

"Jesus," Stosh replied. "Some fancy place he's got."

"Yeah, a real garden of Eden. You gonna go grab him?"

Stosh rubbed his chin and looked perplexed. "Well, we've got a little problem."

"Oh for christ sake. Here we go again. You know the guy is guilty of far more than we could even imagine. Why not go grab him and lock him up and throw away the key?"

"Because we have this little thing called 'due process.' He gets a trial and with what we got, any judge would laugh, that is if we could convince a DA to even charge him."

I rolled my eyes and led Kelly to the couch. "So what's the problem?"

"The problem is we got nothin' to tie him to the kidnapping."

"What do you mean nothin' to tie him? I just identified the place by the smell. Get a warrant and get over there."

He turned to the detectives. "Boys, would you go out and check on the crowds?"

"There aren't any crowds out—"

"Get the hell outta here!" They left.

"So what's the problem?" I asked.

"You're telling me you have identified Ronny's apartment as the place Kelly was kept by the smell."

"Right."

"And you'd be willing to testify to that in court?"

"Right."

"I don't know that smell counts. I assume he didn't invite you over for a beer, so I'd have a better case against you for breaking and entering than against him for kidnapping."

"But Stosh, I..."

"I know, kid. It sucks. But that's the way it is."

"Stosh, I..." Kelly started. But I was too mad to let her finish.

"That's a big crock of crap. You know damn well—"

"Spencer."

I put my hand on her leg. "Kelly, don't try and make sense out of this. The whole damned system is nuts. I—"

"Spencer. Take a rest would you? My turn," Kelly said with authority.

I looked at her with rage but didn't say anything.

"Thank you. Stosh, would it help if there was something of mine in the apartment that was still there when you got there?"

"I think so. We'd have enough suspicion to check the place. If we found something that put you in there, I think that would be enough to squelch any possible questions."

"Okay. Well, I left my ring in the room they dumped me in."

I looked at her with my mouth hanging open. "Your ruby diamond ring?" She had worn it for our first dinner.

She nodded.

"How did you happen to do that?" Stosh asked.

She shrugged. "Seemed to me it might help if I left something behind, kind of like Hansel and Gretel's trail of breadcrumbs. My hands were tied so I didn't have much choice. But I managed to slip the ring off my finger and work it down into whatever it was I was sitting on."

I gave her a big hug.

"Do you have any idea what you were sitting on?"

"It was a pile of something. Soft. I think I felt a pair of pants. I didn't want to poke around too much."

"Ma'am, you are something else. I think you have earned yourself a shower. Leave your clothes by the door, and I'll get them in the washer."

She frowned. "Thanks. But if you don't mind, I think I'd rather they were in the garbage."

"Understood. I'll get you a garbage bag... and a robe."

Stosh took her hand and led her out of the room. I opened all the windows and then walked outside and stood on the front stoop. The fresh air smelled good. It was still warm and the humidity was high. The clouds were breaking, and every once in a while the moon spilled light between the cracks in the clouds. I thought about the situation. Here I was hiding in the safety of the police and lucky enough to have Kelly safe despite the danger I put her in. Sam Spade would be slowly shaking his head and telling me to try a different line of work. But then I realized I had found who Marty's father was; I'd solved my case. It was Stosh's case that was the problem. After a few minutes I heard the screen door open and Stosh joined me.

"That's an amazing woman."

"Yes, sir, she is that. Why did they let her go?"

He waved me to the glider on the porch and we sat.

"I think they were just sending a message. You pissed them off. They were letting you know they could get her if they wanted. Keeping her meant nothing to them. But as long as she was missing we'd be looking and they didn't need that. They have other things to worry about. So they dumped her."

The street was empty, and all but one of the unmarked cars had left. Two detectives sat unmoving in the front seat. All the lights in the neighboring houses were off.

"So how do you like the PI business, kid?"

I gave him a look full of resignation and sorrow and said, "Okay, so it's not all romance. But I did find what I was looking for. That's gotta be worth something."

Stosh shrugged and then turned the shrug into a stretch and a yawn. "Sure. Everybody's gotta make a living. But there are guys out there who just don't care if you are alive or dead. And if you start poking your nose into their business, dead will be the choice. You do what you like with you but you have involved Kelly."

"Yes, I didn't realize." I paused. "Stosh, these guys killed Mom and Dad."

"I know, kid. And we'll get them. But my point here is that Kelly didn't sign on for trouble, and I'm not getting any damned sleep."

"Sorry. I'll call someone else next time."

"No, you won't. You'll call me. But it's possible to call with your suspicions and then let us take care of it. And I don't tell you everything we do."

"Fine. But there are things I can do that you can't."

"Right. But it's not that we can't. We won't. Because it's illegal, and lawyers would be raining down on us."

"So it's better that I take care of it my way."

"No it's not, Spencer. Your way can land you in jail or get you killed. You wouldn't like either option. Although maybe the clothes would be an improvement either way. So you've got the father thing nailed down?"

"Yeah. Ronny is the father, which is not good news."

"I guess that's good for the mayor. You believe the mayor?"

"Yes. There's no way it could have been him."

"How do you know?"

"You'll have to take my word for it. It gets a little complicated and personal."

"Well, good work on that, Spencer."

"What are you going to do about the car accident?"

"You're not going to like this, but I don't think there is much we can do about it. Bobby is not very reliable, and there is no way we could tie him to whoever gave him his orders. And it sounds like it really was just supposed to be an accident."

"Great. So they get away with it?"

"Not if I can help it."

"So?"

"So, they got Capone for tax evasion. We'll see if we can get them for whatever is going on at the track."

"What *is* going on at the track?"

"We're pretty sure there are drugs going in and out, but we don't know how."

"Did you get anything from Bobby?"

"Nothing that makes much sense. Found out that Bobby spends most of his time doing Ronny's work for him. Cleaning stables, pitching hay, all the dirty work."

I shook my head. "The guy is a real prize. Too bad Bobby doesn't tell him to go to hell. But he admires him and is scared of him at the same time."

"Yeah, I noticed that. Bobby expends a lot of energy keeping Ronny from getting mad at him. But he says there have been times he was doing Ronny's job and got yelled at for doing something Ronny had told him Ronny would do himself. The kid's memory isn't that great for details. He'd make a crappy witness."

"What do you mean, yelled at for work Ronny wanted to do? I get the feeling Ronny doesn't want to do anything."

"The kid says there were a few times he was setting up hay for the horses, and Ronny exploded. Wanted to do it himself. Said Ronny kept a list of horses he wanted to hay himself."

I sat for a minute. A car went by. It caught my attention only because it was doing the speed limit which was slow. "Try this on, Stosh. What if the drugs are coming in in the hay bales on certain days? Somehow the bales are marked, and Ronny gets those bales in the stalls of certain horses where they are later opened and picked up."

"Could be. Could not. We've got no proof. We'd have to catch them at it."

"Maybe we can."

He just looked at me. "Continue."

"Ronny had lists of horses in his apartment. They show which horses are supposed to be where on which days. The day a shipment comes in, he simply puts the marked bales in the prearranged stalls and someone later opens the bales and removes the drugs."

Stosh stared at the lawn and then responded evenly. I had expected him to be a little excited. "Seems simple enough. But we'd have to know which horses were marked on which days."

"I think he keeps a list, and I think he keeps track of how much money he makes."

"And how do you come to think this?"

"I've seen the lists."

"Okay." He didn't ask where. "How do we know which days the drugs are coming in?"

"We simply check the list against the race lineups and see when that lineup of horses will be at the track. Kelly could find out when the horses are trailered in and—"

"Whoa, boy. Haven't you risked the little lady enough?"

"Yes. But I don't think that would be a risk."

"Spencer, everything is a risk. Start thinking like that, and you will be a bit ahead of the game."

"Well then maybe there is some other way."

He nodded. "There probably is. But there is another problem."

I waited.

"Ronny isn't apt to just hand us the lists for our viewing pleasure."

"So? We know where they are. Go in and look. Get a warrant."

He shook his head and let out a big sigh. "Kid. It just doesn't work that way. You've heard about all these gangs on the streets. We know they've killed people. We know they're going to kill people again. We know where they are. They don't hide. They stand out in plain view. But we can't just run up and drag them off. They are protected by the same laws that protect you. We treat one of those poor misguided souls badly and the ACLU is filing lawsuits."

"Sure. Let's protect the rights of the bad guys. What about the rights of people to walk down their streets without getting shot at? How about if we get rid of the ACLU first?"

"Kid, I don't disagree. It's just the rules I've gotta play with. Now, your friend Ronny is also protected by the same rules. I have no good reason to search his apartment. No judge would issue a search warrant on the supposition we have."

"Well if you're not going to do anything, then maybe there's another way."

He stood up, turned to face me and said sternly, "Spencer. I didn't say we're not doing anything. We have a watch on several places, his included. I just can't bust in without more reason. And if I see anyone else trying that they will be arrested. Understand?"

I didn't respond.

"Spencer, I'm not kidding. I appreciate your sense of justice, but if you try anything you will be behind bars without my sympathy. Do you understand?"

I nodded with resignation.

"Good." He put his hand on my shoulder and said with compassion, "This isn't easy for me either. But over the years you get used to it. We do what we can and have to settle for that."

"Sure, Stosh. That's why I'm not a cop."

He stretched and yawned. "Our loss, Spencer. Our loss. Good night, kid."

"Good night, Stosh."

The screen door whooshed shut, and I listened to his footsteps on the wooden foyer. I scanned the front yard. It looked like the plain clothes guys were asleep. Probably not. I decided I should be.

Chapter 33

I woke up at six. No one else was up. I showered downstairs so I wouldn't wake anyone and was eating Frosted Flakes with extra sugar when Stosh came down.

"Hey, kid."

"Mornin', Stosh. Hope you got some sleep."

"Slept great. Course I didn't start till three."

I winced. "Sorry."

He got a bowl, pulled out a chair, and joined me, without the extra sugar. "That's okay, kid. Just try and stay out of trouble."

"I always try. I'm just not always successful."

He crunched a mouthful of flakes. "What are your plans?"

"I'm not sure. Is our quarantine over?"

He nodded and crunched. "Unless you do something else crazy, and you're not planning on it are you?" He hesitated.

"No."

"Good. Then my guess is you're safe. They have Bobby back. Leave him alone. Keep bothering him and you may get another warning, or worse."

"Do you think Bobby is okay?"

"I think so. He doesn't know much."

"But do they know that?" I clanged my spoon in the empty bowl and pushed it away.

He shrugged. "These aren't nice people." A few more bites. "Your paternity case is wrapped up, right?"

"Right."

"Then why don't you disappear for awhile? Go up and see Rose and do some fishin'."

"I'd like to. But there are a few things on the agenda."

I got a concerned look.

"Nothing you'd care about," I assured him. "Want to catch an art show, and the mayor has something he wants me to look into."

Another concerned look.

"Don't worry, I'm heading for Wisconsin."

He wiped his mouth and pushed his chair back. "Good, you can be their problem for awhile." He picked up the bowls and put them in the sink.

"Kelly is going to want to get back to the track. Think she's okay?"

His mouth scrunched. "Think so. For the same reasons that you're probably safe. But if she feels nervous, have her take some more time off. I'd have her switch hotels anyway. And give her my direct number."

"Okay. Thanks, Stosh."

He patted my shoulder. "I made a promise, kid. I'm stuck with you. Stay in touch."

I arranged the Trib on the table. Sports section first. Kelly came down halfway through. She declined my Frosted Flake offer and made some wheat toast and sliced a banana. I filled her in on Stosh's opinions. She did indeed want to get to the track to see to her horses. I told her to keep her eyes open and to be careful.

I filled her in on the hay theory and the possibility of the clue being at Ronny's. She agreed that it was a shame that Stosh couldn't just walk right in but was less dismayed than I. She asked about Marty's father. I told her I knew but couldn't say. She congratulated me and said she understood. I told her to switch hotels and to call and let me know where she was.

"Spencer, do you think we're safe?" She was standing at the counter eating.

I gave her a kiss on the forehead and some assurance. "I think so. They've sent their warning. If they're still walking around they have to figure the cops didn't get anything from Bobby. As long as they feel safe everything is okay."

"You aren't planning on doing anything that would make them feel unsafe are you?"

I opened the fridge and poured some orange juice. "That seems to be the question of the day."

She took a sip of my orange juice and asked with raised eyebrows, "And the answer of the day is?"

"A firm no, ma'am. I've got other things to do."

"Good. I don't want to lose you."

"You won't." I wrapped my arms around her and pulled her close. "How about dinner tonight?"

"Sounds good. I'll let you know where I am."

"Call me and we'll work out a time."

She nestled her head into my chest. Her hair smelled like roses.

"Spencer?" she said softly.

"Mmmm." I was thinking of taking her upstairs and falling asleep, but not necessarily right away.

"I hope Bobby is okay. I felt so much better when he was with your friends. He's really a nice kid. I like him."

"Yeah, he seems like a nice kid who got in with the wrong crowd. I like him too."

"Despite...?"

"Yes, despite what happened to my folks. He was just the fall guy. I want the thugs who set it up, which is why I'm so frustrated by Stosh."

"Maybe Stosh has something up his sleeve that you don't know about."

I shrugged. "I hope so."

She looked at her watch. "Gotta go. I arranged for the horses to be taken care of, but I feel better doing it myself. I'll call you." I got a peck on the cheek. "After the last dinner, my expectations are high. See you tonight."

"Bye, green eyes. See you."

I watched her go, resisted the urge to go back to bed, and searched for my keys. After five minutes, I found them in my pocket. Good start to the day.

I had to go back to my apartment, but I shouldn't have. It didn't help my mood. The place was a mess and it just made me angrier. By the time I straightened up, it was noon and I was hungry. I decided to eat some of my fee.

Beef's joint was crowded. The only seats were at the counter. I grabbed a stool and slowly spun forward. Beef saw me from the other end of the counter and gave me a salute. He picked some coins off the counter and carried an armful of dirty dishes to the kitchen. He was back in less than a minute.

"Hey, bigshot. Thought you disappeared. I hope your absence means you've been making progress. How about the special?"

"Sounds good. And yes, I have made progress. I should have something for you in a couple of days." I had something for him now but wasn't sure how to tell him, or even what to tell him. The truth didn't seem like such a great idea. Maybe if I gave it some time I would come up with something better. I guessed I could always tell him I'd come up empty. I didn't want him or anyone else knowing Ronny was Marty's father.

"Good. I can't chat. I've gotta figure out how to pick up Marty. The lady who usually drives her home was in an accident."

"She at day care?" I asked.

"Yep."

"I'll go get her. I've got nothing going on till later." I planned on getting to the gallery sometime midafternoon. "Do I have time to eat?"

"Sure. It'll be right up. She's done at one. It's the Happy Toddler on Western just south of Baylor. I'd really appreciate it."

"No problem. Glad to help."

"I'll have to call and tell them you're going to pick her up. Thanks, Spencer."

In less than a minute, Beef put a plateful of meatloaf and green beans and mashed potatoes in front of me. I covered the meatloaf in a thick layer of ketchup and got a dirty look from Beef. I shrugged. As far as I was concerned, the ketchup was the main course. It was excellent. So was the meatloaf.

Twenty minutes later I parked in front of the Happy Toddler. A swinging sign hanging above the door sported a large smiley face. I waited ten minutes for one o'clock to roll around and then went in. The kids were putting toys away. Marty saw me and came running over.

"Look what I made," she said with a big smile. It was an abstract finger painting that I liked more than some of the stuff I saw the last time I was at the Art Institute.

Marty was loading her backpack when a short woman in a smock came up to me.

"Are you here for Marty?"

"Yes, ma'am. Beef sent me."

"Could I see some identification please?"

I showed her my driver's license. She smiled and handed it back to me.

"Sorry to bother you, but we like to be careful."

I smiled back as I helped Marty sling the pack over her shoulder. "No problem. It's nice to know she's in good hands."

"Oh she certainly is. We have wonderful people here. If you ever need a place for your—"

I stopped her in the middle of her sales pitch and assured her that I wouldn't have a need for her services in the near future.

I held the door for Marty and asked how her day was.

"Oh, okay, I guess." She looked sad.

"Just okay?"

She nodded as I buckled her into the back seat.

"How come?"

"My friend didn't come today. She said she would."

"Your friend?"

"Yes, the balloon lady. Last week she promised to come back and she didn't."

"Well maybe she had some kind of emergency. Maybe she'll come tomorrow."

"I hope so. She said I'm her favorite."

That wasn't hard to believe. Marty was a wonderful kid, especially considering what she had been through. After a short drive, I walked her into the diner and waved at Beef. He waved back and gave me a thumbs up.

Next stop, Kathleen. Traffic was light going up the expressway, and I made it to north Clark Street by three. The gallery was glass-fronted and looked crowded. I drove past and parked in a self-park lot. I wondered how I would fit in. I was dressed in jeans, and not my best jeans at that. I found out as soon as I walked through the door. The room was full of society darlings in designer clothes. I sighed, decided I didn't care, and tried to find Kathleen. Her paintings and drawings of Door County were scattered about the room, and she was standing near one of the largest, a scene of the Cana Island lighthouse framed by the fall colors of the trees. I caught her eye and got a big smile.

While I waited for her to finish chatting with a couple who looked like they just stepped out of a fashion magazine, I scanned the room and wondered how Kathleen and I would react to one another. As far as I was concerned, I was stopping in to see a friend. I had a feeling she might have more on her mind and wasn't quite sure how to handle that. As it turned out, I didn't have to worry about it.

I was admiring a scene of Egg Harbor when she wrapped her arms around me from behind. I turned around and returned the hug.

"Hello, Spencer! I'm so glad you could come."

"Wouldn't miss it, Kathleen. I'm very proud of you. Your work is fabulous."

"Thanks. This is really a big break."

A quick little man with a long nose and beady eyes, whom she introduced as the gallery manager, took her arm from behind and said she was needed to answer some press questions. She told him she would be right there.

"Oh, Spencer, I'm so sorry. This is not a good time to talk. How about dinner when all this is over?"

The little fox man pulled her away before I could answer. I really didn't want the opportunity to have a conversation any deeper than we'd just had; deep conversations with Kathleen had never led to any good. While I was considering how to make a graceful exit, my beeper went off. I went to find a phone. It was Kelly.

"Spencer, I'm so glad I got you."

"Hi, Kelly. What's the matter? You sound upset."

"Spencer, Bobby is dead."

That had to sink in for a second. "Bobby? Our Bobby?"

"Yes. One of the stable boys found him in a stall with his head bashed in. There was blood all over."

"Are the police there?"

"Not yet. We just called them."

"Stay put. I'll be there as soon as I can. It will probably take me forty-five minutes. Make sure you stay with a crowd. I'll call Stosh and make sure he knows if he hasn't already heard. Stay where the police are. I'll find you."

"Spencer, he was such a sweet boy," she said as she started to cry.

"I know. I'm so sorry, Kelly. Will you be okay till I get there?"

"Yes. But hurry."

"I will."

I hung up and called Stosh's private number. He answered on the fourth ring. He was just leaving for the track. He said he'd be there in ten minutes. I heard him yell something that I didn't understand. Then there was a dead line.

I found Kathleen, interrupted politely and quickly explained that I'd received an emergency call, and I would try to get back to her. With people surrounding her, she didn't have a chance to respond. The last impression I had of Kathleen was the hurt look on her face.

Chapter 34

In late afternoon traffic, it took me almost an hour to get to the track. The place was crawling with police and flashing lights. The entrance to the stables was cordoned off, and the patrol officer standing at the yellow tape wouldn't let me in based on my good looks. I started to explain I was looking for Stosh when Rosie drove up. I waited and walked in with her.

Stosh was halfway down the row of stalls which were on both sides of a hayed pathway covered by a roof. Kelly was standing with a group of about ten people in a paddock area next to the stables talking with detectives. When she saw me she ran over, put her arms around my neck, and started to cry. Rosie squeezed my arm and walked to where Stosh was giving orders.

I held Kelly for a minute and then asked if I could take a few minutes to talk to Stosh. She nodded and said she'd wait there.

I walked through little clouds of dust swirling in the light filtering in through cracks in the wooden roof. Most stalls were occupied. The horses didn't care what was going on. They were either eating or asleep or swatting flies with their tails.

Several evidence techs were sifting through the hay in the stall where Bobby lay. He was crumpled against the left side of the stall. The top of his head was caved in and was matted in blood and lay nestled on a pillow of red hay. A medical bag sat open on the other side of the stall where Stosh stood talking with a gray-haired man I assumed was the coroner. Stosh saw me standing outside the stall and held up a finger. A minute later he finished talking and joined me, shaking his head. A uniformed policeman started unzipping a body bag.

"What do you think, Stosh?" I asked.

"I don't think, kid. I just do my job."

"What does the coroner think?"

"Says he was killed anywhere from two to four hours ago. Death caused by a blow to the head."

"Any idea what caused that blow to the head?"

"We didn't find the murder weapon, if that's what you mean."

"Was there a horse in the stall?"

He gave me a *Why are you being such a pain in the ass?* look. "Why am I talking to you? You become a detective when I wasn't looking?"

I stared at him and chewed my bottom lip.

"Aw, what the hell. Full of Pride was in the stall. We had him removed after the techs were done with him."

"So the horse is a suspect?"

"Could be. Blood on his front left foot and shoe."

I watched four cops carry the body bag out of the stall. They were all sweating. The crowd of people gathered at the entrance to the stable parted to let the police through. I watched Kelly as Bobby's body went by. She shuddered and her eyes welled up.

"Stosh, you know as well as I do that the horse didn't do this."

"No? You here when it happened?"

I gave him a disgusted look and said, "I don't like coincidences."

He kicked up a dirt cloud. "I don't either, kid. But I need some evidence, and till I get some I don't want to scare anybody away."

"You know who is guilty. You should be able to lock 'em up."

"Sure. But we're not the gestapo. We do it the legal way so guys like you don't get rounded up too. Although with you, maybe it would be a good idea." He took a handkerchief out of his pocket and wiped his forehead. "Somebody wanted it to look like Bobby got kicked in the head. That is possible, but not likely. Maybe Kelly can help me find out something about this horse. Would you see if she is up to talking?"

"Sure." Leaving me standing alone, Stosh turned and walked back into the stall.

Kelly was glad to help. She didn't say anything about Bobby, but she held my hand tightly. She told Stosh that Full of Pride was ornery if he was treated poorly. But Bobby would never have treated him unkindly. I could tell she was struggling to keep her composure. Stosh thanked her, and we headed back toward the paddock.

Halfway through the stables, she said, "Spencer, Bobby was a nice kid. What kind of person would do that?"

"A mean one—a desperate one."

We walked in silence till she said, "Ronny has to be involved in this. And he gets to walk around like nothing happened. It doesn't make sense. He should be in jail, or, or..."

"Yeah, " I sighed. "I agree with the 'or' part. But Stosh's hands are tied by the law. He needs evidence."

"I hope he finds some."

"Me too. Maybe he needs some help."

She stopped and looked up at me. "Meaning?"

"Nothing. Just that citizens sometimes provide information that leads to convictions."

"By citizen, do you mean you?"

"Maybe."

"Spencer, you stay away from this. I don't want you—"

"Don't worry. I like breathing. But maybe I can help with the evidence."

"You know something about the murder?"

"I know who's involved. So do you and Stosh. But, no I don't have any evidence."

"So how are you going to help?"

"Well, maybe I can help with the drug smuggling."

"And how is that going to help with the murder?"

"Directly, not at all. But, as Stosh pointed out to me, Capone went to prison for tax evasion. Prison is prison."

"Spencer..."

"I'll be careful, Kelly. But I have several scores to settle. I don't like sitting back and waiting for the wheels of justice to turn. Sometimes they need some grease." I walked her to her car, warned her to be careful and to make sure she wasn't followed. I got the name of her new hotel and told her I'd pick her up at seven for dinner.

A hot wind was blowing the dust around in the parking lot. Looking into the glare of the sun in a cloudless sky, I watched Kelly pull away and then stared into the blue until perspiration started to bead on my forehead. The guy who killed my parents was dead, but that gave me no solace. I didn't blame Bobby. I blamed whoever used him to do their dirty work and they were still walking around. I waited till one of the beads ran down my nose, then wiped my forehead with my forearm and made my way back to the stable. I met Stosh at the paddock.

"Thought you left, kid."

"About to. Question."

"Shoot."

"When you do surveillance, do you watch the front *and* back?"

He gave me a long stare and then answered. "That would be the preferred method. But it also depends on how important it is and how much personnel I can free up."

"Well, how much personnel do you have freed up these days?"

Another look. He said, "Things are tight," turned, and walked away.

I watched him go, then slowly walked to my Mustang. After cranking up the air all the way, I drove to the front gate where there was a pay phone and made a call to the Blue Note. I drove away slowly so I wouldn't raise too much gravel dust. When I hit the blacktop, my tires screeched as I made the turn around the corner of the grandstands.

Chapter 35

After I left the track, I stopped at my office to shower and change and then headed for Kelly. We didn't talk much all through dinner. When we did, it was about the weather.

At ten, I parked a block away from Ronny's apartment and was again waiting for Jesse. He tapped on my window fifteen minutes later. We both made our way to the rear of the building and a few seconds later were back inside Ronny's apartment. It looked as though nothing had changed.

I was looking for a list of future races hoping to find one with some indication of a horse that would be getting a hay bale full of cocaine. This time I'd brought gloves. Old racing forms were strewn across the kitchen table and were spattered with what looked to be spaghetti sauce. I moved dirty plates and found nothing but more mess. The telephone was on the back corner of the table. Next to it was a phone book. I picked up the phone book and under it were four sheets of paper. They all had dates starting with Monday and lists of horses. Monday's sheet and several others had a horse circled. Tipsy on Monday. I reburied the sheets under the phone book, and we left as quietly as we had come.

I called Stosh and a half hour later parked in his drive. He was sitting on the front porch waiting. He had on baggy, yellow shorts and a T-shirt and had a fat cigar stuck in the corner of his mouth. He was not happy, but then again neither was I. Maybe he had stubbed his toe getting up to answer the phone. That's the worst. There's that split second of wait between when you know you stubbed your toe and when the nerves finally transmit the pain to the brain. You just stand there and grit your teeth and wait for it. Or maybe he wanted to lock me up and throw away the key. Or just maybe he was angry because his hands were tied behind his back by the law that paid his salary. Whichever, he looked like my dad the first time I was an hour late getting home from a date. He stared out at the street.

"Okay, kid, give it to me."

"Monday. Horse named Tipsy. I talked to Kelly. She says his stall is four to the west of Full of Pride. "

He nodded. "So, for a horse's name, you risk your career, not to mention your life."

I knew he was angry, but I wasn't sure at who, or what. "Nope. To see these guys in hell I risked my career. And if I could trade my career for their arrest, I'd rip up my license right now."

A car drove by, slowed, and pulled into the drive four doors away. Stosh yawned, stretched, and took a long puff on his cigar, exhaling the smoke very slowly. After studying the ash on the end of the cigar, he said, "So the way you see it, somehow the hay is marked. The bales with the stuff get into a prearranged stall. This time it's Tipsy's. Then Ronny retrieves the stuff, and a bunch of guys get rich."

"That's my guess." I tried to lean back in the white plastic chair. It wouldn't lean. "I figure you get some people in there to watch the stall and wait for Ronny to show."

He slowly turned to look at me for the first time since I got there. "No shit."

"Sorry. I didn't mean to imply that you hadn't thought of that, just that maybe you would have trouble actually doing it. Sometimes it seems like there's a lot you can't do cuz you have to follow the rules."

He spat out a piece of leaf. "Yeah, I guess it would seem like that. But not everything we do is readily visible. I'll let our guys at the track know. You said there were four sheets of paper. What were the dates?"

I told him. They were all about six weeks apart.

"No wonder we haven't noticed anything. With that frequency, the odds are against us catching them at random. Now that we have where and when maybe we can make something happen."

I thought about it. It was like having an intermittent electrical problem with your car. Whenever you take it to the mechanic it works fine. "So where do we go from here?"

"You go home and forget you were ever here. I'll try and do the same." We stood up. "I'm going to bed and dream about making it through a night without being woken up by you." He poked me in the chest with his forefinger and pointed at my car.

I nodded and walked away.

As I opened the door, he said, "Hey, Spencer. Thanks."

I nodded again. He was still standing on the porch as I drove away.

My building looked lonely. There wasn't even one light on. I creaked up the stairs and let myself into my humble abode.

My answering machine was flashing. Two messages. They were both from Kathleen, hoping I was okay and asking if we could get together before she left on Friday. I was glad we couldn't. She was still too tempting. But I'd at least call before I left for Wisconsin in the morning to let her know I was okay.

I splashed some water on my face, stripped off my pants and shirt and fell onto the bed hoping I was tired enough to skip the dreams.

Chapter 36

The sound of someone yelling down the hall woke me up a little before seven. I considered going back to sleep, but I had a five-hour drive in front of me and wanted to get there with plenty of daylight left.

I was very familiar with the area around Algoma. It was the last town before Sturgeon Bay and Door County. It took a little longer but I usually drove the lake route up Highway 42 through Algoma when I went to Door. The drive along the lake was always breathtaking. This time was no different. I stopped and got a hot dog at Manny's and ate it sitting on the concrete breakwater that was on the south side of the little harbor. It was about three feet wide and extended out a couple hundred feet into the lake and then turned north for another hundred feet. Across the harbor mouth, about another hundred feet away, was a bright-red breakwall light.

It was a warm, sunny day. A sapphire-blue sky was dotted with fluffy, white clouds. A few years ago, things had been a bit different. I had walked out on the breakwater and, after getting about halfway out, the foghorn had started to sound. Thirty seconds later, I was completely engulfed in fog and couldn't see two feet in front of me. I immediately felt panic as I lost my visual bearings. Even though I knew I would get back to shore if I just turned around, it was still unnerving.

Just north of Algoma, Highway 42 turned northwest. I took the right turn onto County Highway S, which followed the lakeshore. Farmers worked fields to my left, and the blue water of Lake Michigan sparkled to my right. It was a pleasure to be out of the city. I glanced at the map and watched my odometer for the five mile mark and a grove of trees on my right. As I drove up a little hill, I slowed and turned onto a dirt road just past the trees. It was not marked. The mayor said they had not improved or marked it so people would not know the house sat tucked in behind the trees. They had succeeded. There was no hint of the house from the road.

The road wound back into the trees and came out of the relative darkness into bright sunshine and a spectacular view. Ahead on my left was a sprawling ranch house. To the right of the house was a wide view of the lake. As the road exited the trees it became a blacktop driveway. Pulling off onto a bricked pad, I parked the car. At the end of the circular drive, a flagstone pathway, flanked with limestone boulders, led to the front door about fifty feet away. The large entryway was flanked on both sides by wings of the cedar-sided house. The trees formed a large horse-shoe around the house, hiding whatever neighbors were on either side. But up here there tended to be quite a bit of room between neighbors. Without the security system Ronny could have taken his time getting in the house.

I decided to walk down to the lake before going into the house. A newly-mown grassy area behind and to the south of the house gave way to knee-high wild grasses and shrubs that grew at the top of a fifty-foot-high cliff. At the far corner of the grassy area a screened gazebo marked the top of a set of wooden stairs that descended straight down the cliff face to the water. A few lonely birch trees somehow held on to a perch on the cliff. A cool breeze off the lake cut into the midday heat. From the top of the cliff, I scanned the beach. There was very little sand; mostly boulders and driftwood bleached white from the sun. A couple hundred feet offshore a group of gulls played above the waves.

I could hear the rumble of a passing semi as I walked back to the front of the house and punched the code I had memorized into the security pad. The message changed from armed to disabled, and I unlocked the door. A marble entryway blended into thick carpet of almost the same gray color and led into a large living area. The far side was almost all glass and afforded a beautiful view over the lake. Three brightly colored sails billowed their way south toward Algoma.

Standing in front of the center window, I thought about the man who owned this house: mayor of one of the most important cities in the world and all the power that goes with that, married to a rich woman, two splendid houses, more than enough money to satisfy him, influential friends. He had it all, yet he had nothing. I suddenly remembered his eyes. They were empty; emptied by a father who'd beaten him and a mother who'd stood by helplessly and watched; by a half brother whom he'd tried to protect and turned out to be a bum; by a life that took more than it gave where important things were concerned; and by a woman he loved but couldn't have. Most people probably envied him. But if you looked into his eyes, there was only sadness. He was worn out by the fight, worn down by life. He wasn't Marty's father. That was too bad, for both of them. I think he wanted to be somebody's father and perhaps he'd have made a good one if life hadn't cut out his heart. Not that he wasn't a kind man. He just didn't have what it took to go after what was truly important. The power wasn't—Elizabeth was. If he'd had some guts, she would be alive today. Instead, he'd sat by and watched her ruin her life. I wasn't sure whether I despised the man or felt sorry for him, or both. The view here was spectacular, but he would never see it with all that sadness blurring his view.

A sound like the muffled snap of a breaking twig made me turn quickly to my left. I listened, but heard nothing but the whoosh of the air conditioner. I walked toward where the sound had come from and found the bedrooms off to the left of the living area. There was no one there. Must have been the house creaking as it reacted to the heat outside and the cold inside. Suddenly, I felt uneasy being there and got on with my search.

I started with the bedrooms. There were three, all furnished with comfortable, fluffy pillows and chairs and soft, lacy curtains that let the light shimmer into the rooms. Another room was full of kids toys, neat and tidy. That room faced the front of the house. What looked like the master bedroom adjoined a large bathroom with a two-person whirlpool tub. On the side table by the bed, the side away from the windows, was a book, the only sign in the house that a person had ever been there. Otherwise it was like a museum, unchanging and for show, locked behind a glass case. The book was *The Adventures of Augie March* by Saul Bellow. It was a thick book. A bookmark with a teddy bear on it was stuck about halfway through.

The other wing of the house held a kitchen, a media room, and furnace and laundry areas. I took about two hours to do a thorough search, under and behind everything. I found nothing. If Mrs. Grey did have the rest of the checks and pictures, she had them hidden somewhere else. And when I finished the search, I realized I wanted to be somewhere else too. There was a pall that hung over this house that covered the beauty of the setting like a shroud. Normally I would be at home here in the peace and quiet. But right now, I needed the noise of the city.

Chapter 37

I took the quickest route to the interstate and made it back to Chicago by seven. The mayor wasn't in when I tried his private number. I left a message that I would call back.

Driving back, I thought about Ronny and his slimy trail touching all aspects of this case. But if he had been blackmailing Elizabeth, and it certainly looked that way, and she had been paying, he wouldn't want her dead. Unless she'd stopped paying. She'd been planning to move. To get away from him? But what would have changed to make her decide that?

A nice neat detective story would have a clue somewhere. Unfortunately life was not nice and neat. I had evidence to link Ronny to the drugs at the track, but I had nothing to link him to Elizabeth's murder. Was there a link? He was certainly capable, but that didn't mean he did it. In her line of work Elizabeth could have been killed by anybody, which was probably why the police had her case in a drawer.

Was it strange that they hadn't found many personal items in Elizabeth's apartment? Or had she gotten rid of everything that meant anything except for Marty? I remembered Ethyl saying that she had boxes of pictures stored up in the attic. Maybe Elizabeth had stored things up there too. It was worth a shot.

I called Kelly, chatted for a few minutes, made plans for dinner Saturday, pulled off my pants and shirt, flopped on the bed, and read till I fell asleep.

Chapter 38

Friday started off as a gray day. The sky was overcast with some patches darker than others, and the air had the smell of rain. I was planning on going to the Cubs/Mets game by myself so I wanted to get to Elizabeth's apartment relatively early. But I wanted Maxine's help, and I didn't want to wake her. Deciding that eleven would be a good compromise, I next tried to decide whether to stay in bed or have breakfast. Breakfast won. I deserved some retainer, even though I couldn't tell Beef what I had found. I still didn't know what to do about that.

By the time I got to the diner, it was nine thirty. The place was almost empty. I slid into a booth, and Beef joined me with two cups of coffee. I ordered pancakes and eggs sunny-side up.

"So, hotshot, you're still eating your retainer, so you must be doing something. But I don't hear about much."

I smiled with effort. "You watch TV. The good guys spend the first forty-five minutes catching up with the bad guys. It's not till the last fifteen minutes that things start coming together."

"Hmm. I suppose that means something, but couldn't you just say you don't have crap?"

"No, because that's not true."

"So?"

"So what?"

"So, I hired you to find out who this guy is. What do you got?"

I sipped my coffee. "I have loose ends. Till they're tied up, I keep them in my pocket."

"Oh, that's nice. Well maybe I'll just keep your pancakes in my pocket."

I shrugged. "There's other diners."

He folded his arms across his chest and leaned back. "Well, maybe there are other PIs."

"There are. All over the place. Like flies on a cow on a hot day. I'll get you the phone book."

While we chatted, Maria brought my breakfast. A big glob of whipped butter topped the pancakes, and a sprig of parsley colored three strips of bacon. We exchanged hellos with smiles.

I picked up the syrup jug, poised it over the pancakes, and, before pouring, asked, "So, do I eat this or not?"

"What am I going to do now, throw it out?"

I ate. I deserved it. After all, I had done my job.

He watched me with squinty eyes. "Just tell me if you got anything that might get us somewhere here. If you got nothing, I won't hold it against you. You're new at this."

Great. What I had found out, I didn't think anybody wanted to know, especially Marty. And if Beef hadn't killed Elizabeth, he would probably kill Ronny if he knew Ronny was Marty's father. He was certainly capable. But by withholding what I'd learned, I looked like an amateur detective who was getting nowhere.

"I got something, Beef. Trust me for a little bit. It's kinda complicated. I just want to be sure."

"Okay." He wasn't happy. I wouldn't have been either.

I nodded. "How's Marty doing?"

"Aw, she's a good kid. But lately she's been kinda down about the day care joint. She's taken a liking to a new helper who hasn't been there lately."

"That's normal, given her life."

"Yeah, well I don't want her attached to nobody but me."

"That's normal too. But someday your little girl is going to grow up and get detached."

"The guy that tries to detach her is going to have to deal with me. I'm not losing her without a fight. "

I pitied whoever that guy would be. And I wondered again just how far Beef would be willing to go if he found out his sister was leaving. Could he have killed her in a fit of rage? If he had, that was one thing. But if he hadn't, Marty was lucky to have Beef care about her. And if he had, it didn't look like he was going to get caught.

"When I picked Marty up, they asked for ID. I'm glad they're being careful."

"They better be. I remind them every time I drop her off. And I also remind them what is going to happen if they screw up."

"Bet they're happy about that." I didn't think either Kelly or Marty were in danger anymore, but it didn't hurt to be safe. But I also wondered. Most of the help at the center were young girls who probably didn't pay a lot of attention to much of anything.

I sopped up the last bit of runny egg with a corner of toast, wiped my mouth, finished my orange juice, and thanked Beef for breakfast. A wave to Maria as I passed the cash register and I was out on the street. The midmorning traffic was sparse. I crossed the street to my car and headed for Beth's apartment.

Chapter 39

Three kids were sitting on the curb smashing cans. I nodded once and gave them a two finger salute. They nodded back. A mangy black dog sprawled against the trunk of a scrawny tree in the only shade within sight. And it wasn't much.

The inside stairs were covered with pages from a newspaper someone had dropped or thrown down the stairs just for fun. On my way up, I picked up the pages. I knocked on Maxine's door and offered her the newspaper when she opened it.

"Couldn't afford a quarter for a new one?" she teased.

"You know how it is with us struggling PIs. Maybe one of these days I should grow up and get a real job."

Her smile disappeared. "You know, maybe I should too."

I walked in. The blinds and windows were open and sunshine filled the room. "Something happen?" I asked with concern.

"No. Well, not other than me doing some thinking. You made me sit back and take a look at my life."

I grimaced. "Maxine, I didn't mean to judge you. I know you're just trying to get through life along with all the rest of us."

She shook her head. "Don't feel bad. And I know you're not judging me. In fact, maybe it's because you accepted me for who I am that made me want to be better."

"Then I guess that's good. We can all afford to be a little better."

"Sure. But it's not that easy. I have no skills, well at least not that other people would accept. Can't exactly put what I do on a job resumé. I've been sitting and thinking and thinking, and I have no idea. It's kind of depressing that I'm thirty years old and have made nothing of my life."

I gave her a pat on the back. "Maxine, you have something a lot of people don't. You're a good person and you care. That's worth a lot."

"Tell that to the employment office." She took some magazines off the couch so we could sit.

"I bet you could get a job at one of the department stores. You don't need experience. They'll train you."

She scoffed. "They'll also wonder what I did for the last ten years."

"Tell them you were a housewife. Happens all the time."

"Got all the answers, don't you? Maybe I wouldn't want to play that game."

I felt sorry for her. She was trying, but didn't have a lot of options. "That's another story. What game would you want to play?"

"You mean besides president of Sears?"

I didn't answer.

"I'm sorry, Spencer. I know you're trying to help. It's just frustrating. It was easier when I didn't think about it."

I took her hand. "Which is why I feel bad if I started you thinking about it."

I looked at her face. Even with no makeup she was still pretty. I half expected a tear to form, but it didn't. She had been through too much for that.

"I guess I'd like to do something with people. But not in a big store. I couldn't handle corporate America."

I laughed. "I couldn't either."

She squeezed my hand. "So, is this business or pleasure?"

My eyebrows raised.

She smiled. "Not my business. Yours, silly."

"Nuts. I was hoping I was being propositioned."

No more smile. "You wouldn't want me, Spencer."

"Not under these circumstances, no. But if I met you at the library it would be a different story. You are an attractive woman and a nice person." I patted her knee. "But yes, business. Ethyl mentioned that she kept some stuff up in the attic. I was hoping you would accompany me up there to see if Elizabeth stored anything."

"I'd be glad to, but Ethyl has the key. How much time do you have?"

"Why? Is she out?"

She laughed. "No, she's never out. Well, hardly ever. That's why she has the key."

"Couldn't you all have keys?"

"I suppose. But this works. Most in here are so transient that no one keeps anything up there. There's nothing up there that I couldn't wait for Ethyl to come back if I wanted it. Just a box of memories. And besides, Ethyl kind of has squatters rights on the attic."

"So why do I have to wait?"

"You don't. She's home. But she will insist on going with and giving you a guided tour of her life."

I shrugged. "I've got time. If that gives her some pleasure, I'm game."

"Okay. But please remember that I warned you."

"Noted."

We walked down a flight and I knocked on the door. Ethyl asked who it was, then quickly opened the door.

"Why hello, Mr. Manning. And Maxine, you look lovely this morning. Come in and I'll make some lemonade."

"No, thank you, Ethyl, maybe later. I need a favor. I'd like to go up in the attic and see if Elizabeth left anything up there."

Her face lit up and her eyes sparkled.

"Oh, certainly. Let me get the key and I will show you the way."

I figured I could find the top of the stairs by myself and told her so when she returned, but she was determined to come with us no matter what. Maxine gave me a snide look. Ethyl was back in less than a minute with an excited look of adventure on her face.

"Okay, we're off. Young man, if you'll just give me a little bit of help on the stairs." She took hold of the railing with her right hand and offered me the other. I let her intertwine her arm with mine. She looked like a little kid getting into the car for a trip to the zoo.

But this time the car was stuck in low gear. One slow step at a time finally got us to the landing between the second and third floor. I was getting frustrated thinking how long the whole trip would take, Ethyl still had the happy look on her face, and Maxine was trying very hard not to laugh. We finally made it after several stops along the way to rest.

Ethyl fumbled with the key and then slowly pulled open the door. I expected dark and dreary and messy with nests of cobwebs. It was quite the opposite. There were several windows that let in enough sunshine that we didn't need a light and, except for dust, the attic was fairly clean and well organized. Little notecards pinned to the rafters divided the space into areas for each apartment. It was hot but not unbearable. Most areas were empty, but each had a card. There was one box in Maxine's spot, one in Beth's, and nine in Ethyl's. Hers was full. A rickety old wooden chair with upholstery hanging from the back stood neatly aligned in front of Ethyl's area.

"Well, what do you think?" Ethyl beamed with pride.

I was surprised and told her so.

She seemed to get extra energy from the attic and took my hand and led me to her area where she sat on the chair. "Now, if you'll just bring over box number one we can get started." Maxine sat on the floor and leaned back against the hip wall staring straight ahead. I knew that if she would have looked at me she would have burst out laughing.

I didn't want to spend the rest of the day in the attic, but that's where we were headed. I needed to get some control here.

"Ethyl, I'd love to look at your things, but I need to see what's in Elizabeth's box. Maybe we could do it some other time. I'll be sure to come back."

She looked heartbroken.

I felt like I had just kicked a dog and, tired of the smug look on Maxine's face, tried a compromise. "How about if you and Maxine go through your boxes and show me the really important things as I go through Beth's box?" That worked. Ethyl was happy. Maxine wasn't. The smug look was gone. I wasn't sure I liked the replacement. I pulled box number one off the top of the pile and set it on the floor next to Ethyl. Maxine came over and sat cross-legged on the floor next to the box. They were opening it as I walked to the other side, took Beth's box out into the center of the attic, and blew the dust off the top. It was a simple cardboard moving box with the flaps folded under each other.

I don't know what I expected, but I did hope to find something that would help. I didn't. All that was there were memories of a sad life that didn't need to be that way. Almost everything in the box had to do with Marty. There were pictures and little things Marty had made out of popsicle sticks and clay. They were all organized by age, separated into little piles wrapped with pink ribbons.

As I sorted through the piles, Ethyl held up various items and talked constantly. I was sure Maxine had heard these stories before, but she sat and listened patiently. Ethyl insisted I look closely at several items: pictures, postcards, an egg beater her mother used to make chocolate cake with, and a wooden spoon, cracked from old age, that she used to stir lemonade as a child. By the end of the second box, she was pulling out things that had belonged to her great-grandmother and dated back to the 1800s. I oohed and aahed from my spot in the middle of the floor until she made me come over to look at a roll of tickets. With resignation, I got up and sat next to Maxine who now seemed to be having a good time.

"This is one of my favorite things," said Ethyl. It was just a roll of red movie tickets. I guessed there were a couple hundred on the roll. They were nothing special, except to Ethyl, or so I thought at first. "I always dreamed of having the neighborhood kids put on a play of some sort, and I could give out tickets. But no one was ever interested." She ran them through her fingers.

"What's that writing on them?" I asked.

"Oh, that's nothing. I wish he hadn't done that. Kind of ruins the tickets don't you think?"

I took hold of the end tickets and looked at them closely. They were signed "John Wilkes Booth" across the face of the ticket. "Ethyl, where did your great-grandmother get these?"

She sat up straight and answered, "My Great Grandmother was the ticket taker at the McVicker's Theater. My Grandma told me her mom used to go and sneak in with her friends and sit in the back. She told such wonderful stories."

"But these are signed by John Wilkes Booth. Do you know anything about that?"

"Mother said they used to do that. They had the actors sign the tickets to try and get more people to come see the show. Kind of like a souvenir. But she said it didn't work very well, so they stopped. Business wasn't very good."

I wondered if I was missing something. Neither of them seemed very interested in the signatures. "Ethyl, do you know who John Wilkes Booth was?"

"Of course, he was one of the actors at the theater."

"Besides that." Still no response from either of them.

Maxine gave me a puzzled look. "What are you getting at, Spencer?"

"John Wilkes Booth was the man who shot President Lincoln."

Ethyl looked shocked. "Well, that's not very nice is it?" she said as she shook her head in disapproval. "Perhaps I should get rid of these tickets."

"Why would you get rid of them, Ethyl?"

"Weeeell," she drawled out disapprovingly. "I don't want to keep something from a murderer in with my precious things."

I looked at her in disbelief and said, "That's exactly why you *should* keep the tickets."

She was puzzled. "Why?"

"Because he is not just a murderer, he is the murderer of President Lincoln. That makes him famous."

She straightened and jutted out her tiny jaw. "Well, maybe a person like that doesn't deserve to be famous."

I unrolled about a hundred tickets. They were all signed. "Ethyl, whether he should be famous or not is beside the point. He is, and because he is, these tickets are worth a lot of money."

"Oh don't be silly, they're just old tickets."

I shook my head. "Because they are old tickets they are probably worth something in their own right. But because they are signed by Booth, I'd be willing to bet they're worth a fortune."

She didn't react but Maxine did. "How much do you think, Spencer?"

"I have no idea. But I could ask around. Ethyl these could be worth enough that you could move out of here into some nicer place."

Shaking her head, she started to roll up the tickets. "Two things young man. I wouldn't want money from a man like that, and I don't want to move out of here. I have lived here for many a year and this is my home." She relaxed and her eyes twinkled. "And you know, this isn't such a bad place." She lovingly put the tickets back in the box, evidently forgetting that she didn't want them with the rest of her precious things. Maxine gave me a "what are you going to do?" look and patted Ethyl's arm. Ethyl pulled out a doll and started the next story. I went back to Elizabeth's box.

I carefully went through each packet and was down to the bottom of the pile. Lifting up a bundle I saw a small white envelope tucked into a corner of the box. I pulled out the flap, turned the envelope upside down and dumped the contents into my hand. Lifting up a silver chain, I saw a silver cross and a medallion of Jesus dangling from the bottom. It was probably something she had worn most of her life. She'd probably taken it off when she moved into this building. I had been taught that Jesus had sacrificed his life for us. What kind of sacrifices had Elizabeth made, and for whom?

I supposed she'd done it for Jeffrey Grey—to protect his image. And since she ended up living in this building, I accepted the chain of events that may have led here. I had thought I understood, but as I sat in the attic looking at all that was left of her life, I decided I had no idea of what she'd gone through. She had given up everything that had been important to her, well almost. She still had Marty, but the guilt of what she was doing to Marty must have been awful. I tried not to judge but did not understand how moving was her only option. I know Maxine said that Beth felt like a whore anyway and maybe her self esteem was shot, but I think I would have said the hell with the mayor and his image. I would think I'd go to him for help. But I was not Elizabeth, and I was not walking in her shoes. I felt sad and like a failure. I had hoped that Jeffrey Grey was the father and would be willing to support Marty. At least that would add something positive to this story. But now the ending was not so happy. I certainly didn't want anyone else knowing that Ronny was Marty's father—Marty because she deserved better, and Beef because he would end up in jail after he killed Ronny.

I slipped the chain into my pocket for Marty some day and repacked the box. Then I sat and watched Ethyl and Maxine for a bit. Ethyl was very happy; this made her day. And Maxine sat patiently like she was sitting at her grandmother's knee listening to a fairy tale. Maybe it was good for her too. Maybe she needed a grandmother.

As Maxine got down another box, I announced that I had to go. Ethyl looked disappointed. Maxine said she would stay for a bit. Ethyl immediately brightened up. I gave Maxine a kiss on the forehead and a wink and let myself out. When all this was over I'd get the box to Beef.

I spent the afternoon at Wrigley Field but even the sunshine and a Cubs win couldn't erase my sadness. I felt depressed and wished I could make everyone's lives magically improve, including mine. I spent Friday night alone with a bottle of beer and a bag of potato chips and fell asleep watching an old movie. I woke up at two, turned off the TV, and went to bed.

Chapter 40

Saturday night I picked up Kelly, and we went to dinner. We chatted about the track. She was still upset about Bobby. So was I, but not as much as she. She asked about the case, and I gave her a brief rundown, leaving out the mayor's name.

I reviewed a bit and told her to feel free to butt in if she had an opinion. Verbalizing my theory might help me figure out if I believed my own scenario.

I took a long drink of beer and started. "Elizabeth had an affair with a married man who wouldn't leave his wife for whatever reason. She accepted that. Then the man's brother found out about the affair and forced himself on Elizabeth."

"The brother being Ronny," Kelly interrupted.

"Right. Ronny knew his brother wouldn't give him any more money. But then he found pictures and checks and saw other possibilities and blackmailed Elizabeth. The first brother had been giving Elizabeth financial support for Marty even though, as he knew, Marty was not his daughter. Elizabeth is afraid and needs more money to cover the blackmail and so asks for an increase in what the lover has been giving. The lover knew Marty wasn't his kid because he had a vasectomy many years ago. So he has been paying the support out of the kindness of his heart and also because he probably feels somewhat guilty for the position he put Elizabeth in. But that only went so far, and he eventually told Elizabeth he couldn't give her any more." I took another drink.

I continued. "Instead of blowing the whistle on this guy—"

"Wait a minute," Kelly interrupted. "Did Elizabeth know the lover wasn't the father?"

"No. But she didn't know he *was* either. She had sex with both brothers within an hour of each other, the second by rape. I guess she hoped it was the first."

"I would too. And she probably assumed it was when he paid the support."

I nodded. "Probably. Anyway, instead of making all this public—"

She interrupted again. "This is something the public would care about?"

"Yup. But can't tell you why."

"That's okay. But you do have me wondering."

"Promise me one thing, for Marty's sake. If you ever figure it out, keep it to yourself. I've probably already told you more than I should."

She crossed her heart. "I promise."

"So, to protect her daughter, Elizabeth clammed up and decided to accept the consequences. She thought she deserved what she got. After all, she'd been having an affair with a married man, so she had some guilt too. She has to live and she has to pay Ronny, so she moved into a dump and started working nights to make ends meet. She continued to get money from the lover and to get visits from Ronny, probably to pick up money, who befriended Marty and promised her a ride on a horse."

The waiter set down two bowls of cream of roasted tomato soup that smelled wonderful. Draping my napkin in my lap, I took a sip and continued. "So the money she got from night work pays off Ronny. She knows what she is doing to Marty and feels horrible. I'm guessing she was planning on disappearing and starting over—Marty said they were going to move again. That would have devastated her brother who loves Marty and might do anything to not lose her. But before she got that chance, she stopped a bullet. End of a sad story, except that Marty is someday going to wonder why she has no parents, and the answers are not going to be happy."

Kelly wiped soup off her lips with her linen napkin. "Poor little girl. Do you have any idea who killed Elizabeth?"

"I've been told by several people that that is none of my business. But I do have some ideas. Certainly could have been Ronny, but he's an easy answer, and if he was receiving blackmail money, why would he kill her? Could have been the lover, but I don't think so. She wasn't blackmailing him. She asked him for more money but dropped it when he said no. He wasn't paying any more than he already had been. Could have been Beef. The man has a temper and he adores Marty, and if he found out Beth was taking Marty away, who knows what he could do? Or she could have been killed by one of her customers or in a robbery attempt."

"What do you think?"

"I think this soup is delicious."

"About the murder, silly."

"Well, I'm not supposed to think about that. But if I did, I guess I'd lean toward the customer/robber scenario or Ronny just because bad guys tend to act like bad guys. But Beef does have a temper, and in a fit of rage or passion you never know what can happen. He did break down the door. I don't think the lover did it. Despite everything, he did care for Elizabeth. I don't think he would harm her, but you never know."

"But he let her move into that neighborhood."

"Yes. But there is a bit more to it. And that's a lot different than murder."

"Think it will get solved?"

"No, I don't. There are simply no clues to follow, and the police have done all they can." The main course was set in front of us. I had prime rib and Kelly had scallops. Both looked wonderful. We ate and talked of other things. I was dying to tell her about the operation at the track on Monday, but knew that talking about my case and talking about Stosh's were two different things. However, I didn't want her there and suggested we go to the zoo. She said she needed to be at the track, but I insisted and she agreed to let me know on Sunday. I didn't like that and suggested we go away for a few days and come back Tuesday. She gave me a funny look and asked why this sudden interest to get away. I told her I just needed a breather and wanted to spend some time with her. She said it sounded nice and would see if she could get away. It depended on when a horse was being delivered to the track.

We finished and drove south to Jackson Harbor. I parked, and we sat on the breakwater at the entrance to the yacht club. It was about ten o'clock and boats were starting to make their way back into the harbor, but many running lights still sparkled out on the lake. The moon stood about thirty degrees up in the eastern sky and moonlight shimmered across the gently lapping waves. Except where the moonlight hit the water, it was hard to see the horizon as the color of the sky blended in with the water.

"This is beautiful, Spencer," Kelly whispered.

I agreed and added some trivia. "One of Columbus's ships is sunk out there somewhere." I pointed out beyond the breakwater.

"Sure," she laughed. "How gullible do I look?"

I laughed. "Not one of the originals. The Columbian Exposition was held in Chicago in 1893. That's why many of Chicago's museums were built. Anyway, Spain sent over a replica of one of Columbus's ships, and it was anchored here at Jackson Park. It sunk and is still out there."

"Well, get some tanks and we'll go find it."

"I'm sure somebody knows where it is."

"And I know where you are." Kelly turned sideways and wrapped her arms around me, and for the rest of the night I forgot about the mayor and his half brother and the Niña or the Pinta or the Santa Maria.

Sunday morning Kelly called and told me she had to be at the track on Monday. A horse was being trailered in, and she had to be there. I asked her for dinner Sunday night, and she told me she was sorry, but she was flying home for a visit and was coming back late Sunday night. I told her to be careful and to stay away from Ronny. We said goodbye and she promised to call Monday afternoon. I called Stosh to tell him Kelly would be at the track and to watch out for her. He said he would but assured me there should be no problem. The only trouble he expected was from Ronny, and they should be able to contain that pretty well. I asked again if I could be there and he said no, which I expected, but did point out that if I had taken a different path after the academy it could have been different. Right. Thanks. I told him to call me as soon as something happened.

I wasted the rest of the day napping and watching baseball washed down with a few beers.

That night, I drove to my parents' house and faced some memories and ghosts.

Chapter 41

I slept at my folks' house and woke up at six Monday morning. That was an hour I was not used to seeing, but I was very anxious. It was going to be a long day. I wanted to be at the track, and it's hell not being where you want to be.

Sunday I had gone through drawers of papers and made piles that seemed to make some sort of sense. Monday morning I got around to opening the safe. The only thing inside was Dad's weapon and a box of ammo. I picked it up and held it in the palm of my right hand. It had the clean smell of oil to it. I set it on the oak desk and watched the sun glint off the barrel. The gun was wrapped in a heavy cloth in the safe. I took out the cloth, sat at the desk, polished the already shining gun, and set it back in the patch of sun.

At ten I went out for a paper and came home with the Trib and a box of Pop-Tarts. Flopping down on the couch, I read and ate and fell asleep. My pager woke me at twelve thirty. I anxiously looked, expecting it to be Stosh, thrilled that the waiting was over. It wasn't. I dialed the unknown number.

A voice answered, "Happy Toddler," and then Beef came on the line.

"Spencer, Marty is gone."

That stopped me cold.

"Spencer!" he yelled.

"Yes. I heard you. What do you mean she's gone?"

"Missing. As in not here. I got here to pick her up and she's not *here*."

"Beef, she has to be there. Maybe she's out playing."

"We've looked all over. She's not here."

I kept thinking. "Washroom?"

"Spencer. We've checked everywhere. You say one more thing and I'm ripping this phone out of the wall."

I knew he would. "Okay. When was the last time someone saw her?"

Beef yelled away from the mouthpiece, "Hey, you! Yeah, you! When was the last time someone saw my kid? Well find out for chrissake." Back to me. "Jesus, these people are idiots."

That may have been true, but I also realized Beef wasn't the person to be asking the questions. "Beef, let me talk to whoever is in charge." The phone banged down on a hard surface, and I heard more yelling. In just a few seconds, a woman answered. "This is Miss Brown."

"Miss Brown, my name is Spencer Manning. I am a private detective. I understand Marty is missing."

"Well, we don't know that, do we? Just because she isn't here doesn't mean she is missing. I and my staff do not have to take this abuse from Mr. Williams."

"No, you don't. But he is upset, and we would like to find Marty. If she is not there, what other explanation do you have?"

"Mr. Williams does not always pick her up himself. There are several people on his list and sometimes he adds someone else. Just last week a strange man picked her up. If you ask me, he needs to pay more attention to the child. She needs stability, not strange people ferrying her around. If he doesn't have time to—"

"Miss Brown. Please. Give us some help here. The strange man last week was me and who picks her up is beside the point. Would you like me to call the police?"

"Well, no. Of course not. Why would you do that?"

I took a deep breath. "Because a child is missing."

"She is not—"

I interrupted and considered letting her deal with Beef. "She is. We asked you to keep a special eye on her, and now she is gone and we are concerned. Now if you are not going to help I will call the police." I didn't tell her I would anyway.

"Well there's no need to do that."

"Good. Then go ask your personnel and the kids when they last saw Marty and put Mr. Williams back on the line."

She did. I tried to calm him down, and I asked if he couldn't have asked Maria or someone else to pick her up. That didn't calm him down.

"Listen, PI, I know what I did. I'm picking her up and she ain't here. That's what is. And are you just going to ask stupid questions?"

"No, Beef. But we have to start somewhere, and the simplest thing is that a mistake was made and she is already at home." I risked another stupid question. "Have you called home?"

"No, I haven't called home. How would she get home?"

I needed to get him doing something to keep him busy. "Beef, Miss Brown is checking to see when someone last saw Marty. Put me on hold, and you call home to just check, okay?"

"Shit. I know—"

"Beef, we need to rule that out, and I need to wait for Miss Brown, so I would appreciate—"

The phone clicked, and I wondered if I was cut off or was put on hold. The man was one big pain in the ass, and what I really wanted to do was tell him to go to hell. But I was concerned about Marty and would put up with his crap for her sake. A minute later Miss Brown was back on the line.

"Sir?"

"Yes, I'm here."

"Several of the children remember playing with her but don't remember her leaving. And none of my staff remember her leaving either. Miss Donnelley helped her clean up about noon, but then went on to someone else when she was done."

"Okay. Please put me back on hold for Mr. Williams."

She did. Beef came back and said Marty was not at home.

"Beef, here's what I want you to do. I will call the police and—"

"Great, those assholes aren't going to—"

"Beef. Shut up." He did. "Either you do what I say or you can go to hell. Got it?"

"You know the cops don't do anything. They didn't do anything for Elizabeth."

I felt sorry for him, but there was no sense in arguing. "Okay, I *am* going to do something, but we have to let them know so they can start looking."

"What are you going to do?"

"I have some places to look."

"Where? I'll look."

Just what I needed. "No, I'll look. You stay there and wait for the police."

"I'm not—"

I hung up. I called Stosh's direct line and got a Detective O'Malley who told me Stosh wasn't in. I knew where he was. I asked for Rosie. She wasn't there either. I asked who was, and he connected me to Rodriguez. I explained the situation and asked for him to get a car over to the center. He assured me they would be there in a few minutes. I warned him not to expect a happy taxpayer. I didn't envy whoever got the call.

I put on my shoes without lacing them, grabbed my keys, and headed for the door. I was halfway there when I stopped, thought for a second, and went back for Dad's gun. I grabbed it and the bullets.

I ran to the car, stuffed the gun and bullets into the glove compartment and sped off. I was a good half hour from the center. When I got to the Eisenhower Expressway, I should have turned west to go to the center, but continued straight toward the track. If Marty was missing, Ronny was involved. The police would handle things at the center.

I continued down Cicero and, after running a few lights, came to the racetrack. It was crawling with police. The front gate was blocked, and traffic was being turned away. A uniformed officer waved me on.

I pulled onto the sidewalk, and he started yelling at me to move. When I didn't, he drew his weapon and started toward me. I held my hands up in the air.

"Keep your hands up and get out of the car."

Two other officers had joined him. Unfortunately, I didn't recognize anybody. He opened my door and backed away. "Officer, I—"

"Shut up. Slow and easy. Turn around and lean over with your hands on top of the car." I wondered why I was getting the harsh treatment.

I wanted to get back to the stables. I also wanted to avoid getting shot. "Officer, my name is Spencer Manning. I need to get back to the stables to see Searg... Lieutenant Powolski. I know where he is and what he's doing."

He started to respond and was stopped by one of the other officers who asked if I had ID. I said I did. He said to get it out slowly. I did. He got on his radio and got ahold of Stosh and explained the situation. The response was "Shit, send him back."

The second officer handed back my wallet. The first glared at me. I glared back. Tough as nails. The tires spun in the gravel, and I fishtailed through the parking lot. The first cop yelled something after me. I don't think it was very complimentary.

The employee parking area was full of flashing red lights. And more were added as an ambulance came up behind me. This didn't look like something that was under control. I thought of Marty and Kelly. I tried not to think. A throng was gathered at the entrance to the stable area. Whatever had happened was over. Rosie met me as I ran toward the stable.

"Spencer, calm down. It's all over."

"Who is hurt?"

"Ronny Press. Shot. He's not going to make it."

"I need to talk to him." I was glad it was just him, but I needed to get to him while he could talk. "Did you catch him with the stuff?"

"We got him. He moved bales around and then started pulling one apart and pulling out packs of cocaine. He had no clue we were there.

The evidence guys are all over the place. We should really stay out of the way, Spencer."

"There's a little girl missing, Rosie, and I think he knows where she is."

She didn't think twice. She started pushing us through the crowd.

"How did he get shot?" We moved through the crowd.

"One of the detectives told him to drop the stuff and lie down. He pulled a gun and started shooting. He missed. We didn't."

Ronny was lying in the dirt outside the stall. Stosh saw us coming and met us about twenty feet away.

"Spencer, I told you to stay away from here. There's—"

"Stosh, Marty is missing. Beef went to pick her up from day care, and she wasn't there. No one remembers seeing her go with anyone."

His anger dissipated. "And you figure Ronny knows something?"

I nodded. "Can I talk to him?"

"You can try. But you'd better hurry."

I bent down next to a bloody Ronny Press. His clothes were shredded and bloody in too many places to count. I started to feel sorry for him and then remembered Bobby's body. His eyes were closed.

I called his name. No response. I tried again as the paramedics came up and tried to push me out of the way. Stosh told us to work around each other. As a paramedic cut open his shirt, he opened his eyes and looked at me.

"Ronny. Ronny, can you hear me?"

A faint "Yeah" was all I got.

"What did you do with Marty?"

Glazed eyes opened and rolled slowly toward me and tried to focus. They didn't.

"Marty," I repeated. "You remember? Elizabeth's little girl?"

"Sure," he sputtered. "So what?"

"She's missing. I figure you know where she is."

"You're full of..." He coughed and winced with pain.

I wanted to punch him. "Where is she, Ronny?"

"I got no idea. I didn't..." Another cough.

"You like kidnapping. You've done it before. Come on, Ronny. Do something nice before you die. That little girl doesn't deserve to rot wherever you've got her."

He tried again to focus, but he just looked right through me. "Yeah we grabbed your girlfriend," he said with a gurgle as his breath formed words through the blood in his throat. "But I don't mess with kids, man." His breath came in fast spurts. The medic was applying bandages and setting up an IV. "I liked that kid. If she's missing, it wasn't me—it wasn't..." A last gasp of breath rushed out of his mouth. His head slowly rolled to the side and hung at an odd angle with eyes open and staring. A fly landed on the corner of his open mouth and crawled inside his lower lip, probably wondering why it wasn't being swatted—if flies could wonder.

One less bad guy on the earth. And despite how bad this bad guy was, I did feel something that leaned toward sadness. But I didn't have time for sadness. If Ronny wasn't lying, then where was Marty? I told Stosh I was going to Ronny's apartment. He said I wasn't, that they would handle it and he wasn't kidding. I told him to let me know what happened at the apartment and started back to my car. As I walked, I scanned the crowd for Kelly. I didn't see her. Halfway to the car, Rosie caught up to me.

She linked her arm through mine. "Spencer, is there anything I can do to help?"

"No thanks, Rosie. Stosh is checking Ronny's apartment. After that I don't know where she could be. I must be missing something."

"Does this have anything to do with your visit to the mayor?"

"Not unless he's doing a great acting job and is really a kidnapper. No, I don't think so."

"Spencer, sometimes things are not as they seem. I'm not saying he had anything to do with the little girl, but people can be good actors."

I leaned on the car and looked at her. "I'll remember that. But geez, I can't believe he would fool me that easily. If he did, I should find another line of work."

She gave me a hug and a kiss on the cheek. "You'll figure it out. Keep digging. That's all detective work is. Sometimes you get a revelation, but usually it's just talking to everyone you can think of and accumulating piles of data and notes. I've gotta get back to work. If I can do anything, let me know."

"Thanks, Rosie. You're the best."

She waved as she walked back to the stable. I opened the door and sat down. A little dust devil spun in the parking lot as the warm wind picked up from the southwest. As a detective, I had a lot to be happy about; I'd found out who Marty's father was, and I'd fed Stosh the information he needed to shut down the drug ring at the track. So my first case had turned out pretty well. But all that meant nothing if I couldn't find Marty. I felt so helpless. Was there something I was missing or could she have been grabbed by a total stranger for no reason at all? Kids do get kidnapped. But I reminded myself that I didn't believe in coincidences. The dust devil collapsed on itself as it lost its energy source. Despite Stosh's warning, I decided to drive to Ronny's apartment. I couldn't sit and do nothing. As I swung my legs into the car my pager went off. It was Maxine. I found a phone and called her. She answered on the first ring.

"Spencer, I've just had a talk with Ethyl. I think you should talk to her. Can you come over?"

"I'm a little busy, Maxine," I said dejectedly.

"But I think it might be important."

I wasn't interested in Ethyl and almost said so but managed to be polite. "What does she want to talk about? The tickets?"

"No. We were talking about the night Elizabeth was killed. I brought up the fight Elizabeth had with her brother, and Ethyl said, 'Brother? That was no brother!' Spencer, she says it was a woman Beth was fighting with."

"A woman?" I figured Ethyl'd had a few too many sips of lemonade. "But we know it was Beef. He admitted he was there and they fought. What's the problem?"

"Yes. That's what I told her, but listen to this. She says the fight she heard was about one in the morning. Whoever that woman was saw her alive. All you have to do is find out who she was."

I remembered the words Ethyl had said she heard: "You can't have her, she's mine." I knew who the lady was, and I knew who had Marty.

"Maxine you are a doll. I owe you big time. I gotta go. I'll explain it to you later." I called Happy Toddler and asked if the balloon lady had been there today. She had been but she had left.

Leaving the car door open, I headed for the stable at a dead run and pushed my way through the crowd. Stosh was standing with two plain-clothes cops watching the evidence men.

"Stosh, I need to know..." I said breathlessly.

"Spencer, slow down. I told you I'd let you know as soon as I heard about the apartment. We're trying to—"

I put up my hand. "No. I need something else." I pulled him aside.

"Spencer. Am I on your payroll? You want to use my department, join it!" he said with an angry edge to his voice. "In case you haven't noticed, I'm busy here."

"I need to know if the mayor's wife is at home."

He gave me a puzzled look. "And why would that be?"

"I think she has Marty."

"Are you crazy?"

"For the mayor's sake, I hope so. For Marty's, I hope not."

Now he pulled me farther away from the men. "You're saying the mayor's wife grabbed the kid?"

"Well, yes. But there are extenuating circumstances."

He rolled his eyes. "And those are?"

"It's too long to go into. I need to find Marty. If the mayor's wife has her, at least we know she wasn't grabbed by some nut who stuffed her in a dumpster. Given the choices, I'm hoping it's the mayor's wife."

"God. You're out on a limb here with assumptions, Spencer. Do you know what could happen if you're wrong?"

"Yeah, nothing. The only person I'm telling is you. I just want to know if she's home. And you can find out."

"And how is that?"

"Call your surveillance team and ask."

"Surveillance team? You making more assumptions?"

"I guess. But I figure they're pretty good."

"And if she's home, then what?"

"Then I pay a visit."

"And if she isn't?"

"Then we look for her."

"We?"

"Okay, me. But either way, you have no liability."

He shook his head. "Stand here, and don't move and don't bother anybody." He walked away muttering something under his breath.

I watched as two men in plain clothes picked through the straw and placed bits in plastic bags. Stosh was back in less than two minutes.

"She's not there. Left at ten this morning and hasn't returned."

"Thanks." I glanced at my watch. Almost two.

"Now what? I can't—"

"Now I look somewhere else."

"Good. Call me if you find anything. And for chrissake be careful. And watch who you accuse!"

I was already running back between the rows of stalls. There was only one other place I knew to look, and it would take me five hours to get there, if I drove fast. I was stopped by the crowd. Rosie was standing with several uniformed policemen who were trying to keep the workers back.

"Spencer, why the hurry?"

"I'm still looking for Marty, and I think I know where to look." I started to fight back through the crowd.

"Hey, you want help?" she yelled after me.

"Aren't you working?"

"This is pretty well wrapped up, and someone else can do the paper-work. I think I can get some personal time."

"Sure. But I'm in a hurry."

"Let me check and I'll be right with you. Where we going?"

"Wisconsin."

A look of surprise filled her face. "Okay, what the hell." She called Stosh on her radio and asked for some personal time. He said okay and told her not to let me boss her around. Not too dumb, that lieutenant. She turned to her partner and told him she'd be in tomorrow.

"Let's go," she said as she started to clear a path. "We need to stop at my place so I can change. Your car?"

I nodded.

Rolling the windows down to let out the heat, we headed for the track entrance which was still congested. The officer at the gate was having a tough day. This time he was getting an argument from Kelly. When she saw my car she hurried over.

"Spencer, what's going on?"

"The drug ring is in for bad times."

"Did you get him?"

"Well, actually Stosh got him. The important thing is they are got."

She said hi to Rosie. "Can I get back there?"

Rosie said she would talk to the officer and got out of the car.

"Where are you two off to?"

"Marty is missing. Wasn't at the center when Beef went to pick her up."

"Oh, Spencer, I'm so sorry. That poor little girl."

"I think I know where to look."

"Good luck. I hope you find her."

"Me too."

Rosie got back in the car and told Kelly it was okay to go on in.

"Thanks, Rosie. You'll find her, Spence." She leaned down and gave me what she called a good luck kiss. I wondered if it was to let Rosie know who was who. I kinda hoped that anyway.

The officer cleared the crowd for us, and we headed north on Cicero.

Chapter 42

After stopping for gas we got on the tollway and headed north. We had plenty of time to talk, and I figured that Rosie knew enough already to trust her with the whole story. I started at the beginning with my hunt for Marty's father and told her about the mayor and Ronny and about Louise wanting kids, but the mayor being unable to oblige. Somewhere along the way Louise went nuts, or at least half nuts. Then Ronny broke into the safe at the summer house, and Louise found pictures of Marty and the canceled checks. I was again assuming that she had found them but the assumption fit my theory so I kept it. I told her the mayor had sent me up to search the place. From there on, the story was my take on what I thought had happened. And I was betting my take was right. I figured Louise had put two and two together and had gotten four or at least her version of four which added up to the mayor fathering a child with another woman. And Louise figured that she deserved the kid more than Beth and twisted her brain into thinking that the kid was really hers and was willing to commit murder to prove it.

So Louise tracked down Marty and followed her to the day care center where she volunteered to help.

Rosie had been listening quietly up till now. She asked a logical question.

"Doesn't the center think it strange that the mayor's wife is volunteering at their center?"

"No. They are thrilled. Mrs. Grey has a long history of volunteer work with kids and support for kid's organizations. Don't you watch the news?"

"I try not to. Politics isn't one of my favorite topics."

"Mine either. Before this, I was lucky to know the mayor's name."

"Okay, so she volunteers and buddies up with Marty."

"Right. Marty said there was some woman at the center who she liked a lot. Must have been Louise. She has a perfect chance to sneak out with the kid. No one would question her being there or paying special attention to Marty, and Marty would go off with her without a fuss."

"Should we notify the Wisconsin cops?" Rosie asked.

"I don't think so. Marty is safe unless Louise feels threatened. The cops would want to get involved and would scare her."

We were both quiet as I slowed down for the tollbooth before the Wisconsin border.

As I pulled away, hitting seventy as fast as I could, I asked, "So what do you think?"

She pulled one foot up under her on the seat and laid her hand on my leg. "I think your reasoning is pretty sound. It's kind of scary that that could happen. But there is one good thing about it."

"And that is?"

"If Mrs. Grey thinks Marty is hers, she isn't going to hurt her."

"I hope not, Rosie. But if this turns out to be the way it looks, she is a dangerous woman and a good shot. If she was willing to kill to get Marty, she'll be willing to kill to keep her." I took her hand. "You still want to come?"

"Well, I'm not going to let you go alone. Tell me how the place is laid out."

I did. She made me promise I would let her run the show. I did.

We were passing the turnoff to Billy Mitchell Airfield and coming up on Milwaukee. "Spencer, you realize I have no jurisdiction in Wisconsin, and your license is no good there either."

"Yes, it is. I didn't know where I wanted to set up practice so I got a license in both states."

"Well we're going up against someone who probably has a gun."

"Right. But we've got her outnumbered."

"What are we going to do, share my gun?"

I told her to open the glove compartment and told her whose it was.

"Did you change the registration?"

"No. I've been meaning to."

"Meaning to doesn't count. You can't use that, Spencer. Do you have any idea how badly screwed we are if something bad goes down here? I can see the headline now—'Mayor's Wife Killed by Ex-Police Chief's Gun.' Sounds great doesn't it? Spencer, I think we should call somebody if she is there."

"Okay. But if Marty is in trouble, I'm not waiting for the troops to arrive."

"Okay. But remember, I make the decisions."

I didn't answer.

"Right?"

"Right. Don't worry, Rosie, this could be nothing."

"Nothing?"

"Sure, she could not be there, or she could not have Marty, or she could and it could be real easy."

"Or not."

"Boy, aren't you Little Miss Positive Thinking."

"Being prepared for the worst and then being pleasantly surprised in this business gives you better odds of staying alive, especially when you're dealing with someone violent."

"I agree."

We drove in silence for the next two hours, turned right at Highway 10 and headed toward the lake. Rosie took in the scenery. About an hour later we drove into Algoma. I pointed out the red lighthouse and told her we'd be there in ten minutes.

We climbed a hill, and I watched for the thicket of trees as I slowed and turned into the drive at ten to seven. As planned, we stopped half-way through the trees. I walked to the edge of the trees while Rosie watched over the car. A large, dark red Buick was parked at the end of the brick drive. There were no lights on in the house, but it was still early enough that they weren't needed. I watched for ten minutes and saw no sign of activity. Making my way back to the car, I tried to keep a positive thought about Marty.

As I reached the car, Rosie moved out of the trees.

"Looking for acorns?" I asked.

"Yup. Thought I'd hunt up some dinner."

"Oh yeah, sorry."

"You owe me. So?"

"Big red car on the drive. I assume it's hers. No sign of anybody, but they could be around back. Most of the living space faces the lake, so we wouldn't see them from the front."

"So?"

"You're the boss, remember?"

"At the moment, I'll defer to you. Got a plan?"

I didn't, at least not a good one. "Two choices. We can wait for dark and some lights to go on and move around the house and get a good idea of who is there. Or we can go knock on the door."

"Yup, just a couple of lost lovers looking for directions. Problem is, unless you know this house is here, you wouldn't know this house is here. So it's not a place where lost lovers would stop to ask directions."

"Okay, so I knock on the door and you cover me. Which do you like?"

"At the moment we don't have the advantage. Dark gives us that. We get knowledge and surprise."

"Yeah, but maybe Marty can't wait till dark."

"Not an easy decision, Spencer. But we do have an advantage cops don't always get."

"And that is?"

"Time to think."

I looked at her and took a deep breath.

"So we're back to choices."

A dog barked. Could have come from anywhere. I figured Marty was probably okay but didn't like thinking about the other possibilities, and my imagination was running away with me, including murder/suicide. After all, the woman was not all there.

I looked up as the deep-throated groan of a semi downshifting to make the grade filtered through the trees. "We gotta do something, Rosie. I have to know she's alive and okay. Once we know that we can afford to wait."

"Okay. How?"

"How about if I go to the door and tell her her husband sent me to check the security system?"

"Better, but I don't think she'd believe you. Got anything else?"

I tried to find a bird I heard chirping up in one of the oak trees. Every time I thought I knew where it was, the chirp came from a different spot. I gave up.

Both of us jumped as we heard a car door slam and the engine start.

"Damn, she's leaving," I said.

"And this is the only way out," added Rosie.

"And we've got no place to hide."

We both ran to the car hoping to beat Mrs. Grey out of the drive. We didn't have a chance. I was pulling my door closed, and Rosie was getting in when the red Buick cruised into the wooded part of the drive, Louise Grey at the wheel. When she saw my car, the Buick stopped. I started to get out, trying to come up with a good excuse for being there. Before I cleared the door, she put the car in reverse, floored the accelerator and raced back out of the woods. I thought I saw the top of Marty's head in the back seat. As the right rear tire slipped off the blacktop, stones and dirt spit up into the air. Once she'd backed out of the woods, she spun the wheel, turning the car perpendicular to the road, scraped the left rear fender against a tree, and raced out of our line of sight.

Rosie slammed her door shut. "Get down to the house. Fast."

I floored the Mustang and followed Louise to the house. We cleared the trees in time to see Louise hurrying Marty into the house.

"She obviously assumes we're here because of Marty, and now she feels trapped," Rosie explained.

"Isn't this going to make her feel more trapped?"

"I don't care how she feels anymore. Let's think about Marty. Louise is a dangerous woman, and she wants Marty with her. If she thinks she's trapped, there's only one way of keeping Marty."

I felt fear and helplessness. "So what do we do?"

"Pray you don't hear any shots. Stop behind her car." She took my father's gun out of the glove compartment and handed it to me along with the extra bullets. "Who goes to the door, you or me?"

"Maybe we should wait and see what happens."

She unholstered her gun and said emphatically, "No. We have to get her attention on us before she has a chance to do anything. Decide, you or me."

This was my case. "Me."

"Get going. Tell her we had car trouble. Doesn't matter if she believes it or not. I'll cover you from here." She reached over and honked the horn. "Attention getter."

I got out.

"Spencer."

I turned my head.

"She's not the mayor's wife. She's a woman with a gun. Be ready."

I nodded and started toward the front door which was about eighty feet away. I moved slowly, hugging the boulders along the side of the gravel path and trying to catch sight of either Louise or Marty through the windows on the side of the door. I didn't see anything. The sun had dipped below the trees, and the house was in shadows. A few lights were on in the house, but the foyer was not lit. As I watched, the double-hung window on the left side of the door slowly slid up. I was trying to think of a better excuse than car trouble. I didn't need one. I was about a third of the way to the door when a shot rang out. I immediately dropped as a bullet ricocheted off a boulder to my left. I squeezed in between two boulders.

"The shot came from that open window on the left of the door, Spencer." Rosie was on the other side of the path behind a large, pink hunk of rock. I had no idea how she'd gotten there that quickly.

"We can't shoot, Rosie. I don't know where Marty is."

"Right. Gotta try and talk her out. You talk. See if you can get her calmed down. I'll see if I can get closer. Fire only if you have to. This will change if she knows we have guns."

I squeezed tighter into the space between boulders. "Mrs. Grey. My name is Spencer. I'm a friend of your husband. He sent me to look at the security system. I just want to talk to you." I watched Rosie move to the next boulder. Louise watched too. She fired again. This time there were two pings as the bullet bounced off of rocks. All of a sudden, I didn't feel too safe behind my boulder. Bullets could turn corners if they bounced off of rocks. Rosie had crouched and flattened against a rock. Another shot and more pings. It was bad when you didn't know where the shots were coming from. It was twice as bad when you didn't know where they were going. I didn't like being a duck in a shooting gallery, especially when I couldn't shoot back.

There was enough light for Rosie and I to see each other. She motioned me to stay behind the rock. I wasn't going anywhere, but I also realized the rock wasn't much cover. I tried again. "Louise, we just want to talk to you. Please—"

She fired again, at nothing. Neither of us were giving her a target. I remembered the bullet that went right through Elizabeth's heart and hoped that was just a lucky shot. Another shot. The ping was off the boulder to my left. A shard of rock hit my left arm. I thought of firing into the air, but, remembering what Rosie had said, decided that might make her more desperate. As long as she thought she had the upper hand I hoped she would stay with us. If she thought she was in danger, she might end it with two shots inside the house. I had to keep her attention by talking.

"Mrs. Grey, Louise, you haven't hurt anyone. Stop shooting and we can talk. Open the front door and—" Another shot. This one didn't ping.

I looked desperately at Rosie. She mouthed "keep talking" and then suddenly pointed toward the left side of the house. I twisted and looked. Marty's face was framed in the window. I gave her a small wave. She waved back. I thought of trying to get her to climb out the window but didn't want to put her where Louise could see her. I remembered the last words Elizabeth heard: "You can't have her, she's mine." If Louise was crazy she might do anything to keep someone else from getting Marty, including killing her. As long as Marty was in the bedroom and Louise was in the foyer we were okay. I just had to keep her there. I motioned to Marty to stay put.

"Louise, I'd like to come in and talk. We can work this—"

Two pings. Sounded like one on each side of the path. Great, she could get both of us with one shot. She obviously didn't want to talk. I saw the flashes to the left of the door. I wondered how much ammo she had and figured I'd better assume she had plenty. She was firing at my voice, but as the sunlight faded we became tougher targets. As long as we didn't stand up, we were hard to see.

From the other side of the path, I heard Rosie whisper my name. "Spencer, let me get in position where I can see that window. Then..." She stopped as the porch lights went on. "Shit," Rosie spat. As she said it, she popped above the rock, shot the lights out, and was back down before the next three shots rang out.

I wondered how long our luck would hold out. If she threw enough bullets into the rocks, sooner or later one would find us. Or two. Then things got worse. Far off in the distance, I heard a muted siren. Normally I wouldn't mind the cops showing up, but in this case I thought it would do more harm than good. Louise obviously thought she could handle both of us. But if the troops rolled in, even a crazy person would have to feel overwhelmed. And if she felt overwhelmed, I was afraid she would use her last option. We had to end this before they got here. But I had no idea how.

Rosie got my attention again. She pointed toward the road. I nodded. "Count to five, then put a couple of shots through the window. I'll get a couple of shots off to the left," she whispered.

I counted and fired. Rosie had flattened out on the path hugging the boulder. She fired as Louise fired from the house. I heard more glass break and heard a muffled yell from Rosie. Her gun was lying in the path, and she was holding her left wrist. She nodded she was okay. As the sirens got louder, two more shots came from the house. I reloaded. I glanced toward the left and saw Marty with a frozen look of fear on her face and realized I was afraid too. But I was also angry. I wished I knew whether the shot that killed Beth was pure luck or skill. Then I decided it didn't matter. I was out of time. I needed to get her to fire and, so far, talking had worked. As I started a sentence, I rolled into the path and fired into the window just above the ledge. I have no idea what I said, and I didn't take time to think. I heard the ping before I felt the pain in my leg. A sharp searing stab just below my left knee. I rolled back into the rocks and listened. Marty was still in the window. The sirens sounded right next door. I put another shot into the window. Quiet. I tried to stand and couldn't.

"Cover me, Spencer," Rosie said.

I rolled into the path and fired from a prone position as Rosie grabbed her gun and sprinted for the door. She flattened against the wall and banged on the door with the butt of her gun. I kept my gun trained on the window. There was no movement inside. Rosie called to Louise. No answer.

Holding her gun with both hands at her chest, Rosie yelled, "Can you walk?"

"I can limp."

"Get over to Marty and get her out of the house." She pointed out the drive. "We'll have company soon. Get her out before they get here."

I tried to stand and didn't do too well. Looking at Marty, I moved as fast as I could trying to hop on my good leg. The sirens were deafening, and I could see headlights slicing through the trees. When I was about ten feet from the house, I yelled to Marty to open the window. She slid it up as I reached the house, and I pushed in the screen. I reached through the opening and helped her climb out. I pulled her to me and flattened against the wall as the first squad car came out of the trees and stopped at the edge of the brick drive. Two more were right behind. Spotlights played over the yard. I dropped my gun and put my hands high in the air as one light found me. Marty kept both arms wrapped around my waist.

As another light focused on Rosie, a deep voice bellowed, "Drop the weapon and turn and place your hands against the door."

She did, and yelled as loud as she could, "I'm a police officer. There's a woman with a gun inside the house."

I tried to see what the cops were doing, but with the light in my eyes I couldn't see a thing.

"Both of you keep still while we sort this out. Where is this woman with the gun?"

"She may be just inside this door to my left. I'm pretty sure she's hit. But she may also be anywhere else in there."

"Do you have ID?"

"My purse is in the Mustang, passenger's side. Rosie Lonnigan, Chicago detective."

I heard a car door open.

"Who are the guy and the kid?" asked the cop.

"He's a private detective."

Great, I thought. Two things a small town cop loves, cops from the big city and private detectives.

Rosie continued. "The girl was missing. We came up to see if she was here. She was, kidnapped by the lady in the house. The lady opened fire. We shot back. The shots have stopped. And both of us are hit. Could you get an ambulance?"

A few seconds later, "Okay, Miss Lonnigan, keep your hands in the air and walk back to us. And there is an ambulance out on the road. As soon as we get this area secured, we'll bring it in."

"Okay, but if you don't mind, I'd like to live to see another day. I'd like to find out where the woman is and if she is still alive before I walk out into the open."

The cop thought for a minute. One of those tough decisions. I thought I could help. "The back of the house is mostly glass. If the drapes are open, you can see the front door through the living room."

"Hey. I don't need help from you, fellow." But a few seconds later I heard the sound of running footsteps heading around the back of the house.

"Okay. I'm going to send two officers around the back of the house and see what there is to see. You two stay put."

I didn't feel good about staying put. "Officer, if the woman is still alive she's trying to get to this bedroom to get this kid. I'd rather not be standing here."

"Okay. Walk out to us slowly."

"Let me send the girl while I make sure the lady doesn't get into this bedroom."

"Okay. But keep your hands up."

I told Marty to run toward the light and that I would be with her in a minute. She didn't have to be told twice. As she ran away, I peered into the room. It was still empty. I gave her enough time to get to the cars and then limped after her as fast as I could. She made it in a ten seconds. It took me two minutes. As I reached the cars, Marty again wrapped herself around me. One of the officers asked her to stand back. She looked up at me. I said it was okay, and she reluctantly moved away. As she did, he moved in and frisked me.

"Okay, Chief. He's clean."

"Sit, Mr. Detective. Put your hands behind you. Cuff him, Charlie. You hurt bad?"

"Bullet in my leg. On the whole, I'd say it's not one of my better days. Do we need the cuffs?"

"Till I get this figured out, we do. If it turns out we didn't, I'll apologize. Charlie, put him in the back seat, and take him out to the ambulance."

Charlie started to walk me away. Marty put her arm around my waist.

"What about the kid?" Charlie asked.

"Take her with. If he's going to the hospital, you go too."

"I'm not going anywhere without her." I nodded toward Rosie.

"Not my call. The doc says you go, you go. I don't know if you're a bad guy or a good guy, but either way, I don't want you bleeding to death in my county."

His radio sounded. "Chief, I can see up to the front door. There's nobody there. But the sliding door back here is open. Want us to go in?" The radio crackled.

"Yup, but be mighty careful. Might have a crazy woman with a gun."

Charlie tried to lead me to the car. "Listen, Chief, I'd like to stay. It's not bleeding much. A few more minutes isn't going to hurt. Take Marty out and I'll go if it gets worse."

"Suit yourself, tough guy. Take the kid, Charlie, and then get back here."

I assured Marty I would be with her very soon and felt my heart break as she walked to the car with Charlie.

"Mind if I sit?"

"Be my guest. You know whose house this is Mr. PI?"

"Yup."

He blew air out his mouth and shook his head. "Just what I needed."

The radio crackled again. "We're inside. I'm gonna turn another light on." The foyer brightened. "Holy shit, Chief. There's a bunch of blood here, and a smeared trail goes around the wall and down the hall to the north."

"Follow it, slowly and carefully."

We all waited for the next crackle. It seemed like ages before it came. "She's dead, Chief. Lying in the hall just outside the second room on the left. With all this blood, I have no idea how she made it this far."

"Okay, Sanders. Check the rest of the house. Make sure nobody else is in there. Then open up the front door and let us in." He waved to two other officers to move up and told Charlie to bring the ambulance in. He and two officers walked to the front door. He patted down Rosie. "Hands behind your back please, ma'am."

"Do you think we could skip the cuffs?" She held up her wounded wrist.

"Billy, cuff her good wrist to yours and take her back to the car. I'm going in."

By the time Rosie got to me, the ambulance had pulled up and two medics got out. They looked like teenagers. Rosie said her wrist was just a scratch, but one of the medics insisted on taking a look. The other concentrated on me.

The medic cut my pantleg and cleaned some of the blood away. "Looks like the bullet is still in there."

"I figured."

"We'll have you at the hospital in fifteen minutes."

As the medics gathered their supplies, the chief walked out of the house and back to the cars. Charlie filled him in, and he told Charlie to ride with me and babysit at the hospital.

"How about you, miss?" he asked.

"I'm okay," said Rosie. "But can I go with him?"

"No, ma'am. Sorry. Doc, is he going to live?"

The medic said sure. I'd be fine as soon as the bullet was yanked.

"He'll live, ma'am. You can see him after we get this straightened out. You're going to the station."

The medics got a stretcher and helped me onto it. Marty was coming with me.

The chief got on his radio and gave orders to get Doc Pritchard and an evidence tech out here. I assumed Doc was the coroner.

As they loaded me into the ambulance, the chief walked over and said, "One quick question. Please tell me that's not the mayor's wife in there."

"That's not a question," I said. "And I'd love to tell you that. But I can't. And I'd like to keep this quiet till he is contacted."

"Shit. I'll be up all night keeping this quiet. There goes my fishing trip. Haul him away, guys."

I stopped the medic who was closing the door. "Rosie, will you call Stosh? I'll call Beef and tell him Marty is okay."

"Oh, you bet. I'll have Stosh get someone to clean out my locker too."

I turned to the chief and told him my gun was by the window.

"We'll get it," he said.

The door slammed. I hadn't thought about Rosie. I had just thought about Marty. I didn't want to think about the wall that might fall on her for helping me. But we had been fired on first and just done what we had to do. And I didn't think the mayor would be looking for heads to roll. He'd want this kept as quiet as possible. Marty held my hand all the way to the hospital and right up to when a nurse gave me a shot, and I drifted off.

Chapter 43

When I came to, I was in a sunny room under a crisp white sheet, my leg hurt like hell, and the room was kind of blurry. A television hung on the wall in front of me. Beneath it were two chairs. One of the chairs was occupied by the chief. It took a minute for me to struggle through both memories and sedatives to remember where I had seen him before. Then it took another minute, as I struggled to remember his name, for me to remember that I didn't know his name.

I took a deep breath, winced, and said, with a voice that was mostly air, "Hi, Chief."

"Hi, tough guy."

I figured by this time he knew my name, but I kinda liked tough guy even though I didn't feel so tough. "Am I under arrest?"

"Nope. I pulled my man out of here last night after a talk with a Lieutenant Powolski. He sends his regards."

I winced again. "I bet. Suppose he wants to talk to me."

"That's a good bet. He said he would like to run on up here, but he was busy with something else you had stirred up."

"Was he blaming me or thanking me?" I glanced at the clock. I couldn't focus well enough to see the hands.

"Didn't sound like either. Just telling me why he wasn't coming. He did convince me that you were not worth paying Charlie overtime to guard. Said if I had no problem with what went down, I should send you home."

"And do you have a problem?"

"Not yet. Hopefully it will stay that way, and I can still catch some fish. You mind telling me what happened after you drove into my county?"

I did. I left out the part about being scared, but related the rest exactly as it had happened.

He stood and tucked in his loose shirt. "Have a nice day."

"That's it? I'm free to go?"

"Yup. Your story matches with Detective Lonnigan's. I'm happy. Right now I don't need talk, I need fish. If I want you, I'll call, but don't hold your breath."

"Did Lieutenant Powolski explain the situation to you?"

"Nope. After talking to more Chicago brass than I've seen in a Pullman car, I could tell they didn't want to talk about the situation, and if I didn't need to know, I didn't want to listen. Whatever brought you here is none of my concern. What happened after is, but so far it looks just like what you said. If it stays that way, we're done talking." He turned to go and stopped. "Oh, Powolski says you've got a date with the mayor tonight at eight. Same place. See ya, tough guy."

He walked out and that was that. My eyes could finally focus on the clock hands. It was a little after nine thirty. I was wondering if I should get up and get dressed when a woman in a white coat walked in and picked a clipboard out of a tray at the foot of my bed. I wanted to guess she was a doctor, but there was no stethoscope around her neck. She was a doctor nonetheless.

"Good morning, Mr. Manning," she said with a smile. "I am Doctor Johnson."

I gave what little smile I could and returned the greeting.

"How's the leg?"

"Hurts."

"Ah, yes. That's the plan. Lets you know something is wrong."

"Wonderful. Kudos to the designer. What's my status?"

"They pulled a bullet out last night. Lots of tissue damage but missed the muscle and bone. So, considering, you are fine, even though it may not feel that way. A few days on crutches and you're on your way to a complete recovery."

"Great. How about Detective Lonnigan?"

"She also is fine. Abrasion on her wrist. She's waiting out in the hall."

I nodded. "So I can go?"

"Yes, sir. Stop at the desk at the end of the hall and sign out and you are a free man. Here's a prescription for pain pills." She handed me a slip of paper. "Don't think you can do without them. The drugs are still wearing off. What you feel now is only going to get worse. When you're ready, call a therapist, and they'll get you back on your feet. Good luck." She smiled again. Well, actually her original smile just got bigger. She had a constant smile that seemed a part of her. I thought of staying awhile. She made a note on my clipboard, replaced it, and headed for the door. I noticed a pair of aluminum crutches in the corner.

"Hey, Doc."

She stopped with her hand on the door handle. "Yes, sir?"

"Where's your stethoscope?"

With a laugh, she answered, "Run over by a gurney. It wasn't pretty." And she left. Ten seconds later, Rosie came in. I needed a revolving door.

"Well, well, you're alive."

"Yup. Alive and well but kicking might be a little tough. All in all, I wish I were in Philadelphia," I said with my best W.C. Fields accent.

She laughed, but not for long. "You'll wish that even more when we get back. So will I."

I tried a deep breath and didn't get as much air as I would have liked. "Yeah, I'm sorry about that, Rosie. I'll take all the heat."

"Thanks for the offer, but you are not a cop. We will both get heat. The difference is you can go home after."

"What did Stosh say?"

"He made sure we were okay and then said to say nothing about anything. He had the chief and the mayor on the phone within ten minutes."

"That was it?"

"That was it. But I've got a feeling the 'in-person' version will be a bit more in depth."

I sat up but it wasn't easy. I adjusted the bed and replied. "I bet you're right. How's Marty?"

Rosie pulled a chair over to the side of the bed and sat. "She's as fine as she can be. She's waiting in the lounge. Hasn't said a word about last night. I think it should stay that way till we get her someone to talk to who knows what to say."

"I agree. God, what that little girl has been through."

She nodded. "Not exactly your ordinary fun childhood. But the worst should be over."

"Should be, at least for her." I thought for a minute and realized for the first time what I had done. "My God, Rosie, I killed the mayor's wife." I felt sick.

She took my hand. "You killed a crazy, dangerous woman who was shooting at us and probably would have killed Marty and herself if given the chance. You did what you had to do. Never think otherwise."

I knew that was true, but it didn't help much. "I can imagine the headlines in the papers: 'Ex-Police Chief's Son Kills Mayor's Wife.'" I rubbed my forehead with the hand that wasn't being held by Rosie.

"I don't think you'll see that headline, Spencer."

"Why not?"

"There was nothing in the paper here this morning. I don't know how, but I think this will be buried. There were a lot of telephone calls made last night. A lot of important people didn't get much sleep."

"But she's dead. People are going to want to know why she isn't showing up at parties."

"Yeah. There will have to be something, but I don't think our names will pop up. Remember, the mayor has a story he doesn't exactly want told. I'm not fond of covering up the truth, but how would the truth serve the common good?"

"Seems like a big thing to cover up."

"I agree. But bigger things have been covered up and with bigger people involved."

"Whew. Politics. You can have it."

"I don't want it. I just want to do my job."

I squeezed her hand. "I hope you still have one, Rosie."

"Me too. But I think it will be all right. Bottom line is we did what anyone else would have done. We got the bad guy and saved the kid. Hard to argue with the results. The most we will get is heat over the procedure. And I can handle that. Well, are you up to getting dressed? You have an appointment with the mayor at eight."

"I heard. Sure. Let's go."

"Oh. Got something for you." She reached in her pocket and pulled out the remains of a bullet. "We got lucky, Spencer. The gods were on our side."

I took it and rolled it between my fingers. We did get lucky. It could just as easily have been in my heart, or Rosie's. I laid it on the table.

"I'll get dressed, and we'll hit the road. Where's my car?"

"Right outside. Marty and I will be in the lounge." She draped my clothes on the bed. "And Spencer?"

"Yes, ma'am?"

"If you ever change your mind about the force, I'd be proud to ride with you."

"Thanks, Rosie. Same here." I gave her a kiss on the cheek.

Rosie left, and I slowly got out of bed. Pulling my pants on was tough, but I struggled through it. I stopped in the bathroom, washed up, and tried the crutches. Figured I didn't need the therapist. I made a couple of slow trips across the room. Even with crutches, going was slow. Hobbling over to the table, I looked at the bullet. After a minute, I picked it up and dropped it in my pocket. I stopped at the desk and, after signing out, headed for the lounge. Ten minutes later, we were on our way home.

Rosie drove. I stretched out as much as I could in the back seat and, for the first time, wished I had a bigger car.

Chapter 44

Tuesday night I nervously entered a room full of stone-faced people at the mayor's house that included Stosh, Chief Ranek, Captain Daniels, and the mayor. I expected to be raked over the coals. I wasn't. At the most I was debriefed. I was also told to take a vacation and forget about what happened and what the outfall would be. It didn't last more than an hour. The mayor asked to talk with me alone. Stosh said he'd wait outside. I figured that would be when the axe fell. It didn't.

Jeffrey looked and sounded very sad. He simply wanted to assure me that I had acted responsibly and to thank me for my discretion in the matter. He emphasized that if anything ever came out and I was questioned I was to tell the truth. He also wanted me to help him set up a trust fund for Marty. He wanted to remain anonymous, but he wanted to at least provide for her college education and would like to start sending monthly checks. He asked me to work that out with Beef. The money could be used however Beef and I decided. I could make up any story I wanted. We parted with him promising to call if he ever needed help and me wishing him luck. He would need it if he was ever going to forget this unhappy chain of events in his life. I knew he never would.

Outside, Stosh was leaning against his unmarked car. He told me to get in. He didn't help with my crutches. I expected a tongue-lashing. He suggested a beer at the Blue Note. I didn't refuse. On the way there, we talked. Or rather *he* talked. I listened. He was mostly concerned about my involving Rosie. When I pointed out that she had volunteered to come along, he said it was a good thing she did because I had needed help. He suggested maybe Mrs. Grey wouldn't be dead if I had gone through official channels. As I started to protest, he stopped me. He had spent several hours with Rosie and, unofficially, he said I had done a good job under the circumstances. He didn't come right out and say it, but he did hint that I had been able to move faster on suspicion than he would have been able to in his official capacity and maybe that had saved Marty's life. He also pointed out that, besides finding Marty's father, I had helped to wrap up a drug ring and solved a murder and that he was proud of me. He reminded me that there was always a spot on the force if I wanted it. I asked how much I would have to change my style. He said quite a bit. I reminded him that following rules and regulations wasn't exactly my style. He said he noticed.

We closed the Blue Note at one a.m. after a few beers and filling the boys in on the events at the track. Ronny was dead and twelve others were in custody, everybody accusing everybody else trying to save their own necks. I thanked Jesse for his help. Stosh quickly changed the subject.

On the way back to the car, Stosh suggested I head north for a few weeks. Said I looked tired. I said it sounded like a good idea. He said I might have more fun if I took a friend. I agreed.

Chapter 45

Wednesday morning I filled my prescription and took a few pills. I couldn't tell much difference. It probably would have helped if I had gone to bed instead of out on the town. I headed for Beef's and ordered a big breakfast.

It was almost ten so the place was empty except for a few regular coffee drinkers. Beef sat with me in a booth, and I filled him in on all he needed to know. I had struggled over the father issue and finally decided to tell him I had found who the father was but that he was dead and the family was willing to provide support for Marty if it was kept quiet. I certainly didn't want Marty, or anyone else, knowing that Ronny was her father. I told Beef that I had located an attorney of the father's family. They didn't want any publicity, and in return for anonymity they would provide a trust fund for Marty's college and a monthly check. Beef insisted that if I knew who the attorney was he could find who the father was. I convinced him that it was more to Marty's benefit to have the trust fund than the name of the father, and this way *he* could be Marty's father. He finally agreed.

I drove around the block to my office, called Aunt Rose, collapsed on the bed, and slept till two. When I woke up, I called that friend and invited her to Door County for as long as she wanted to stay. She was thrilled. I said I'd pick her up Thursday morning at nine and asked her to meet me in front. I was having a little trouble getting around.

Thursday morning I pulled up five minutes early, and she was waiting with one suitcase. She gave me a big hug and told me to switch seats. She'd drive. I offered to help with the suitcase, but she gave me a scowl and told me to "get real." Liberated women. Whose idea was that? She pulled away from the curb with me giving directions.

On the way, I told the whole story. She already knew quite a bit. After swearing her to secrecy, I started with Elizabeth going to work for the mayor and falling in love and ending with me waking up in a hospital room in Algoma. There was a lot of head shaking and wondering why people do the things they do. We didn't have the answers.

We talked about the case all the way to the bridge at Sturgeon Bay where the talk then turned to the scenery. Less than an hour later, we rounded the bend in Ephraim and headed up the hill to the inn. She parked the car in front facing the harbor and stared with her mouth open. Multi-colored sailboats speckled the harbor and green, turtle-backed islands dotted Green Bay in the distance.

"Spencer, this is gorgeous."

"It is that. There's more. You get settled and we'll take a drive."

"It can't be better than this, Spencer."

We got out and she retrieved her suitcase. Before she could set it on the ground, Aunt Rose was running to meet us. Her gray hair was pulled back in a bun, and her flowered apron was blowing in the breeze that always blew in off the harbor. Her face looked a bit tired, but there was that sparkle in her eyes that had been there for as long as I could remember.

"Spencer, what in the world happened to you?" I struggled with my bags. "Leave those be. I'll have one of the boys get them. And this must be Maxine." She held out her arms and gave her a hug. "Spencer has told me so much about you." Aunt Rose linked her arm through Maxine's and led her away. "I don't know why you would want to give up an exciting life in the big city, but you are a blessing to me, dear. I could sure use help with this place. And good help is so hard to find. It doesn't pay a lot but, if you want to stay, we can work out some kind of benefits. I'll show you to your room and then give you a tour."

I leaned on the car and watched them walk up the stairs to the front porch. The place never changed. At least it never seemed to. Maybe I just didn't want it to. The same flowers were in the window planters, the same rockers were scattered along the wide porch that wrapped around three sides of the white building, and the same cat slept on the cushion of the wicker chair by the door. As I watched, Maxine pulled away from Aunt Rose and ran back to me.

She threw her arms around me and almost knocked me over. When she leaned back there were tears in her eyes. "Spencer... I... I can't believe I'm here. This can't be real."

I wiped her tears with my finger and pinched her arm.

"Ouch!"

"Yup. It's real."

She rubbed her arm with a smile on her face. "I don't know how to thank you."

"No need. You're doing us a favor. Aunt Rose really needs some help. I think you two will get along fine."

"I think so too. She is such a sweet lady."

She looked at me and started to cry again.

"Hey. I just wiped all those off."

She laughed. "I'm sorry. This is just so amazing. I don't know why you did this for me."

"Because you are a wonderful lady, and you deserve a break and so does Rose."

"Thanks, Spencer."

"You are welcome."

She gave me a kiss on the cheek and started back up the hill. She stopped and tentatively turned back.

"You didn't tell her, did you?" It was more a statement than a question.

I shook my head. "No reason to. I told her all she needs to know and that is that you have a good heart and you are my friend."

She slowly shook her head. "You are amazing."

"No. I'm not. But sometimes life is. Now get, before I start blubbering too." Didn't want to lose my tough guy nickname.

I watched her make her way back up the hill. Then I tucked the crutches under my arms and half tripped and skidded down the hill and across the road to an old, faded-green wooden bench next to the rocks at the edge of the harbor.

A duck swam at the water's edge looking for food. Leaning the crutches against the side of the bench, I sat and took a deep breath. That old fishy smell brought back a flood of memories of days spent with nothing more important to do than watch the clouds drift by.

The sputter of an outboard engine brought me back to reality and thoughts of the last couple of weeks.

I figured I had done pretty well. I had found the father. And, despite breaking a few laws, I had helped Stosh get information he needed to bust the drug ring, and I had solved Elizabeth's murder. Not bad for my first case. You'd think for all that I'd have more to show for it than meatloaf and a couple of pieces of chocolate cake. Oh well. I was feeling pretty good till I started to think about the wake of sadness all this had left.

Elizabeth, Louise, Ronny, and Bobby were dead. As far as I was concerned, Louise and Ronny had gotten what they deserved. Life had dealt Elizabeth a bad hand. Falling in love had led to an early grave. Bobby was an innocent bystander caught up in Ronny's schemes.

The mayor was left with a pretty empty life and a lot of guilt. And there were so many "ifs." If only he had leveled with his wife about the children and the vasectomy. If only love were more important than money. If only Ronny hadn't been so greedy and had not burgled the safe. If only Louise hadn't come home and surprised him before he could close it, leaving the evidence of Marty behind. And, if only Elizabeth hadn't felt so damned guilty, then maybe she wouldn't have moved and would have found some other way out.

The duck walked up on the grass, and I thought about Kelly. I had talked with her on Wednesday. After hearing about what happened at the track, her father wanted her to come home and she had agreed. She promised if she ever got to Chicago again, she would call. If. Too many "ifs" lately. I needed to forget all of them, and I was in the right place to do that. As I made my way back up the hill, my thoughts switched to Aunt Rose's homemade Door County cherry pie.

* * *

If you liked this book, please post a review at:
Amazon.com/dp/1939548039

To be notified of future Rick Polad books,
go to rickpolad.com and click on "JoinMailList"
and/or
"Like" my Facebook page and post a comment at:
Facebook.com/SpencerManningMysteries

www.ingramcontent.com/pod-product-compliance
Lightning Source LLC
Chambersburg PA
CBHW021954010726
47494CB00003B/736